I0600105

Beneath Your Lies

Nicole J. Owens

MOONLIT
GRAVES
PUBLISHING

Moonlit Graves Publishing

Copyright © 2025 by Nicole J. Owens. All rights reserved, including the right to repro-
duce, distribute, or transmit in any form or by any means. For information regarding
subsidiary rights, please contact the Publisher.

No part of this publication may be reproduced, stored or transmitted in any form or
by any means, electronic, mechanical, photocopying, recording, scanning, or otherwise
without written permission from the Publisher. It is illegal to copy this book, post it to
a website, or distribute it by any other means without permission.

No portion of this book may be reproduced in any form without written permission
from the publisher or author, except as permitted by U.S. copyright law.

This novel is a work of fiction. The names, characters and incidents portrayed in it are
the work of the author's imagination. Any resemblance to actual persons, living or dead,
events or localities is entirely coincidental.

Designations used by companies to distinguish their products are often claimed as
trademarks. All brand names and product names used in this book and on its cover are
trade names, service marks, trademarks, and registered trademarks of their respective
owners. The publishers and the book are not associated with any product or vendor
mentioned in this book. None of the companies referenced within the book have
endorsed the book.

First edition

Developmental editing by Laura Apgar
Copy editing by Victoria Bell
Proofreading by Victoria Straw
Cover design by Samantha Sanderson-Marshall with Smash Designs
Chapter icons designed by Emma from Designolio – Book Cover & Illustration Studio

BENEATH
YOUR
LIES

Nicole J. Owens

Trigger Warnings

Before you dive into BENEATH YOUR LIES, I wanted to take a moment to speak with you. Not just as the author of these pages, but as a fellow human being and a passionate advocate for mental health and emotional well-being.

This book explores themes that may be distressing or emotionally triggering for some readers. Though none are described in heavy detail, I believe it's important to be proactive and share these ahead of time:

– Infidelity
– Domestic abuse
– Mention of miscarriage
– Drug/alcohol abuse
– Loss of parents
– Murder
– Explicit sex scenes

If at any point you feel uncomfortable, anxious, or distressed, please know that it's okay to pause, to put the book down, or to step away entirely. Your well-being will always be more important than turning the next page.

You are not alone. You are seen. You are valued.

With compassion,
Nicole J. Owens

Prologue
Fifteen Years Earlier

I don't remember the sound, just the silence after. It felt thick and wrong, like the world had forgotten to breathe.

Steam rises as I press my fingertips to my throbbing forehead just beneath the hairline. Loose strands of my pulled-back hair dance in the slight breeze moving toward me. The silence is unsettling, interrupted only by the ringing in my ears and a lingering hiss like a venomous snake.

My movements are slow, and my mouth hangs open. Pain surges through my skull as the pads of my fingers dig deeper into my flesh. Peeling my hand away, I see a thick, red liquid dripping down.

Blood.

But is it mine?

I blink rapidly, straining to focus as I survey the scene before me. Sweat trickles down my brows and the burning sensation makes it unbearable to keep my eyelids open.

I pick up my phone and dial without thinking as panic builds in my chest. I take a few steps forward; my legs functioning solely on muscle memory. I'm only feet away from the chaos that erupted mere moments ago—close enough to crouch down and touch the body sprawled across the concrete. Bloodied and mangled, a once-attractive face is now unrecognizable. The body's limbs curve and bend at unnatural angles.

I did this.

This is my fault.

The chime of an outgoing call abruptly stops, and I strain for the familiar voice.

"Sorry I missed your call..."

Voicemail.

Anxiety fills my lungs. If I can't get hold of him, there is no one else I can call. No one else can help me.

I end the call and immediately tap the number to redial.

My breaths come in heavy rasps. A tidal wave of impatience cascades over me. I'm so fucked. So absolutely fucked.

A groggy, muffled voice answers after the fourth ring. For a fleeting second, relief washes through me, but then I remember why I'm calling. The reason I'm standing here, covered in blood.

The familiar voice is thick with sleep and lined with irritation. "Why are you calling so late—"

I don't let him finish before blurting out what I hope are coherent words.

"I need your help," I whisper, my voice breaking as I choke back sobs. "I think I killed him."

Now

"The rage of a woman is not to be underestimated—it is a force to be reckoned with, a storm that demands respect."

Unknown

1

Veronica

The first thought that crosses my mind is: *How much physical exertion would it take to sever a human head from its body?*

The blood beneath my skin hums as an unfamiliar perfume fills my nostrils. And that's when the second thought quickly follows: *That's not something a loving wife would think.*

I should be screaming. I should be crying.

I should be throwing things across the room, shattering them into millions of pieces. Tearing apart this goddamn house, one overpriced name-brand item at a time. Hurling insults that cut to the core. Hell, there should be spit shooting from my lips as I fuse together words that tear through the heavy silence.

I should be scratching, punching, and kicking until I draw blood. Until I feel an ounce of satisfaction at the pain I've inflicted.

I should be delivering physical pain to match the internal pain. Because there should be internal pain ravaging my body.

I should feel something.

I should feel *anything*.

But at this moment, there is only numbness.

My chest is hollow. My tongue is thick, and the inside of my mouth feels like sandpaper. If I had saliva to spare, I'd spit every drop between his eyes just to see his reaction. Just to feel something.

But the truth is, I feel no emotion when I look at this man groveling on his knees in front of me. It's as if I'm looking at a stranger, watching this story unfold through someone else's eyes, like I'm watching a heartbreaking conclusion for the first time. This is the part where everyone cries for the heroine.

But what if the heroine's undoing is her own fault?

The stranger's face is blood red and tears spill down his cheeks. I think he's choking on apologies, but I can't seem to focus long enough to hear his words. His dyed brown hair is speckled with grays and his forehead glistens with perspiration. The balding spot he tries so desperately to hide is on full display. His too-thin lips quiver. His gray eyes are trying their best to appear apologetic.

This stranger that I know all too well. My usually controlling husband.

The only two feelings fighting their way to the surface are disgust and disappointment. It's unclear whether I'm more disappointed in him or in myself.

This man is supposed to be the personification of power and cunning, but he kneels before me, drenched in the scent of another woman. A lip print stains the collar of his white dress shirt. It's a cheap plum-purple shade that I would never be caught dead in.

The dumbass couldn't even take the time to change before coming home.

This man thought he was untouchable, that his secret would never be discovered. But that's the problem with people who believe they're untouchable: They get sloppy.

The thing about secrets is that they always come out, no matter how hard someone tries to conceal them.

He's crawling on his knees like a fucking child, and he reaches for me with his slightly wrinkled hands. I try to back away, but my legs refuse to follow any command. It's as if the numbness in my core is paralyzing me. He closes the small distance between us, and I silently curse my body for not complying.

He wraps his too-thick arms around my waist, burying his face in my abdomen as he continues to cry. His blubbering makes my body shake. Maybe that gives him the impression I'm emotional. Betrayed. Devastated. All the things he wants. All the things he expects. Anything but what I'm actually feeling.

And that annoys the shit out of me.

"I'm so sorry, honey," he cries out, his voice cracking.

I continue to stand motionless, unaffected by the continuous lies pouring from his mouth. I know he's not sorry. He's only sorry he was caught.

"I-I don't know how I let it go so far. She means nothing to me."

She. I flinch at the final admission of guilt. My stomach clenches and bile fights to exit my throat via my pursed lips.

The "she" he is referring to is the busty brunette his firm hired as his replacement secretary. How fucking clichéd could he be?

Even more tragic, she's only nineteen years old.

She's one year younger than I was when I met him five years ago. He was fifty back then. Old enough to be my father. He still is.

Shit, he's old enough to be her grandfather.

My stomach turns. The urge to retch is almost undeniable. I should've known his preferences in age wouldn't change and that one day, I'd grow too old for him and the inevitable search for someone younger would begin.

He's ruining everything I've worked for.

I should be surprised, but I'm not.

Should. Should. Should.

The word is swimming in my head, drowning me with expectations of how a loving wife should feel in this moment of betrayal.

"Veronica, please. Baby, please, I'll do anything."

Another sob pillages his body. He buries his face deeper in my stomach, his hands pressing tighter on my back.

"Anything," he whispers between sobs.

2

Veronica

The door slams behind him, and only then do I allow myself to break down. I feel the pieces of my blackened heart fracture, cracking so intensely I'm afraid I won't survive the impact.

This is not how everything was supposed to go.

I collapse to the floor with a sob and slap a trembling hand to my mouth to silence my cries. I wait until he's had enough time to reach the elevator before I let the sounds of my pain out. I've always been one to control a situation; I always have the upper hand. Very few times have things pivoted out of my control.

This is one of those few times.

Hearing the faint sound of the closing elevator doors, I let a scream rip through my lips. A scream so feral, I can't believe it's coming from my own throat. The sound bounces off every surface. My eyes bulge and tears trail down my face. My muscles ache from tensing for an extended period, but the sound carries on despite my body's desperate pleas. I scream until my voice is hoarse and my lungs are desperate to pull in more air.

I'm not sad. I'm furious.

I clench my fists, and the red-hot fury pulsates throughout my body. I gasp for breath as the world around me blurs into chaotic swirls of red and black, mirroring the wrath deep within me. My ego has taken a major hit.

At this moment, I'm a little girl again, a child whose perfect life is slipping through her bony fingers. I'm plagued by the painful reminder of what consequences can come from my unrestrained wrath. I fight to regain control, desperately clinging to lessons I have taught myself in my past.

With a sharp inhalation, I steady myself and push back against the tide of anger. I'm determined not to let history repeat itself. I won't go back there. With just a few moments to gather myself, I'll get everything under control.

Among the fits of rage, there is something blossoming. Something I haven't felt in a long time; it's a kernel of something to hold on to.

Relief. I feel relieved.

I had a feeling this day might come. The revelation sank in a long time ago, nestling its way into my bones. This new life roped me in quickly, and I was a fool to let it. A young, stupid fool. Twenty years old and easily captivated by the life he could give me. My escape plan.

His head was turned by the lovely broken toy he had found, desperate for affection. That's what Richard is, after all—a fixer, a problem solver. When he found me, I became his next conquest.

And in time, he became mine.

I was a small-town girl, hoping to become someone different in a new city, looking to settle a score. I was desperate to leave my past behind, a past I still refuse to speak of. Those secrets I spent my whole life guarding so fiercely threatened to consume me. I needed to make a choice—face my demons or continue to conceal the haunting truth.

Here is where our love story begins.

When we met, our chemistry was instant. We both knew immediately what we wanted from each other.

It was *almost* as if I had moved here to find him.

Oh, the irony.

I close my eyes, drawing in my trembling bottom lip. This isn't how things are supposed to end. I made sure of it. Swallowing the lump in my throat, I wipe tears from my cheeks, making sure I position myself in view of our in-home security cameras.

Richard's first wife, Lillian, had passed away right before we met. We bonded instantly over our grief. He had lost his wife, and I had lost my parents. Two broken hearts brought together to become whole again. Sounds like a happy story, doesn't it?

That's what someone might think.

Richard became my lifeline, and I fell right into his trap.

But at the same time, he fell, unknowingly, into mine.

I didn't even put up a fight as he sucked the life from me. A fly caught in the web of a spider—but then again, I had walked right into that web, begging to be consumed.

I had my suspicions about him being unfaithful. Being the dutiful wife, I chalked it up to the stress of work and the lull of being together for half a decade.

Honestly, I'm surprised it took this long.

A few times, I turned up at his office, only to be told by someone who was *not* his new secretary that he was unavailable. I thought it was suspicious when his other secretary, Gertrude, was let go. She was an older woman with a kind face and graying hair. She made everyone feel comfortable and had decades of experience, coming highly recommended to Richard as someone who would be essential in his role as the state's new district attorney. I can still so vividly see her adjusting her metal glasses on the bridge of her nose before glancing down to check Richard's schedule with a smile. A pang of emotion flitters through my chest as I think about Gertrude. Another woman discarded by Richard because of her age.

A "misunderstanding," Richard had called it. But what kind of misunderstanding could there have been? That she wasn't aging backward?

I wasn't the least bit shocked when I walked in one day to see a new girl grinning up at me from the large oak desk strategically placed outside Richard's office.

She was significantly younger than Gertrude. My eyes grazed over her slowly, taking in her tight-fitting dress, her perfect boobs on display, and the deep-purple lipstick accenting her mouth. The same color as the one on Richard's collar.

I quickly glanced at the name plate adorning her desk. Even her name was pretty.

"Hi, Olivia." I smiled at her. "I'm Veronica, Richard's wife."

Keeping secrets must not have been a strength of hers, as her frown gave her away immediately. She'd probably hoped she wouldn't have to look into the eyes of the wife of the man she was fucking.

Yep, this is the one.

After that, everything started to show up right underneath my nose. He'd come home after dinner wearing different clothes than the ones he'd left in that morning. Everything in his wardrobe is similar enough that only the most watchful eye would catch these inconsistencies. He'd tell me one thing in the morning and something different in the evening.

I started paying closer attention to him, creating an invisible tally of the discrepancies in our daily life.

The number of his high-profile cases increased, though I never heard details about them beyond the fact that he said they existed. Nothing on the news channels seemed to corroborate his claims. I assumed he was busy with the case about the murdered women, but he never spoke much about his work. I knew there weren't any suspects in custody. He gave me only little snippets, so I tried to fill in the missing dots.

He became even more secretive when news reporters began covering "the real Richard Sullivan," growing more suspicious of those around him. But not wary enough to pause his affair.

The number of overnight stays at the office also increased for these so-called high-profile cases. Our credit cards showed charges for Michelin star restaurants I had never stepped foot in. I didn't know that the higher profile a case is, the more expensive a dinner needs to be.

As women, we are taught to second-guess ourselves and down-play our suspicions and emotions. That gut feeling is often attributed to "being sensitive" or "overthinking."

Let this be another reminder to other women that you should always lean into those feelings. They are never wrong.

When things kept popping up, I didn't know how to address them. I didn't know if I even *wanted* to address them. A man like Richard does not take lightly to being questioned or accused. I also had my own agenda and needed to proceed with caution.

This morning, he pulled the same routine. His existence was enough to get under my skin. His voice was unusually shrill as he lied through his teeth yet again. That was when I decided I'd had enough. As soon as he was out the door, I looked through his text messages synced on his iPad. He wasn't even trying to conceal what he was doing behind closed doors.

An ungodly amount of *I miss you* and *I'm horny* messages were stacked up there, with some crude pictures to top them off. A few times, a very telling question was asked: *is your wife home?* These dated back for months, starting well before our fifth wedding anniversary. We'd celebrated that anniversary three months ago with a night together at our favorite hotel, a fancy dinner, and some very vanilla sex. I was a bit surprised at how reluctant he was to have sex with me. It wasn't like I wanted to any more than he did, but I put on a satisfactory performance. That was the role I was playing—the happy, pleasing wife.

Now I see why he wasn't up for more action. He was busy getting it somewhere else.

If he regretted what he was doing, he sure as shit didn't act like it.

So today was that day. I had the necessary ammunition to shoot him down from the sky. I sent him a message with only three words. Three words that led us to where we are now. His final admission of guilt. His tears. His desperate pleas for forgiveness. The inevitable imploding of our marriage. Three words to set fire to the life we've built together, while I stepped back and watched it burn to the ground.

Veronica: Who is Olivia?

Of course, that was a rhetorical question. I knew exactly who Olivia was. I just wanted to make him squirm. I wanted to see how far he would go.

I look down and find that I'm tapping a familiar pattern with my pointer finger on my right hand. An involuntary tic I haven't done in years, but it seems to have clawed its way to the surface again.

My mask is slipping.

I rise to my feet and tread across the wooden floors of our penthouse apartment. Landing in front of our fully stocked bar, I pour myself a glass from my lying and cheating husband's favorite collection. His Woodford Reserve Baccarat. I toss it back, then quickly pour myself another before repeating the series of actions two more times until I'm satisfied with the churning in my stomach.

I really should call Lauren, but I'm not prepared for the shit-storm that would bring. Most of my other friends are through acquaintances or colleagues of his. He would be furious if I let anyone know what we are going through. He'd run the risk of yet another scandal surfacing right before the election.

As the state's district attorney, he has an image to uphold. He certainly has techniques for keeping his dirty laundry from becoming public knowledge. People are always willing to look the other way when you're rich and powerful. That's how we got to where we are now.

But after all, money can't fix everything, especially not when there is a snake in the henhouse.

The room resonates with the ominous creaking of my tightening grip, the sounds mirroring the tension building as I close my fingers tighter around the whiskey glass.

The amber liquid, once calmly contained within the glass, is trembling under pressure. I squeeze the glass with such force that it shatters in my hand, fragments scattering like confetti raining down.

I look down at my sliced-up hand. Tiny, irregular cuts dot my palm and fingers like miniature constellations. Blood seeps out of my wounds and onto the floor. The throbbing sensation is a reminder of what happens when I don't bottle up my rage.

I remain standing among the wreckage, breathing heavily, my anger momentarily spent. But still, it leaves a trail of broken fragments as real as the shards of glass.

***

I sit on our couch, staring at our ghostly white walls. The condominium I once called "too big for the two of us" is now threatening to suffocate me. The walls wrap around me like a straitjacket, the seemingly tangible hands closing around my throat.

My hand is bandaged, but Richard doesn't seem to notice. Or he doesn't care to notice.

Richard returned an hour after our initial confrontation. He looks even more disheveled than when he left. When he walks through the door, the first thing I notice is that he is out of breath. His eyes are still bloodshot from his tears earlier. One of his fists is gripped tightly around a ridiculously large flower bouquet stuffed with red roses and pink lilies. I huff a laugh at his predictability. Red roses for love and pink lilies to remind me of our wedding.

This gift only intensifies my disdain.

I didn't want to get married in July. No one wants to attend a wedding in July, especially an outdoor wedding. It's disgustingly hot here. Plus, people were very vocal in their dislike for Richard moving on so quickly and with someone so much younger than him. Lillian had been an active member of the community and loved by all who knew her. They were together for thirty years, a match made by their families at the age of twenty. Lillian was the picture-perfect image of a stay-at-home mom who was supportive of her husband's successful career.

With this backlash, Richard wanted to hurry the wedding along so he could claim it was true love and healing. "It was what Lillian would have wanted for me," he would say. "I truly believe Lillian sent Veronica to me to help me grieve her loss."

Always the performer.

Given his stature, he needed to have a very public wedding, and there was only one venue that would do: The Homewood Grounds and Vineyard. A stunning historical estate with acres of land and some of the state's most popular wines. The only upcoming availability was Saturday, July 22. If we'd declined to move forward with that date, we would have had to wait until January for their next opening.

Richard refused to wait that long. I was fine with waiting. I mean, I had other things to tend to. But once again, I gave up on what I wanted to make him happy. I gave up a lot of things for Richard. The lines between each of our desires started to fade. *We* became more important than *me*.

After the paperwork had been signed and the deposit was made, he returned home with a bundle of pink lilies. He reminded me that water lilies were not only my favorite flower, but July's flower. He told me it was a sign that we'd live happily ever after.

I had the same thought then that I do now, when looking at those flowers he currently holds in his hand: *What a crock of shit.*

"Listen, honey," he says, gently placing the flowers down on the island in the kitchen before walking over to where I sit. "I did a lot of thinking while I was gone."

I tap my thumb to each one of my fingers, a more subtle way to conceal my tic.

He clears his throat before speaking again.

"I have an idea for something that could save our marriage."

I raise my eyebrows, and heat creeps up my cheeks. I know better than to believe anything that comes from his mouth, but my curiosity piques. Desperation can guide a man to do anything.

The knot in the center of his throat bobs.

"What if you have sex with someone else?"

A cough sputters through my mouth as my stomach drops.

For fuck's sake, Richard.

The laugh slips out—light and real—but the second I hear it, I catch myself and clear my throat, casting a quick glance his way to gauge the damage.

Fear is a luxury I can't afford when his jaw is already tightening like that.

"I'm not kidding," he snaps. "Do not laugh at me. I'm your husband."

His facade fades momentarily before he remembers that he is acting a part. A part that requires him to be soft and sympathetic, two traits he's always lacked. His facial features soften as he shifts back to being the heartbroken husband who is hysterical over the thought that he could lose his wife.

There he is. In that moment where his own mask fell, that was the Richard I've grown more accustomed to seeing over the last few years.

He presses his middle fingers to the inner corner of his eyes before blowing a breath out of his mouth.

"I'm serious, Veronica." His eyes rise to meet mine. "I made a mistake, a huge mistake. Don't act like this is any easier for me."

Oh, boo-fucking-hoo. Poor you, I dare to think.

"I think if you retaliate, it'll be easier to forgive me," he says, ending the painful silence between us.

So, he's not kidding. This man is truly delusional. When I take a mental step back to think about what he's proposing, this psychotic belief of his, it could be a wonderful opportunity for me. Knowing if I appear too eager, he'll change his mind, I hold on tightly to my wariness and amp up my performance just slightly.

"Richard, that is ridiculous," I scoff. "You think sleeping with someone else will make this problem go away?"

Pain glistens in his eyes, and he shifts uneasily on his feet.

He's desperate.

"This campaign has me so stressed out. I wasn't thinking when I slept with her. I can't go through a separation this close to the election. My PR team already has all hands on deck, trying to put a positive spin on my last little issue."

I purse my lips. That's what this is all about—his image. Not our marriage. It's an unfortunate coincidence that I uncovered his infidelity this close to a pivotal moment in his career. And so close to another scandal muddying his name.

Richard won by a landslide in the previous election. He was the newcomer, with an impressive plan for the state's criminal justice program. He had a long history of being a merciless criminal prosecutor. He was incredibly vocal about the need to increase conviction rates while still maintaining integrity. He spoke diligently about how we wanted to see more convictions, but he wouldn't tolerate wrongful convictions for the sake of cases closed. The voters devoured his words and couldn't get him into office fast enough.

Getting elected was easy, with his loud words and big promises, but it's ensuring that he stays in office that's stressing him out. His team is having to do some major damage control as of late.

Reporters can't seem to get enough of him, and not in a good way. Rumors of tampering with evidence, misconduct in trials, corruption, and abuse of power are plaguing the upcoming election. Many are calling for his immediate removal from office and the ballot. As scandals unfold and the election approaches, pressure mounts for transparency and swift action to restore faith in the integrity of the District Attorney's office.

Let me be clear, timing is never an accident.

"I can't lose you either, honey," he quickly adds, recognizing the discontent that must be showing on my face at his previous sentence. "We've built so much together."

Where the hell did he even get this idea? If his PR team is responsible for this, then they need to be fired at once. This man wants me to indulge in my own affair. The thought sends a shiver down my spine, followed by that tiny little blossom of relief that continues to grow. I fight to keep my smile contained.

"You should go away for a few weeks," he says. "Give you some space."

Space. That *is* something I could use right now. I'm not sure I can stand to look at his fucking face any longer.

At my continued silence, he pulls out his cell phone and begins tapping on the screen.

"I need to get some things done for the campaign, so I'll be busy. I can easily tell everyone you're away for a little while, readying things for my next term." He continues tapping on his screen in a hurry, as if there is no one else in the room.

As if the state of our marriage wasn't dependent on this conversation.

"I know this may sound overwhelming at first, but if you forgive me, you can have your own affair."

His eyes glance up at me, though his face still points down at his phone, clearly analyzing my every move. Using this moment, I throw a calculated jab at him just to see him writhe.

"There is an active killer out there, murdering women, and you want me to go sleep with some random guy?"

His face reddens further as fury erupts in him like molten lava.

"Don't you dare," he seethes. His voice is trembling, and his eyes burn with an intensity that could scorch the air between us. "I warned you to never bring up that case," he says through his teeth, each word dripping with venom.

I stand my ground, but a quiet tremor of fear curls low in my stomach.

It seems I hit below the belt this time, and I bite back the smile curling on my lips. This man is too predictable.

He clears his throat again before speaking. "Your affair will need to be very discreet. I can set you up on some dates with men I think you'll enjoy." His face stays composed, like he's suggesting a new restaurant for dinner.

I take a few deep breaths to steady my voice before speaking. "Let me make sure I'm understanding this correctly, Richard," I snap, his name coming out with more aggression than I intend.

"You have sex with a nineteen-year-old and then you think you can just cover it up by whoring me out to some buddies of yours?"

Disgust feels sour in my stomach.

"Don't use that kind of language. I'm not whoring you out—you're my wife."

"Was I your wife when you fucked her?"

The words spill out of my mouth.

He's moving toward me more quickly than I can register. As soon as the words leave my lips, he slaps me hard across the face. Black dots cloud my vision from the impact. My palm rises to soothe the burning tingle, the heat pulsing against my hand like a heartbeat. There is no remorse in the eyes staring back at me; they're cold as steel. He hovers above me, staring down with distaste. Only then do I realize he's been standing throughout this entire conversation while I remained seated. It's just another way to assert his dominance over me.

His nostrils flare, and his top lip quivers as he shakes his hand out, trying to relieve his own pain from striking me.

Poor baby.

He's challenging me. Reminding me I'm nothing without him. Everything about this man is tactical.

He straightens his spine before taking a few hesitant steps back, creating more physical distance between us to match the emotional.

"You can spend a few weeks with someone new, blow off some steam. Then when I get back, you'll come home, and we'll never speak of this again." The bite in his tone stings more than my cheek.

His face softens only slightly, and he doesn't give me a chance to speak before he heads toward the front door. It's as if he's finally realizing that striking his wife isn't going to help him get his way.

"I promise, honey. We'll be better than ever."

His words are light, airy. Like we're on the closing statements of a minor argument.

Cautiously, he treads back to the couch where I'm sitting and presses a kiss into the cheek he smacked, as if it had never happened. His lips are dry and cold to the touch. There is no warmth.

Just like our already-dead-in-the-water marriage.

"I made you a reservation at the Addingham Hotel. Kevin will be here to pick you up in an hour."

I remain motionless on the couch, never meeting his eyes as he speaks.

"I won't let us end like this," he says. His voice is as cold as his lips. "I won't lose you like I lost Lillian."

He strides out of the door without another word.

As soon as he's gone, a surge of exhilaration courses through my veins, though I keep my face stoic. My heart pounds against my chest as a sly smile creeps out.

Freedom is just around the corner.

3
Ronan

With a subtle flick of my wrist, the last remaining fingernail separates from its nail bed, hitting the concrete floor with a satisfying clink. The now fingernail-less hand drops to its owner's side as he thrashes against the rope restraints knotted tightly around his shoulders, abdomen, and shins. Blood pools around his bare feet.

My lips curl up into a smile.

We've been here for only an hour.

The room we're holed up in is on the top floor of an abandoned apartment building. It stinks of mold and the walls are stained. The once brightly colored wallpaper hangs in strips. The only light in this room comes from the moon through the one uncovered window.

A solitary battered chair sits in the middle of the room on top of the puddle of blood courtesy of today's guest. Many have seen this room, but none have left alive.

I take a step back and stare at the man's broken nose, highlighted by an angry shade of purple beneath his left eye. While his bruised eye is almost swollen shut, the other is wide and deranged, frantically searching around the room.

I rip the soggy cloth from his mouth.

"Just give me the name and this will all be over." I wipe the blood from my knife on the cloth before pocketing it.

He stifles a sob, then chokes out his reply. His only visible eye pleads with me to spare his life.

"I told you...I—I—I don't have any idea what you're talking about," he croaks. His voice is hoarse from his continuous screaming.

Not so tough now that he's bleeding out.

I shake my head and run my fingers through my hair. I'd love nothing more than to get the fuck out of here to go and shower, but this asshole is making that difficult for me. It's going to be a long night.

"Guess I'll have to get a little more creative to help you remember, then."

I walk over to the metal table that holds a tray of utensils. As I run my hand along the clean blades, visions of the different opportunities to cause pain dance in my mind. I've always preferred a more hands-on approach to my kills.

I single out the tool I've been itching to use. Wrapping my fingers around it, I turn to face him. My smile stretches wide as I relish the terror staring back at me.

I bring up the blade in one swift motion and his screaming begins anew.

Shoving open a metal door, I'm met with the smell of decay in this old, empty warehouse. The first things I see are the dust particles suspended in the dim light and a single flickering bulb dangling from the ceiling, the cord it hangs from swaying back and forth delicately.

Lifeless.

These are the kinds of places where I do business, and I've visited one too many of these shitholes today.

I don't pretend that I'm a good person and I know my job is unconventional.

The job itself isn't difficult to understand, but I don't think most people would agree with what I do.

I remove people for people, easy enough.

It's a path "less traveled" that I stumbled upon in my desperation for survival. My childhood was full of relentless bullying because of my smaller size and rough upbringing. I was always the smallest and the weakest, an easy target. Each day brought fresh taunts and ass-beatings, leaving scars that still run deep.

As I got older, I grew out of being the smallest or the weakest. Letting go of my former identity, I became the very thing I was afraid of. The irony isn't lost on me that I became exactly what I used to hate, but you do what you have to in order to survive.

For me, killing is the only way to stay sane. Younger me might even view what I do as heroic, in a fucked-up kind of way.

As I walk throughout the maze of dust-covered crates and dangling wires, my eyes fall to a figure in the corner. I stop, letting the reason I'm here come and face me.

Footsteps echo as the shadow paces across the floor, drawing closer. The large black shape separates into three silhouettes, one smaller frame flanked by two much larger ones. I cross my arms and lean against the closest wall.

"Death's Shadow," a deep voice croaks as the distance between us grows smaller. "We finally meet."

The owner of the voice steps into the light. His gray hair shines beneath the faint bulb. He's smaller than I imagined, but he tries to overcompensate with his presence. He reeks of arrogance and his brown eyes gleam with a cold intensity, as an emotionless smirk is painted on his face. The jagged scar that cuts across his left cheek is made more noticeable by his grin.

Mark Williams. My new client.

My new filthy-fucking-rich client.

Head of the city's drug ring. The one person who could make me look like a saint.

Or, well, almost like a saint.

He's ruthless, getting his reputation by stabbing the backs of anyone dumb enough to get in his way. A person like him rarely gets his hands dirty.

Which brings up the question: *Why the fuck am I here?*

Part of me is too curious for my own good. I needed to see what he is offering. Working with a man like Mark could open up some solid streams of revenue, no matter how dirty they are. But it could also make people hesitant to work with me.

It's not like the world is exploding with opportunities for a vigilante hit man. Sometimes I have to make decisions even if I don't like them.

Behind Mark, two colossal men stand like sentinels. The faces beneath their shaved heads convey unwavering focus on the role they are playing in this meeting. Protectors. Their proximity acts as an unspoken deterrent, a reminder of the barrier surrounding their mark. Well, both Marks, I guess.

Death's Shadow. I hate the stupid fucking nickname, but it caught everyone's attention, thanks to whoever started it. It is said that wherever death lurks, I'm nearby, hidden in the shadows.

Death is dark, but its shadow is darker.

"In the flesh," I say.

He inflates his chest and stands a bit taller as his eyes survey me. "You're the only person in this city who could rival my notoriety,"

Mark Williams drawls. His eyes examine me before returning to meet mine. "And you're bigger than I thought."

I don't even bother hiding my eye roll. I'm used to people gawking at me for my size. I arch an eyebrow at his first remark, though I'm wondering what he stands to gain in calling this out. Maybe he's testing me. I know him and he knows me. We're aware of each other's...*extracurricular activities.* The fact that we've never been brought together before now is surprising. An inevitable pair of two morally corrupt individuals plaguing the city in our own creative ways.

Maybe destiny does play a role in our dark world.

He continues glaring at me, no doubt wondering how much he can trust me. He hesitates briefly before speaking again.

"Apologies for the..." He flicks his hand toward the space. "The choice in location. I needed to ensure confidentiality. I own this piece of junk."

"All a part of business." I nod.

Mark stays calm, no doubt due to his steadfast confidence. But this persona he holds doesn't hide everything. His uneasiness is obvious by the way his eyes dart around the room every few seconds. With how many enemies he's made, he always has to be on the defense. But here he is, looking at me with something in his eyes I recognize all too well.

Fear.

I can't remember the last time anyone looked at me without fear burning in their eyes.

Actually, it was probably before that night years ago. That night changed everything. I subtly shake away the thoughts before they cloud my vision.

"What can I do for you, Mark?"

Mark clears his throat and places his hands behind his back. One of his henchmen grabs a manila folder from his jacket and puts it into Mark's hands. The towering man's face is still cold and expressionless.

Pulling his arms back in front, Mark steps forward to hand it to me. "This includes minimal information on the list of targets. I know you'll be able to fill in the gaps and do what you do best."

After he's passed the folder to me, he reaches into his jacket pocket, and I tense at the sudden movement and grip the gun in my waistband. The two men behind him step closer, displaying handguns of their own.

"Easy there, Shadow," Mark says, putting up his unoccupied hand to steady his men. "Just a phone for us to stay in contact. No need for anyone to get trigger-happy."

Slowly, he pulls a small rectangle from his jacket pocket and extends his hand for me to see.

I grab it and stuff it into the back pocket of my jeans.

"Come on, man. We've got to trust each other here," Mark says. "I'll be in touch."

He slowly walks toward the exit. Before disappearing, he turns to me and says, "The list is in order of priority." He shoots a pointer finger up in the air before dragging it down.

I stare at him, unmoving, and we stay like this for a minute before he drops his gaze and vanishes into the night.

Waiting until the warehouse returns to complete silence, I turn on my heels and walk in a different direction. When I'm inside my car, I pull out the folder and a list of names stares up at me in bold capital letters.

My next targets.

I read over the list typed on a piece of paper. Most names I recognize. A bunch of nobodies who won't be missed—easy enough. As I dip lower into the list, I see the names have more prominence. Glancing at the last name, a breath catches in my chest.

Shit.

I tuck the folder securely into my back pocket before heading into the city. It's not going to be easy proving myself to Mark fucking Williams.

4

Taylor

Six Years Earlier

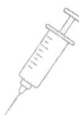

"**W**elcome," an older, cheery-faced woman says to me. Her cheeks are round and look as if they are permanently flushed. Her gray hair is swept back into a low bun, and her eyes are covered by small, wire-framed glasses. "We're excited for your first day. It's been a long time since we've had someone fresh start here, especially someone your age."

I give her a small smile and pretend I'm appreciative of the comment, though I'm smart enough to know it's a backhanded compliment at best.

I can imagine it was a surprise for someone my age to apply to be an administrative assistant at a rehabilitation clinic, but to be honest, the pay and hours are pretty great.

But that's not why I'm here.

I told them I was interested in pursuing healthcare administration, which sounds impressive enough, and they knew this experience would pad my resume nicely. It wasn't a lie—just a convenient detail that made everything else seem more official.

They also probably considered that having an attractive young woman at the front desk would make it easier to coax in hesitant patients, especially the men with too much money and too little self-control. Most of them didn't care about the rules anyway; they just wanted the illusion of recovery wrapped in something pretty.

A checkbox that could be ticked off.

"I'm happy to be here, Mrs. Young," I say, extending my hand to shake hers. My hair is a dull brown, and I'm wearing a pair of glasses I don't need. My tan slacks are crisply ironed and paired with a white button-down. "I know I have a lot to learn, but I'm eager and excited."

I offer her a genuine smile this time.

Tranquility Rehabilitation Center is exactly what it sounds like: A luxury rehab clinic that provides comprehensive treatment programs for individuals dealing with substance abuse, addiction, mental health disorders, and other behavioral issues. Clinics like these pride themselves on their high level of comfort, privacy, and personalized care, along with a range of amenities and services not found in more traditional rehabilitation centers.

Basically, these types of centers cater only to those with money. And lots of it.

Facilities such as this one typically employ a team of experienced and credentialed professionals. It wasn't easy getting the job as a young, inexperienced applicant, but here we are.

You can always make things happen when you're motivated enough.

"Please, call me Linda." The old woman's eyes crinkle as she returns my smile. "And you're, uh—" She glances down at the folder she's holding, likely to confirm my name, concern crossing her face for her forgetfulness.

I interject before she can speak. "You can call me Taylor."

She smiles brightly at me. "We just know you'll be a great addition to the team, Taylor."

5
Veronica

I step out of the black sedan's back seat while Kevin grabs
my beige overnight bag from the trunk. Using my forearm to
shield the sun from my eyes, I look at the hotel with its wings extending to me in a welcome greeting. The air is blissfully warm for
an October day, and surprisingly, the city hums with life despite
it being a weekday afternoon.

Shortly after Richard left the condo, I received an email confirmation for a stay at the Addingham Hotel, like he promised. I
took that as my cue to shove as many of my belongings as I could
into a bag. This would be the start of our time apart.

Though people are striding down the sidewalk, tension hangs
in the air, no doubt from the unsolved murders across the city.
A series of women has gone missing without a whisper of what
happened to them. There's a delicate balance between the city's

visible facade and the darkness tucked away. Despite the danger echoing in the back of my mind, a strange calm settles over me as I remember that even though the killer hasn't been caught, there haven't been any new victims as of late.

As people swirl past me, I'm suddenly self-conscious. I glance down at my gray joggers and oversized white T-shirt. My outfit is an outright contrast to the smart clothing of the business professionals and sleek youth surrounding me. Though my wardrobe choice feels unlike myself, it's what I need to slip into character and become invisible. I am just another member of the city. I'm nothing special, not anymore. It's a persona I'm used to playing.

Even with my attire, the eyes of those passing by swirl in my direction. I need to not draw too much attention. I blow out a breath before shrinking further into myself.

Kevin takes a step toward the entrance of the hotel, his reddish-brown hair shining in the sunlight.

"I've got it, but thank you." I smile weakly, extending my arm for my bag.

He nods a little. "Let me know if you need anything, Veronica."

He bows slightly at the waist before returning to the driver's seat and disappearing into the busy city streets.

A wave of sadness washes over me as I realize it's probably the last time I'll see Kevin. He's a good man, and I've always enjoyed his company. He loves to tell me about his twin girls and the mischief they cause. I've often imagined my own dad telling people stories about me. In a way, Kevin reminds me of my father. He is gentle and kind. The love for his wife and girls is evident in his eyes when he speaks about them.

Though things were never rainbows and butterflies for Richard and me, this has been my life for the last five years. I've grown comfortable with those around me. Of course, I care about them and their well-being.

But I always knew it would come to an end one day.

Another sigh escapes before I turn and stare back at the hotel. It's the same one Richard and I stay at for our anniversary each year.

I bet he made a reservation here as a reminder of our agreement. A reminder that he is watching and everything is on the line. The text I sent him shortly after he'd left today:

Veronica: I'll agree to this arrangement, but I want you to keep your distance from me.

Veronica: You're not making the calls anymore.

Veronica: I am.

I think about Richard and my last stay here in July, and how uncomfortable I was on that trip. Time passes so quickly when you're lost in a daze. Almost six years have gone by since I first met Richard.

The familiar surge of relief washes over me as I remind myself that I won't need to put on a mask for the next few weeks.

Or for the rest of my life, if I'm lucky.

Two large columns highlight the entrance to the hotel. Standing twenty-one floors high, it looks like it disappears into the sky.

The windows are gilded with gold trim that catches the sunlight and casts prisms on the sidewalk. A small but manicured garden envelops the building in a lush entrance.

I swirl through the rotating glass door and step into the lobby. The air is infused with a bouquet of floral scents. I inhale deeply and close my eyes to fully enjoy it. The scent is almost an immediate resolve to the lingering uncomfortable feelings.

To my right is a towering staircase leading to the upper level of the lobby. Past the staircase is a bar that commands attention, an oasis of refinement with gleaming glassware and a symphony of spirits on display. I catch the eyes of the pretty bartender, and she flashes me a quick smile.

God, I could use a drink.

The lobby and bar area are bathed in a soft, golden glow from the crystal chandeliers hanging overhead. A warm ambiance floats around the plush seating dispersed throughout the area.

Pushing my shoulders back to stand tall, I walk toward the check-in desk at the heart of the lavish lobby. Every detail speaks of elegance, from the rich furnishings to the soft glow of ambient lighting, creating a relaxing atmosphere.

This hotel is my favorite in the city. It is a modern take on the classic hotel structure. The reminder that Richard has muddied a lot of my good memories here sours the fuzzy feeling. I try to shove those thoughts to the back of my mind.

A lovely woman with big brown eyes smiles warmly at me from behind the desk. Her hair is tied back in a neat bun and her face is effortlessly beautiful. Her beige uniform shirt is crisp and highlights her bronzed features.

Her face lights up as I approach. "Welcome to the Addingham Hotel." She glances down briefly at my luggage, her smile never faltering. "Checking in?"

I offer her a meek smile and nod. Reaching into my purse, I retrieve my wallet after glancing at my phone. I see a text from Richard and the pit of anger hardens in my stomach. His reply to my agreement.

I turn back to hand over my ID and a credit card for incidentals.

Richard's credit card, to be exact.

She retrieves the items from me and begins clicking on her computer screen as I glance back at the mostly empty bar. I wonder how it would look if the district attorney's wife was spotted drinking alone in the hotel bar on a Tuesday afternoon. Maybe I'll just request a bottle to be sent up to my room, where I'll feel less condemned. Plus, everything is going on Richard's card. It's the least he can do after everything he's put me through.

The infidelity doesn't even begin to scratch the surface.

"Here you go, Mrs. Sullivan."

I stiffen at the formal use of my married name, reminding me why I'm here.

"Would you like some help with your belongings?"

I shake my head before replying, "No, thank you, I'll be all right."

She hands over a key card and says, "You'll be in room twenty-one-oh-nine." Her smile grows brighter as she recites the familiar words, "We hope you enjoy your stay."

Turning away from the desk, I walk toward the elevator with a deliberate slowness, each step echoing slightly in the quiet lobby. My shoes make a soft, rhythmic tapping sound as I approach the sleek, metallic doors of the elevator. I reach out to press the call button, feeling the coolness of the metal against my fingertip. The button glows softly in response.

I glance up at the illuminated floor indicator above the doors, watching as the numbers descend slowly. As I wait, my mind races, a mess of thoughts and emotions swirling together in a chaotic dance. I focus on my breathing, anchoring myself in the current moment, and pushing back against everything that tries to surface.

Closing my eyes, I wait until I hear the mellow sound of the elevator's arrival.

I step into the elevator; the low buzz comforts me, and I press into the back wall, glancing at my reflection in the polished metal of the closing doors. Just before the two doors tap in unison, I see a muscular arm pop through, halting the doors quickly.

In steps a beautiful man with black hair that hangs loosely down his forehead, though the sides of his scalp are visible. His brown eyes twinkle with the lighting of the hotel, and his boyish face is both careless and kind. His eyes scan me from head to toe slowly, as if he's taking his time, lingering in the places he appreciates the most.

As the elevator doors slide shut, I glance over this man, noticing the mischievous sparkle in his eyes. He stands with easy confidence. His lips curve into a slight, knowing smile that makes me wonder what thoughts are running through his head.

"Staying here long?" he asks, placing a hand on the bar behind him after pressing the button for floor twelve.

"For a little bit," I shoot back, raising one of my eyebrows and pursing my lips, my tone playful.

He leans casually against the wall, another smile tugging at his lips. "Well, I certainly don't mind being stuck here with such captivating company," he replies, his voice smooth as silk.

I chuckle softly at his response, meeting his gaze.

"I suppose I'll be seeing you around, then." He raises his eyebrows, stepping a little closer as the elevator jolts to a stop.

"I sure hope so." I tilt my head, letting a smile dance across my lips.

Lingering only a moment longer, he nods before stepping off the elevator, keeping his eyes trained on me until the door closes, finalizing his departure.

Well, shit, this might go even better than I expected. Richard thought he would have the upper hand in this scenario. We both know I'll never forgive him, no matter what happens over these next few weeks. It's not just about the cheating; it's about everything he's done. It's about who he is.

Forgiveness was never what this was about.

The elevator finally dings with its arrival on the top floor. I exit and begin to wander aimlessly in the general direction of the new place I'll call home for a period of time.

My room is at the end of the hallway to the left. The lock blinks green with recognition at my key and I swing the door open before tossing my bag inside. The suite is all windows with a surplus of natural light funneling in. The living room has a white sofa and a matching love seat. The carpet is a mixture of light brown, red, and green.

I see this room for what it truly represents: A well-decorated cage to hold me hostage.

But what happens when you let an animal out of its cage? A ferocity long suppressed takes over and primal fury surges through its veins. It snarls and lashes out at anything in its path, taking no prisoners.

I place the "do not disturb" sign on the door handle, then slam it shut with enough force to rattle the paintings on the walls. As soon as the dead bolt is tucked tightly in place, I push off the door and walk toward the phone to order an obscene amount of room service.

As I await the delivery, I climb into the king-sized bed and pull the airy white comforter over my head. The darkness in the light space is a physical manifestation of me in this beautiful, bright hotel room.

6

Ronan

I drive around the city in my blacked-out Audi. The engine's growl matches the intensity of my thoughts as I'm trying to come down from today's festivities. I glance at myself in the rearview mirror while my fingers wrap tighter around the steering wheel.

There is a small smudge of something dark red on the upper part of my right cheek. I lick the pad of my thumb to brush it off.

Blood, but it's not mine.

I thought Mark's targets might be difficult to crack, given who he is, but I was really fucking wrong. I replay the events in my mind, featuring two lowly dealers who were caught selling secrets about their buyers and suppliers to listening ears. They tried to throw a few people under the bus to save themselves, but those names were on the list already.

No surprise. Mark did his homework.

It's funny how weak someone is when you're holding a knife to their throat. They'll tell you anything to try to save themselves.

I call Mark as I press on the gas. He answers before the first ring finishes, and I'm met with silence.

"Number one and number two." It's a subtle way to let him know which names to cross off. Given the hold he has on this city, he probably already knew they were dead.

"You keep this up and you got a customer for life." Mark says. "You work fast, Shadow."

I press the end button before tossing my phone into the passenger seat. Adrenaline is still surging through my veins. The pulsating energy I feel after each kill is like no other. Every nerve in my body is vibrating.

With my windows down, I inhale deeply, letting the cooling air fill my lungs. The adrenaline slows with each exhale. The rush is addicting, but now I'm desperate for the calm that follows the storm.

I pick up my personal phone to make another call to my partner-in-crime and my tech wizard. The only person on this planet who knows more about me beyond my name and what I do. The only person I've ever really allowed into my life since that night.

The ring rolls in my ear before I hear a familiar airy voice.

"What's up, Ro?" Sylvie says.

Sylvie is a twenty-five-year-old college dropout who could've taught courses herself, even without a degree. She graduated from high school at seventeen and was accepted to every college she applied to. She was excited for what would come next for her, but the excitement quickly faded when she realized she hated college.

To her, her professors moved through the material at a snail's pace. She felt like her class schedule was demeaning and her adviser wouldn't let her skip levels. It was a dead end.

She lasted two weeks before she withdrew. Even without a degree, she's made a name for herself as someone to watch out for.

She's fucking smart and has an attitude to match. She's the little sister I never wanted.

"I need you to get me some information on the last target on the list," I reply. That one is going to require some effort.

"You took out two within twelve hours of your assignment. Surely you can take a day off?"

I laugh silently at her words. As if she ever takes a day off, either.

I can't recall exactly how Sylvie and I met. It was one of those unique encounters where we both needed something that was conveniently dropped in front of us. She probably approached me, made some snarky comment about me brooding but then continued talking to me like I had welcomed it. She never needs a response when talking, often joking that she has great conversations with inanimate objects.

She told me about how she was making money currently—hacking big corporations' websites and forcing them to pay large sums of money to regain access to their own domain. She requested a little extra on the top if they didn't want their employees' dirty laundry to be hung out to dry.

This concept got my attention. Her tone was laced with disgust when she talked about the greed of these businesses.

After learning how good she was at hacking, I offered her an unconventional well-paying position where we both win. She gets to use her niche skill set to help me do my job efficiently, and she gets to continue sticking it to the people who deserve it, plus my protection.

I knew more about her in the first five minutes of meeting her than I've let anyone know in the last five years of my life. After we reached an agreement on working together, I scolded her for showing such personal information to a total stranger and to never do that shit again.

She laughed in response and told me she had a feeling we were kindred spirits, whatever the hell that means. She said she could see the sadness in my eyes and knew I felt similarly to her.

Sylvie has been with me through the ups and downs in my life. She's never betrayed me, and I know she never would. It's impossible to find that kind of loyalty and I don't give people the chance to prove themselves to me. Sylvie was the only person I gave the opportunity to. There is no reason to do it again for anyone else.

"Listen, I hired you because you're stealthy. I didn't hire you to be my therapist," I tell her coolly.

"Well, you most definitely need a therapist, bro." She grunts as I hear her typing on the computer.

There's a brief pause before she speaks again. "It's kind of weird, huh?"

"What's weird?" I shift the phone to hold it between my ear and my shoulder, stopping at a red light.

"The fact that Mark comes out of the woodwork now to give you a list of people he wants gone." She hesitates before she speaks again, letting her words simmer. "He's been running this city for years. Why so much uncertainty now?"

I shrug, as if Sylvie can see my response. It's not my business to know or care what Mark's motives are.

Sylvie knows me well enough and doesn't wait for the answer she knows won't come.

"I heard some key players want him gone. They want to replace him with someone they own; someone they can use for their own bidding. They don't like how unpredictable he is. Higher-ups in the city are getting more corrupt. Greedier..." She trails off like this isn't one of the main reasons why we do what we do.

"Also, it's way too much of a coincidence with the uptick in recent disappearances." Her voice is faint, only a step above a whisper.

It's no doubt that every woman in this city is on edge with the murders. The killer strikes without warning, targeting different neighborhoods, never sticking to the same location. Everyone is at risk.

I've made it clear to Sylvie that she needs to be safe. There are some things out there that even I can't protect her from.

"You listen to too much gossip." I smile as I respond, trying to lighten the conversation as much as a pessimist can.

She snorts a sound that could be considered a laugh, and I know I've won for now.

"You know, I didn't think anyone could be a bigger asshole than you, but I'm surprised every day." She lengthens the last two words for emphasis.

Then she purrs, "Interesting."

"What's that?"

The click of her fingers on her keyboard continues before another pause as the stoplight finally flips to green.

"Looks like you're heading to your favorite hotel bar for the night," she says. "I'll shoot over some details to your email, Ro."

I don't know which nickname I hate more—Death's Shadow or Ro.

7

Veronica

Grasping the wine bottle by its neck, I shove myself up from the king-sized bed. My anxiety is now a dull throbbing instead of an overwhelming wave.

After all I've done to get here, I can't lose myself now.

I lie down on the white love seat and instinctively reach for the remote control on the walnut coffee table. I pulse through the channels, pausing momentarily on the local news. The words flashing across the screen take me by surprise, and I jolt up suddenly. The anchor's solemn voice narrates the latest development in a new missing person's case, adding to the unsettling string of unsolved mysteries that have plagued the city for over a year.

It's been months since the last disappearance, and as far as I know, the case has remained cold. The city was finally taking a small breath after a year of brutal murders. If this latest disappearance is related, that would make it six victims. The police hadn't arrested a suspect, but there were rumors that justice was delivered in another way. This new victim is a reminder that we still aren't safe. And it's a dark cloud over Richard's reputation. I'm sure, more than ever, he's feeling the pressure to close this case swiftly, especially before the upcoming election.

Did he know this body had been found when we spoke earlier today? Maybe that was another reason why he sent me away.

A shiver runs down my spine as images of the missing person flash on the screen.

The victim is stunning, with bright red hair and big hazel eyes. Her smile is bright, and she looks like someone I would have been friends with. Someone who is overly kind to every person she meets—the type of person who would voluntarily help you find your car when you're lost in a parking deck, or pay for your order when you don't have enough money to cover your bill. My stomach flips with the realization that this killer is preying on those who are too trusting. The innocent.

The women's disappearances are only the first of many horrors. A few days after they are reported missing, their bodies are found. Strangled to death with an object, suspected to be a belt or something similar, they were left in rough areas of the city. Even the locations of the bodies had been forgotten, like these women might too be forgotten, buried like trash. Someone wanted to degrade these women even in death. Somebody who must really hate them, or hates themselves.

The thought is too much. Shifting uncomfortably, I pulse my thumb on the remote until I find some show about housewives. I pick up the bottle of wine from the floor and take a swig straight from its mouth, feeling the warmth of numbness spreading throughout my body.

My phone pings and I roll over to see a message from the last person I want to think about right now.

Richard: I hope all went well with check-in. Take some time to rest. I've set up a date tonight for you with a young gentleman named Jacob.

My eyes roll swiftly at the message. It appears he wasted no time in getting the ball rolling.

Richard: Meet him at the hotel bar at 8 p.m.

Not a request. A command. My phone vibrates with an incoming message in the same chat.

Richard: Have fun.

I scoff. "Have fun?" I mockingly repeat. "Fuck you," I shout, throwing my phone across the room. I glance at the clock on the bedroom nightstand and see it's already seven o'clock. I have only an hour before this so-called date.

My heart pounds in my chest as the sounds from the TV hang in the air. The hum of anticipation grips me. Richard's compromise caught me off guard, but I can't lie and say this doesn't present me with some new advantages.

Despite my hesitation, I know I have to move forward. It's the only solution to finding my way out. I walk over to the bedroom's vanity and take a seat, my hands trembling slightly as I apply a coat of lipstick. This entire situation feels surreal and I'm having a hard time separating the feelings that are swirling around in my belly.

On one side of the coin, I'm second-guessing the fact that I agreed to this. It's risky, putting myself in this situation. I can take precautions to ensure this information does not end up with the public but there is no way to guarantee my secrecy. Trying to paint myself as a victim will be a lot more difficult with pictures of me with other men floating around. Men are forgiven much more quickly than women are. I'll be brandished a whore, someone who married Richard for the wrong reasons while Richard will gain sympathy from the world, despite the fact that he was unfaithful first. People around the world will begin comparing me to Lillian all over again. The witch hunt will be revitalized.

He better not be setting me up to fail. I'm going to have to be extra-careful to not get caught.

But again, this is the first bit of freedom I've been given in years. Those people would also be forgetting that I'm only twenty-five years old and I have way more life to live. When I think more about this opportunity, it feels like a heavy weight is being lifted from my shoulders. Of course, I despise Richard for what he's done and for pushing me into this situation, but I'll be the one to truly benefit from this. The hope of finding closure nudges me forward and lessens my hesitancy.

With one last glance in the mirror, I steel myself for the night ahead. I'll entertain this guy for a little and see what Richard is playing at. He probably didn't expect me to go along with this plan. Joke's on him. Getting underneath Richard's skin is an art I've perfected.

My phone buzzes with a phone call and I let it vibrate until it silences itself. Seconds after it stops, it starts again. I tread slowly across the room. I glance down at the screen and a wave of relief washes over me. It's not Richard. But then I stiffen at the realization that this will be an even more difficult conversation.

"Lauren, hi," I say breathlessly, mentally preparing myself for the hurricane that is my best friend. She's the only friend who has stuck with me through it all. We've known each other since we were kids.

"Bitch, are you dead?" she all but yells into the phone.

I laugh at her greeting. "You know I'm not dead because I answered the phone."

She scoffs. "I went to your place today, and no one answered the door. I thought they were going to have to escort me out after I almost beat it down. We were supposed to grab dinner tonight."

"It's, uh…" I pause, knowing Lauren's reaction is going to be over the top. Plus, I want to make sure not to slur my words after all that wine. She'd be offended that I had the audacity to drink without her. Lauren may very well find Richard and kill him herself after I tell her everything. It needs to be done in person so I can check her reaction. Besides, this is the last thing I need before this date tonight. "It's a long story. Can we meet tomorrow?"

"Tomorrow?" She snorts. "What's wrong with now?"

"Like I said..." I wet my lips, letting out a quick sigh before continuing, preparing myself for what might follow. "It's a long story. Trust me, you're going to want to talk about it in person and over drinks tomorrow night. I'll catch you up on everything."

A sense of dread creeps into my stomach as I wait for her response.

"Veronica," her voice is sincere, "you're scaring me. Are you okay?"

"Yeah, yeah," I reply. "I'm okay, I promise."

"You pinky-promise?"

A laugh escapes my lips, and I find myself lifting my pinky in the air at her words. "Pinky-promise."

"Your pinky better be up in the air because mine is!"

I extend my pinky further, as if she can see the evidence. "I love you, Lauren."

"I love you too, Veronica. With everything I have. As long as you promise you're okay, I'll text you tomorrow."

"I'll see you tomorrow." I smile at the calmness she's managed to settle over me even from a distance. Part of me hoped I could dodge her for a week or two, at least until all this blew over a tiny bit. But after hearing her voice, I'm grateful to have ripped off the Band-Aid.

I exhale slowly before pressing my fingers into my closed eyes. I rub upward with pressure, fingers gliding over my forehead and into my scalp.

Standing in front of the vanity mirror, I take one last glance at myself and pull in a deep breath as I square my shoulders.

"Ready or not, let's do this," I mutter to myself, a mixture of determination and apprehension swirling in my chest.

8

Ronan

The single ice cube in my drink clinks against the class as I sit at a corner booth in the Addingham Hotel's main bar. This hotel lies in a popular neighborhood, at the corner of Kings Street and Sixth Avenue.

Positioned strategically, my usual booth offers a vantage point on the hotel's activity while still keeping a sense of detachment. The high back seat of this booth creates an added wall of privacy.

I come here enough that the staff know not to bother me. But the thing about a hotel bar is the crowd is always unpredictable.

I'm surprised at how many tables are filled on a Tuesday night. A table to my left is a group of girls obnoxiously celebrating something. Every time a new round of drinks is brought out, they aggressively knock their glasses together. On the right is a couple who looks miserable. They barely speak to one another and seem checked out. They probably had a canceled flight and are now forced to make the most of an unexpected overnight in their layover city.

I'm here to keep an eye on one of Mark's more difficult targets. Sylvie saw that one of his credit cards was used to make a reservation here.

I glance down at my phone; I've been here for almost two hours, and I haven't even caught a glimpse of the old prick I'm keeping tabs on. Why Mark wants him out of the picture is not my business. What scares the shit out of me is that this is going to be the highest-profile kill I've ever been asked to do. I need to be smart about it.

In the world of contract killing, there is no room for error, especially not when the stakes are this high.

I sit back and look under the table where my feet rest, my ankles crossed over one another. A thick drop of blood stains my usually crisp black boots. I'm going to have to incinerate these shitkickers when I get home.

What a fucking waste.

I roll my eyes and pick up what's left of my old-fashioned. After swirling the remaining liquid in the glass, I toss it back.

Thinking back to my conversation with Sylvie, I would be stupid to not at least recognize her doubt in this assignment, but you don't say no to Mark Williams and remain alive in this city.

As far as tonight goes, I'm not going to waste another goddamn minute on this asshole. I reach over to grab my suit jacket from the booth's seat and slide out to stand. I wipe my hands down my shirt when an overwhelming feeling pulls my gaze up.

That's when I see her.

A woman walks confidently to an open stool at the bar. Her long blond hair swoops over her shoulders, bangs cupping the sides of her face. Her eyes are a green that shines in the light of the chandeliers. Her eyes dart around the room like she's looking for someone. Her eyes settle onto mine for the briefest second.

Her full lips are painted as red as the blood on my boots. She's showing a little cleavage in a black dress. Her dress stops above the middle of her thighs, and from there, she's all legs to her black heels.

I keep my gaze on her as she settles on her desired chair, turning around slightly to pull it out. Her delicate fingers wrap around the metal of the bar stool. Her hips are perfect, with a small waist and a round ass to complement it.

A small growl erupts unintentionally from the back of my throat. She's fucking beautiful.

My eyes stay locked onto her as she sits down. She adjusts her dress and then leans slightly forward to grab the bartender's attention. For a moment, the world seems to blur. A strange feeling sweeps over me—a mixture of curiosity and arousal.

My usual guarded demeanor slips, and I take a sharp inhale of breath. This feeling burning its way through my chest is unlike anything I've ever experienced with other women. It's like a dormant part of me has woken up, a part of me I forgot existed.

Who the hell is this woman?

My eyes stay trained on her as I notice that she stills for a moment. Without time for hesitation, she sits up straighter before raising a hand over her shoulder and sticking up her middle finger.

I snort out a laugh. This one is feisty.

My instincts draw my eyes to her left hand, resting on the bar.

No ring. She's here alone and maybe she wants to be left alone.

A smile stretches across my mouth, and I have a feeling that this night is about to change drastically.

Looks like I'll be sticking around a little bit longer.

9

Veronica

There is something to be said about the intoxication of a first date, even when it's orchestrated by your cheating husband. Maybe it's the power I feel in being a nameless person. The thought of someone watching me come into a room and trying to figure out my story is dizzying. An ominous presence settles around me, pushing me into infamy.

Tonight, I can be anything I want to be.

I drop my raised middle finger and return my hand gently to the bar, admiring my manicured nails. If Richard is here, I want him to know I'm aware of his presence.

I want him to know I don't give a shit.

After I get the bartender's attention, she nods her head in silent recognition that she'll be over soon. I tap my fingers against the marble bar counter. The feeling that I'm being watched simmers.

It takes every muscle in my body to keep myself seated on this bar stool.

I see a figure move behind me, lingering slightly.

I wonder if Jacob is already here. I arrived fifteen minutes early in hopes of having a few moments to gather myself—and to give myself time to change my mind, just in case.

The bartender floats over to me. She's petite and can't be more than five feet tall. Her brown hair is cropped short at her chin with purple highlights coursing through it. Her eyes are wide and serious, but she has a small smile across her dark lips. Her embroidered collared shirt bears her name on the left side pocket: Miranda.

Before Miranda takes my order, I see her glance briefly over my shoulder and her smile fades. It's a subtle action, but I notice it because of the hesitation painted all over her face. Her brow furrows slightly while her gaze stays glued on the figure poised just behind me. I breathe in an unfamiliar scent of well-balanced notes like spices and amber. The scent leaves me breathless. I shake my head slightly to clear my thoughts.

"Glass of pinot noir," I say, trying to read Miranda's expression at what she sees over my shoulder. "Oh, and a shot of tequila with a lime, thanks." I offer my most convincing smile.

Miranda raises one eyebrow and moves toward the glasses, barely acknowledging she heard my request.

The figure hovering behind me makes its way to my right and sits a few chairs down. I let out a sigh of relief knowing it's likely not Jacob. I know Richard wouldn't be so brazen as to sit this closely and watch, though my little act of defiance could've pissed him enough to forgo his usual script.

I keep an eye on the man without turning my head to confirm my suspicions. I don't recognize him. The bartender sets the shot in front of me with a smirk before she goes to pour my glass of wine. Whatever concerned her before has vanished.

I throw back the shot without hesitation, hoping that my air of perceived anonymity remains. If only these innocent bystanders knew what my home life looked like right now, I doubt they'd have as much faith in the DA they elected.

I turn my head slowly to face the man to my right, who's now perched atop a bar stool. He rests his hand on the side of his face, his eyes cutting to the side, gazing over at me. His eyes dip down before slowly rising the length of my body, settling on my face. The intensity of his stare makes my skin tingle. His eyes are piercingly blue, and those beautiful eyes are surrounded by a thick set of long, dark eyelashes. His hair is jet black and slightly disheveled in an intentional way. It looks like he just rolled out of bed, ran a hand through his hair, and was ready to leave. He's effortlessly sexy.

The arm holding up his head is muscled, and that's putting it simply. He's dressed from head to toe in black. The sleeves of his dress shirt are rolled up just slightly enough that I can see tattoos peeking out from underneath. Swirls of colors cascade into intricate designs that stop at his wrists.

I can't see the rest of his face, but I can tell he's stunning, with strong cheekbones poking out over his resting hand. The energy around him almost seems to crackle, sending a jolt through me.

Behind his hand, I see his lips break out into a slight smile that makes my breath hitch.

Could that be Jacob? Maybe that's why he's staring at me, trying to decide whether I'm the woman he's here to meet. Surely Richard is not stupid enough to set me up with a man who looks like *that*.

I realize how desperately I want him to be the man I'm spending tonight with, the need building between my thighs. The urge to feel his large hands on my body, his lips pressed against mine, pumps through my core. A strange feeling burns between us, and it only intensifies the longer our eyes stay on one another.

I'm ripped from the sensation when I feel a warm hand on my shoulder.

"Veronica?"

I turn around to face the intruder. My face feeling flushed from the other stranger's attention, I let out a small pant, aware of the visceral effect our staring competition had on me.

Before me stands an attractive male who can best be described as approachable. He's handsome. He has kind eyes that are a soft brown, and his white teeth are visible in an inviting smile. He has an athletic build, but he's on the slimmer side. He's giving much less of the "throw me hard against a wall and fuck me" vibe I got from the stranger at the bar.

I try to regain my composure before I speak.

"Hi, Jacob? Uh, please, sit down." I'm surprised at how breathless I am. The nerves kicking in are intertwined with the slight arousal coursing through my body from my neighbor's sultry smile. Unfortunately, though, he is not the man I'm here to meet.

"We're going for liquor already?" Jacob chuckles before sitting down next to me.

And as he settles in, the overwhelming gaze of the beautiful man next to me still lingers on my skin.

10
Ronan

Of fucking course some douchebag shows up just as her gaze settles onto mine.

In the seconds leading up to his unwanted arrival, I saw it. The longing in her eyes, begging me to come closer, like it's been a long time since she felt wanted.

Another growl catches in my throat as I recall the look in her eyes. I want to be the one buried between her legs tonight. My cock stiffens at the thought. The pull toward her is impossible to ignore.

I adjust in my seat as I catch her name. Veronica. It feels warm on my tongue.

I glance at the two of them, wrapped in an awkward conversation. A first date, I guess. Her tanned back is now facing me, but I have a clear view of the kid. His face is lit up, like he knows the prize he's won tonight. He's looking her up and down like a starving animal.

Seriously, how old is this kid?

As if on cue, he says, "I'm twenty-two. Just graduated from MIT." He beams at his own accomplishment. He takes a long pull of his beer bottle that the bartender has set down in front of him. He smacks his lips while placing the half-empty bottle back down on the bar. If I wasn't judging him before, I'm judging him now for his poor taste in alcohol.

"I'm planning to attend law school, but for now, I'm taking some time off to enjoy myself." He gives her a wink before placing an elbow on the bar. He leans in slightly, resting some of his weight on his elbow.

This kid is a fucking clown. I think about drawing the knife from my jacket's inner pocket to stab him a few times before letting his lifeless body drop to the floor.

One less asshole to fill this world.

She swirls her wine in her glass and takes a deep breath before looking back up at the person accompanying her.

"Do you have any siblings?" he asks.

The small talk makes me want to gouge my own eyes out.

She shakes her head. "Nope, just me. What about you?"

"The oldest of three boys," he says with a proud smile plastered across his face.

She continues feigning interest, but I notice her eyes darting in my direction whenever she turns to face the bar, which is often.

When I'm about to say fuck it and go home, she leans in more closely to him. I'm barely hanging on. If I have to see her kiss him, I will crack his skull open on the bar.

Her voice is low when she speaks next, barely louder than a whisper.

"How much of this situation do you know about?"

Her voice is unstable, breaking in the middle of her question. I see her back muscles tense as she waits for his response.

Interesting.

His eyes dart around the room, and he clears his throat before responding. He drops his arm from the bar and lowers his hands to his thighs. He peers over her shoulder at me, and I twist away to give the illusion I'm not listening.

"I know enough, I suppose." He looks down at his hands in his lap. He fidgets, using his right hand to press on his other hand's fingernails. Something that looks like sadness shines in his eyes. "I'm sorry about what happened. I won't say anything, of course."

She looks at the bar, and I can just barely see the side of her face. Her shoulders move up and down with her unsteady breaths. Her face is pinched in annoyance. She takes another moment before reaching for her glass of wine. Without turning back to face him, she asks another question.

"So why are you here?"

The kid fumbles his response before saying, "My dad owes Mr. Sullivan a favor. Plus, he said he'd write a recommendation for me

—

for law school and that would go a long way, coming from the DA."

The DA. Mr. Sullivan. Recognition blazes in my thoughts. Could she be Veronica Sullivan?

She slams her hands down on either side of her wine glass before picking it back up to swirl. The noise catches the attention of everyone else in the room. A shudder runs through her body, and she appears to choose her next words wisely.

"I can't do this."

She abruptly stands up and her bar stool lets out a screech against the marble floor. She tosses back the rest of her wine before pushing the stool back underneath the bar. All eyes remain glued to her, trying to figure out the situation. Her eyes cut to me for a split second. There is something behind them, something I can't quite put my finger on.

"I'm sure you're a nice kid, but I'm not doing this." She peels her eyes from me and turns back to face him.

He flinches at the word "kid." Before he even has a chance to respond, she's strutting off quickly, heels clicking as she makes her way across the bar and then into the lobby. My eyes are locked on her ass as I watch her walk away. I can feel the rage pulsating from her body. Her shoulders are hunched slightly forward. An attendant from the hotel approaches her but retreats after seeing the look on her face.

She is a force to be reckoned with.

Well, that was something. At least I know she won't be fucking anyone else tonight. I was afraid I'd have to kill the kid.

My head is buzzing. There is so much I need to learn about her.

But now that I've found her, she's mine.

And I won't let her walk away from me that easily.

11

Veronica

Well, that was embarrassing.

I make it into the elevator without any more mishaps and hold it together long enough for the doors to shut. I drop my ass to the elevator floor and stretch my limp legs out in front of me. Richard actually told him everything that happened. I was *not* expecting that. It's like I'm a raw steak that he dangled out in front of a dog.

My skin flushes further when I think about the handsome stranger watching all of this unfold.

Every ounce of confidence I had before this was completely squashed by the pity party put together for me downstairs. Unfortunately, I was the only person to RSVP to said party. I let out a shriek of frustration as I realize I've underestimated Richard.

Well played, fucker.

He knows I cannot stand pity. I've spent my entire life being the person people felt sorry for. Nothing is a bigger turnoff than a man trying to do me a favor because he feels bad. Sympathy has gotten me nowhere.

Returning to my room, I strip off my clothes and let the bathtub fill with water hot enough to scald my skin. I sink into the large porcelain tub and hiss at the sting as I submerge my body beneath the surface. I drown my frustration in the water, letting the heat calm my nerves.

Tonight is another memory I'll spend years trying to eradicate from my brain. Going to meet someone my husband set me up with in hopes I'd have sex with him. Telling Jacob every detail about our situation reminds me that I'm nothing. I'm an afterthought. I'm another stepping stone for his career. Everything is a game to Richard. This was another reminder of how dirty he can be.

My phone pings at the exact wrong moment and I know it can be only one person.

Richard: Good night with Jacob?

A fucking winking emoji accompanies this text message.

He's baiting me. He must already know how tonight ended, assuming his little pet ran to call him as soon as I left the bar.

What does all of this say about how Richard perceives me? He still assumes I'm just a pawn on the chessboard that he can maneuver to get what he wants.

Two can play this game. He can choke on his fucking words.

I jump out of the tub, then dress quickly in my discarded clothes and double-check my reflection in the mirror. My eyes are slightly bloodshot, but not much has changed from earlier. I slip my feet back into my heels and rush downstairs, hoping my luck is improving and that tonight could be the turning point I've been waiting for.

I'm restless in the elevator, bouncing from one heeled foot to the other. I think back to the moments before Jacob arrived. The electric charge that crackled in the air between me and that beautiful stranger—I can still feel it. Something forbidden beckons me to unleash myself. My breath hitches as I think about how his gaze lingered, tracing the details of my face with a hunger that mirrored my own. Neither of us made a move, but the intensity in his eyes spoke volumes. My heart continues to pound in my chest as I remember the magnetic pull, each beat synchronized with my growing desire.

"C'mon, c'mon," I chant to the elevator, knowing time is of the essence here, watching the numbers slowly tick down.

As the doors open to the familiar lobby, I jog slightly toward the bar. I am filled only with disappointment to find that the blue-eyed stranger is nowhere to be seen.

12

Taylor

Six Years Earlier

"This is where we keep the patients' files and personal information," Linda calls out to me.

She walks along a row of file cabinets. Each one is locked and requires a specific key. In addition to the physical keys needed to access patient information, this room is locked by a security code on the door. Linda covered it up with her other hand while typing it in.

"Each employee who needs access to this room will be given their own personal code so entry can be tracked." She turns to face me and gives me a toothy grin. "Surely you understand the importance of that."

"Of course," I reply, offering a responding smile and subtle nod of my head.

As soon as she turns back around, I mimic her while rolling my eyes. Another insufferable moment with this woman, and I may very well quit on my very first day.

A key responsibility of an administrative assistant is to ensure the clinic runs in compliance with regulatory standards and supports the confidentiality of client and staff information. I must adhere to privacy protocols, too.

I've been studying *HIPAA* regulations so often that I probably talk about them in my sleep.

You see, it's no surprise that this is where I ended up.

After all, this is exactly where I want to be.

13

Ronan

I haven't been able to stop thinking about her. Her large green eyes and the way they pleaded with me. The secret hidden behind those eyes, something I couldn't quite place, like a darkness to match my own.

The way her eyes held mine. It was the first time I've seen someone look at me without fear. She almost seemed to hold a challenge in the way she looked at me, as if she was trying to say, "come and get me."

She doesn't know that I've never wanted anything else in my life as badly as I want her.

I'm desperate for answers. I need more of her. There is something different about her—something that tugs at me in a way I've never felt before. I have an extreme desire to own her. I want her to be mine.

And I will have her.

No matter the cost.

As soon as I confirmed that the Jacob character wasn't going to chase after Veronica in a grand gesture, I left. Though something gnawed at my gut, telling me to stick around just a little bit longer, I had to get out of there and blow off some steam. The only way to curb my adrenaline was to take out another of Mark's targets.

Unfortunately for the next guy on that list, I took my time with him, rather enjoying myself. I savored the familiar feeling of breaking someone, watching the light leave their eyes as they begged for their life. Though the target's final words were still ringing in my ears...

"You really think this ends with me?"

I'd expected most of those on the list to be clueless. It's clear they knew more than I thought they would.

Mark will be thrilled with my progress if I can't get Veronica out of my mind.

Knowing she's staying at the hotel makes it a bit easier for me to track her. She obviously lives in the city, so why is she staying at the hotel?

I lightly shake my head, trying to clear my mind. I don't even know her, and here I am, waiting like a dog for its owner to come home, ears perked and eyes fixated on the door. I'm desperate for even just a glimpse of her.

I stand across the street, leaning against the brick wall littered with black and red graffiti. My back rests on a wall next to the coffee shop, Brew Bliss, and she entered it ten minutes ago.

She's dressed in black joggers with a black tank, covered by a light gray zip-up. Her hair is pulled back at the top and the rest hangs down behind her back. She's sitting alone at a small circular table for two, her fingers tracing the rim of her coffee cup.

I feel the pull to be next to her, even if just to watch her.

It looks like she's meeting someone, but they haven't shown up yet. I should leave and stop acting like a fucking stalker over a woman I don't even know, but curiosity wins this round.

I prop up my left foot and press it against the brick wall behind me. I cross my arms across my chest and wait. I hope she's not meeting up with that shit bag from last night.

My phone buzzes in my pocket, but I ignore it long enough to let my thoughts stray. Tonight, I'll get closer to her, even if just a brush of my fingertips against the small of her back. The thoughts don't silence the vibration against my chest.

I tug my phone from my jacket pocket, silencing it with a swift gesture. Everything else can wait. My focus narrows, and the cool metal of the phone in my hand serves as a temporary anchor.

My eyes stay trained on every man who enters the coffee shop. She's oblivious to every pair of eyes that glance in her direction. She has no idea how much she stands out.

The moment any man begins to approach her, I push off the wall and stride toward her, but quickly settle back into my position as they pass by her to another empty seat.

I'm starting to think my possessiveness is making me jump to conclusions when a petite woman with black hair lands in front of

Veronica. Veronica stands, and the other woman offers her a quick one-armed hug. There isn't much friendliness in the encounter.

I tilt my head to the side, analyzing the situation unfolding before me as the woman turns to look out onto the street. I catch a glimpse of her face.

This woman looks familiar, but why the fuck is Veronica meeting with her?

14
Veronica

We untangle ourselves from one another, and I glance into those familiar gray eyes I know all too well.

"How are you doing, Claire?" I ask.

She purses her lips into a small smile. It's not quite convincing, but an effort, nonetheless. Her eyes are distant. She has never been very affectionate to anyone, especially her father.

Claire Sullivan. Richard's daughter. The only child from his first marriage to Lillian.

The sharp angles of her features hint at more weight loss, leaving her looking even more fragile. Her mousy-brown hair, once the color of fall leaves, is now transformed into a defiant curtain of jet-black strands. Dark circles underline her gray eyes, which are a spitting image of her father's.

Her gaze holds a guarded caution, no doubt hesitant that I'll notice the drastic changes in her appearance.

I was surprised to receive a text from her this morning, asking to meet.

Our relationship has never been easy, but I can't say I blame her. She was seventeen when I met Richard. Her distaste at the fact that her father was marrying someone only three years older than her was always palpable.

I was so consumed with Richard's lifestyle that I never stopped to consider what our relationship might do to a teenage girl. One who had just lost her mother and whose father was remarrying a total stranger—a stranger who was closer in age to be an older sister, not a stepmother.

I've always felt sorry for Claire, though she'd be pissed if she ever heard me say that. Her mom passed away unexpectedly, and her father's coping mechanism was to move on and marry someone else within a year. Richard expected her to accept me as a new part of their lives without question. Of course she was boiling over with resentment at both of us.

When Richard and I first started dating, she mostly kept to herself. One day after I had officially moved in and we told her the news that we were getting married, I trudged to our bedroom after a cycling class, spent and dead set on taking a nap. Sweat still glistening on my brow, I pushed open the door to our bedroom. The comforting familiarity of my space greeted me, but as I stepped inside, I froze. My breath caught in my throat as I saw our once-immaculate bed now a mess of tangled sheets, a mangled, bloody rabbit carcass laid across my silk-white pillow. Its lifeless eyes stared up blankly at me.

I'm not sure I'll ever be able to get that image out of my head. The sheer shock and revulsion left me paralyzed for a moment. My heart pounded in my chest as I backed away, desperate to escape the grisly sight that would surely haunt me.

With trembling hands, I scrambled to clean up the scene. Panic surged through me as I crammed our bedding into a trash bag, frantic to erase all evidence of the incident.

I never told Richard about it, and when he returned home, he never asked why we had new bedding. I'm not even sure he noticed. I understood why Claire had taunted me. I felt like I deserved it. I was once her age, and I could relate. I know what it's like to lose someone close to you.

After all, Claire and I both have our secrets.

Things softened slightly between Claire and me after that day. As she got older, she began noticing more of our similarities.

Her left hand stretches out to grip the back of the metal chair. She tugs it toward her before sitting down across from me, then sets her paper coffee cup on the table. Her right elbow rises and rests on the table; she presses her pointer and middle finger to her temple delicately while her other fingers go slack. Her eyes drop quickly to examine me completely.

"I'm guessing your father told—"

She waves her hand before returning her two fingers to her temple, a sign to tell me I don't need to finish my sentence. She knows enough.

"I'm sorry." She sighs, her eyes looking sad though her flat tone conveys no emotion. "I heard he cheated with someone even younger than me." The sadness disappears and her upper lip twitches.

Another woman in his life who continues to age.

Claire has been in Europe these last few months and returned only a few days ago, no doubt noticing that things between her father and me are exceptionally tense.

She grew up fortunate, for the most part, but no one ever thinks about how money affects a child's upbringing. She didn't speak much about her mother, with whom she had a similarly estranged relationship but of a different nature. Her mother was a strict woman, one who focused too much on their family image and cited her vices as a way to disconnect from the rest of the world. With Lilian as a mother and a harsh and disciplinarian father, it's no surprise Claire morphed into the person she is now.

Though Richard chose to disclose little about his previous marriage, he did tell me that Claire had been a troubled child, often stepping out of line. She had a tough time making friends and blamed her parents for keeping her secluded. Her mother tried her best, but she wasn't a stable woman, using her alcoholism as a way to disconnect. No one ever thinks about how dysfunction affects a child's upbringing.

Claire crosses her legs before sipping from her cup. She pulls back with her lips pressed together tightly.

"I wish I could say I was surprised, but unfortunately, I'm not." Her voice trails off before she clears her throat and straightens her back in her chair.

Even though I feel sorry for her in so many ways, I also find myself feeling envious of her. I wish I'd had more time with my father but of course, my father was nothing like Richard.

As Claire got older, she did grow into herself a bit more. For most of her life, she was going through the motions, doing as little as she could to get by. Once high school ended and the opportunity to get away from her father was presented, she started showing more initiative. She opted to attend college on the other side of the country, adding physical distance to the already apparent emotional distance that had only grown larger over the last few years.

I remember how shocked I was when she told Richard and me that she was going to major in political science during her undergraduate years and apply to law school after. I can't recall ever seeing Richard as happy as he was at that moment. His only child was following in his footsteps. Secretly, I wondered what Claire was trying to achieve by putting on this act, but I played nice and let it go.

This dream of Richard's lasted for an entire semester and that was it. A few weeks before finals, Richard received a phone call to let him know Claire had not been turning up for classes and her

GPA currently sat at 0.8 and she would not be allowed to return for the spring semester.

I'll always remember that day for how furious Richard was. It was terrifying. Veins bulged at his temples as he screamed at Claire, holding his phone a foot away from his mouth. Even after the call, he paced the room, his eyes wild and his face beet red. He continued yelling about what a fuck-up Claire was and how it was her mother's fault. The fury in his eyes was unlike anything I'd ever seen. How I managed to stay out of his rage that night is a miracle. It was a side of him I rarely saw, one he reserved mostly for Claire.

A few days later, she let him know via text message that she would be transferring to a smaller college and changing her major to creative writing. After all of that, she graduated with a 3.4 GPA and has made a name for herself as a travel writer. She has been featured in dozens of popular magazines and has even had a few segments on talk shows.

With this job, she's always gone somewhere, which was probably most of the appeal. She returns home for quick trips, but she has always avoided bigger occasions like holidays.

Throughout the last year, we have maintained a tenuous relationship. I think at the end of the day, she felt as sad for me as I did for her. We're like two caged animals who finally realized we're not each other's enemy. We could be each other's key to survival.

"He's an asshole." She shrugs and takes another sip of her coffee. "We know better than most what he's capable of."

Her stare intensifies as her eyes glaze over. Her jaw clenches as she grits her teeth. Her fingers are white from how tightly she's squeezing her nails into her palm. She always seems to be on edge recently, especially when she is around her father.

I nod my head quickly and offer her a weak smile. She reaches across the table and lays her hand atop mine.

As if noticing my gaze, she lightly shakes her head before tilting it slowly to the side.

"I just wanted to see how you were doing," she says, her voice low. "Didn't want you to act irrationally about anything."

"I'm okay." My eyes drop to her lingering hand. "Thank you for checking on me."

The silence between us hangs in the air. She pulls her hand away and tucks it into her lap, like she's trying to hide our contact.

"If you need something, just let me know," she adds. "I know people in other countries if you want to get away for a while."

"I appreciate it, Claire." I'm not sure who I'm trying to convince more, her or myself. "I'm guessing he doesn't know you're meeting me?"

She shakes her head again. "I would prefer it to stay that way; I don't need another reason to fight with him. He doesn't even know I'm back in town yet."

Her eyes cut to the sides, as if she knows it's possible we're being watched. Richard won't like that, visible proof that he does not have as much control over the women in his life as he thought.

Looking at Claire now, it's like I'm staring at my own reflection. She and I are more similar than I ever could've imagined. The two latest women to be cast aside by Richard, no longer considered worthy of his time and affection.

"This doesn't change our understanding," she replies coolly, as she tilts her head to the side.

Taken aback by the shock of her acknowledging it aloud, I quickly shake my head, dropping my eyes to the table. There could be eyes anywhere.

"No, of course not," I reply in no more than a whisper.

"Good," she says, leaning back in her chair, then clasping her fingers together atop the table. "I'd hate for something to come to light during all of this."

My eyes raise to meet hers. I let my shoulders slump, and I nod.

As if recognizing the thoughts swirling in my head, Claire stands abruptly. She stops next to me and presses her lips to my cheek.

"Be careful." She curls her lip upward in a smile. "Lots of dangerous things out there."

She nods before spinning gracefully to exit the coffee shop.

15

Taylor

Six Years Earlier

"We've got a new patient coming in today," calls Linda. I can't see her, but I can always hear her. Her voice is like a megaphone, always commanding whoever she is speaking to. "Or, well, not new. A repeat visitor."

At this comment, I sit up straighter in my chair and my eyes widen with anticipation. I frantically search for her, hoping she'll continue talking.

"Oh?" My voice cracks, and I clear my throat to try to cover up the change in my tone. She peeks her head out from an open door and walks to my desk. I feign disinterest in the topic, knowing she'll only scold me for taking part in gossip if I act intrigued. The best way to get her to keep talking is to act like I couldn't care less.

My ears prick up at the sound of the name I was hoping for.

It takes every ounce of energy I can muster to keep a stupid smile from spreading across my face. I have been so patient these last few months while working here. My life has been all about being patient, especially if I want to carry out what needs to be done.

"Kind of a big deal," she says, leaning closer so that no one can hear what she's telling me. "Confidentiality is even more important when someone like that is checked in here. If a reporter calls or stops by, you must deny that you know anyone in our facility by that name."

Linda stands up straighter and hands me the file she has behind her crossed arms.

"Here's the file—it'll give you all the information you need," she says before turning to walk away.

My fingers are trembling around the file I hold with both hands. The paper crinkles beneath the small tremors.

Linda just handed me everything I needed.

16
Ronan

A poorly made paper airplane socks me right in the nose, ripping me from my thoughts.

"Earth to Ro," Sylvie calls out, waving her hands dramatically in front of my face. "Sheesh, where do you go when you're stuck in there?" She raises a pointer finger to tap her temple.

I chuckle. Sylvie has always let me know I don't need to be so serious all the time. "Let loose and enjoy yourself" is what she is always preaching to me. But causing pain is what I do to enjoy myself.

As different as we are, I'm grateful for her. Over the last few years that we've worked together, she's become the only family I have left. I care about her enough that I once let her convince me to go to her family's house for dinner.

Huge mistake on my part.

She comes from what you'd consider a picture-perfect family. Don't get me wrong, her parents have had their struggles with Sylvie and the path she has chosen for herself, but they are still happy. Weekly family dinners are still a requirement, especially as their children have started to move out.

As soon as I pulled up in front of the two-story brick house, a feeling of regret hardened in the pit of my stomach.

What am I doing here? This is a terrible idea.

The blue front door swung open with such force that I knew Sylvie had sensed my presence before I even stepped out of my car.

Sylvie is the oldest of five children: two younger sisters and two younger brothers. She's always joked about being the matriarch of the children. She says that's why she's so smart, by helping them with their homework. Her dad can be a hard-ass—according to Sylvie, of course—but he's a hard-ass built by love and protection. He was a veteran, and it shows.

The night I arrived, he was sitting on the front porch in a rocking chair, posture straight and shoulders squared with discipline. A grin was smeared across his face as he stood to welcome their new guest.

Behind Sylvie, a woman came out of the door; she had a bright smile and crinkling eyes to match. The resemblance was too much to ignore, and I knew this was her mother.

It felt like a happy home, even though I had no experience with one.

I let out a deep sigh before opening my car door and letting my boot-clad feet drop to the pavement. Ready or not.

The evening was casual. I tried my best to make sure I was never invited back, spending most of the evening letting Sylvie's oldest sister flirt with me. She couldn't stop smiling from ear to ear. I'd never cross the line with family because believe me, a swift kick to the dick from Sylvie is very possible—if her dad didn't try to kick my ass first.

Unfortunately, I was the main event of the evening. Every single pair of eyes was glued to me as the questions seemed never-ending.

"So, Sylvie says you're her boss. What do you do exactly?" her dad asked before shoving a forkful of mashed potatoes into his mouth.

Oh, shit. I should've known they would ask me this. Why was I not more prepared?

Luckily, Sylvie interjected before I ruined this entire dinner with my brutal honesty.

"He's the CISO." Sylvie beamed with food visible in her mouth.

What the fuck is a CISO?

Not giving anyone a chance to speak, she continued, "Which stands for Chief Information Security Officer." She plopped another bite of baked chicken into her mouth. "He oversees the security strategy for the whole company, ensures protection of all assets, and leads the security teams."

Well. That was one way to put what I do, I guess.

She offered me a knowing glance, having given this question more thought than I did.

"Yeah." I cleared my throat. "That pretty much sums up everything."

Mrs. Garcia smiled at me. "That's very impressive. We know Sylvie has loved working for you and it sounds like you all do a fantastic job."

My eyes cut to Sylvie's for a quick second. "Yeah, protection is definitely our top priority."

Sylvie dropped her eyes to her plate and let out a snicker.

"Ronan," Andrea said softly. She is the second oldest daughter, second to Sylvie, fourteen months younger than her. She batted her eyelashes before continuing. "Do you have a girlfriend?"

I choked on a sip of water, caught off guard by the invasion of privacy.

"Jesus, Andrea," Sylvie spat as she slammed a fist down on the table.

"Sylvie!" her mother yelled before sighing and rubbing her hands down her lap. Her cheeks blushed, and it was clear she regretted yelling at her daughter in front of company. "You know better than to use the Lord's name in vain."

"Yeah, well, Andrea knows better than to ask ridiculous questions like that to my boss." Sylvie rolled her eyes, and Andrea stuck her tongue at her.

"It's not like you're even into guys, Sylvie. Plus, he's not *my* boss."

Sylvie's jaw twitched in irritation ,and I saw her grip close around her fork.

Please don't throw the fork at your sister's face over me.

"It's okay, Sylvie. I swear." I winked at her, and the tension at the table eased slightly. I turned to Sylvie's sister and said, "No, Andrea. I don't have a girlfriend. My work makes it...difficult to have a personal life."

She continued looking at me and batted her eyelashes a few more times for good measure, and I decided it was best to ignore her for the rest of the evening, to avoid any family violence.

The rest of the evening was less awkward, and I actually enjoyed myself. I thanked them for hosting me. Later that night, I texted Sylvie to let her know that once was more than enough.

I come out of the memory as I lounge on a worn-out leather couch, likely a hand-me-down from Sylvie's parents for her new place. Every window in this room is covered with floor-length blackout curtains. Her personality can be seen throughout the room. Miniature statues of anime characters cover her large desk.

Sylvie is hunched over a group of computer screens, eyes focused on the middle one. Her long, black hair is pulled on top of her head in a messy bun. She's in her usual attire of gray sweatpants and sneakers that look like they've never seen the outside. Her fingers move effortlessly across the keyboard, the room echoing with her clicks and the hum of electronic devices as she focuses more intensely on whatever it is she's looking at.

After I finally left the coffee shop, I came over here to get more information on Veronica and Richard. I need all the distractions I can get. Rising to my feet, I join Sylvie next to her computer screens. I lean over to look at the collection of documents displayed on one screen. They list details on Richard Sullivan.

Richard is as dirty as they come. He's everything you'd expect from a politician. Ties to illegal things that have flown under the radar for years. He has a list of criminals who are at his disposal. I have my own history with Richard and how he handles his dealings. It's a vendetta of sorts that will make this kill all that more rewarding.

I can't help but wonder how much Veronica knows about her husband's extracurricular activities.

"Anything new?" I say, my tone casual. I place my palms on the back of my head and stretch.

Sylvie looks up from her screens, a mischievous grin playing on her lips. "Oh, you know, just the usual. Corrupt CEOs, shady politicians, the works." She raises her shoulder and dips her chin while batting her eyelashes in a playful manner.

She lowers her eyes back to the screens.

"Did you find anything on the DA's wife?" I ask, keeping my voice quiet as I drop my arms back down to my sides. I try not to involve Sylvie in anything outside of work, because I don't need her getting more involved than she already is. I'd never forgive myself if something happened to her.

She glances at me inquisitively, eyes flitting only briefly to the side without turning her head fully to face me. She knows it's unusual for me to ask about a target's personal life. If she sees through me, she doesn't convey it.

"Not much of interest." She chomps on the gum she's been chewing since I arrived. She quickly blows a small bubble that pops before she continues. "She grew up in Lexington, Pennsylvania. Her parents died when she was ten. Went to the University of New York for a year before dropping out. Not long after that, she became Mrs. Sullivan." Her tone changes as she says the final two words, as if she's mocking the title.

She scoffs as her eyes continue flitting across the screen.

"Seriously, she was twenty years old when she married his crusty ass." She scrunches her nose and shivers. "She's a hottie, and she's wasting years on that douchebag."

The sides of my mouth peel upward.

'Hot' doesn't even begin to describe her accurately.

"How did her parents die?" I feign a true lack of interest and glance at my feet.

Sylvie crooks her mouth to the side like she's remembering. "They were killed in a car accident," she says as she leans closer to the computer screen. She shifts awkwardly in her seat before clearing her throat. "Looks like Veronica was in the car when her parents died." Her voice is somber.

A beat of silence hangs over us as I digest her words. Veronica's past is more like mine than I thought. Maybe we are both made up of dark pieces.

Sylvie glances to her side, and I look down at her face. The evidence of my past is pouring off me. She notices the awkward silence and probably has a good idea of what is spinning around in my head. She gazes at me with an infinite amount of understanding in her eyes.

"Don't give me that look," I say flatly.

"Sorry." Her voice is softer, less snarky. "I know it's still tough."

I swiftly shake my head but don't comment. She knows about my childhood and what happened to me. And she also knows I don't care to speak about it.

"You're abnormally interested in his wife."

Her chair whirls around and she comes to face me directly. It's a deliberate change in topics, and I know that she's hoping to catch me off guard.

She purses her lips as she stares me down before giving my shoulder a small shove, a calculating look smeared across her face. Her eyebrows rise in recognition as she analyzes my face. She's trying to find a gap in my armor, a small pressure point of weakness.

But you can't find what doesn't exist.

Veronica has stirred up something inside me that was buried long ago. My job makes me dangerous and having a weak spot would only hurt us both, eventually. Still, no matter how much I try to fight it, the thoughts of her never disappear for long.

"Any reason why that is, Ro?" She puffs a thick breath through her nose. Clearly, she noticed my lack of reply.

I match her stare, daring her to press the situation further. I'd rather stay silent about my infatuation; it wouldn't serve Sylvie for her to know Veronica's involvement in what's coming next.

I tilt my head to each side and crack my knuckles. I shoot her one more intense glance before turning to walk to the door.

"Don't worry about me, Sylvie," I reply, offering her a subtle smile as I turn to leave.

She groans loudly in disgust, and I hear her chair squeak as she turns back to her screens.

"Trust me, Ro," she yells as she stuffs a hand into a bag of chips. She crams the handful of chips in her mouth, and she says in a muffled voice, "I don't care where you put your dick, but good luck."

17

Veronica

My phone vibrates with another call, and the movement makes me jerk as I apply nail polish to my pinky toe.

"Shit," I yell, my annoyance casting a shadowy light over the mindless activity.

I was indulging in it to distract myself. I close my eyes and scratch the top of my head with the hand not holding the polish applicator. I take a deep inhale to try to drown out the incessant noises coming from my phone. The call ends, and I lean forward to glance at the screen as my phone is lying on the coffee table.

> 8 missed calls from Richard
> 1 voicemail

So much for Richard agreeing to give me space. He is even more insufferable now that I'm not under his thumb twenty-four-seven. He's not going to give up until I finally talk to him about last night. He wants me to admit defeat, ask him why he felt the need to disclose the full situation to my suitor. He wants to see how embarrassed and battered I am, ready to tuck my tail between my legs and return home.

Knowing my luck, he somehow found out that Claire and I met for coffee, and he wants to grill me on that interaction.

With a heavy sigh, I tap the new voicemail and let it play through the speaker on my phone. Silence rolls through my eardrums before I hear a light breath and his hauntingly familiar voice.

"Hey, baby, I know you're avoiding me, but I just wanted to talk to you about everything. I heard you walked out on Jacob. I figured you may need some time to yourself, so I'm hoping you can meet up soon and try again when everything has settled down. Let me know what you think. Love you."

The voicemail ends, and I sit in silence for a moment before pressing the trash icon, erasing any trace of his voice. His words sounded empty, as if he were the one feeling defeated. He knows he can't control me and it's eating him inside. His pathetic inabilities are festering inside him like an old wound that won't heal.

For a moment, I see an all-too-familiar shade of red clouding my vision. I shake my head, knowing another outburst is not something I can handle right now. There are some things that should stay buried.

Maybe it's time to finish what I've started.

I stand from my bed and walk to the closet. Opening the door, I push aside the neatly hung clothes to find my hidden bag—a physical representation of the skeletons buried in my closet.

I grab the burner phone tucked away in the bag and dial the only number in the phone. It rings only once before the call is answered with silence.

"It's me," I say, my voice sounding hoarse. "I've got something you want."

I glance around the bar as conversations buzz and glasses clink. The cocktail bar Lauren chose hums with electric energy. The polished concrete floor leads to a bar decorated with geometric accents. The bartenders there ask about your preferred flavor profile and mix up a drink just for you. The entire place is dripping with contemporary artwork. It's *very* trendy and *very* Lauren. I'm not surprised that this is where she chose to meet, and I have to admit the change of scenery is nice.

I sip my cocktail, the bartender's spin on the classic Clover Club, and try to clear my mind. My meeting with Claire has left me feeling uneasy since this morning. Between her and Richard's never-ending contact, I feel more stressed out than I did before. Plus, I'm still reeling from my missed opportunity last night with the beautiful man from the bar. While I had the chance, I should've pranced right over and shoved my tongue down his throat with Jacob still there. That would've given Richard a reason to blow up my phone.

Placing my drink down on the table, I look back at the front door at the exact moment Lauren glides in. Her graceful movements allow her to weave through the space with an effortlessness most people have difficulty achieving, and heads turn in her direction. Her long, brown hair falls in huge curls, and her hazel eyes are hidden by a pair of large designer sunglasses. She waves her hand at the host before striding over to my table as she spots me.

I laugh at the sheer "Lauren-ness" of her entrance. It's like she called ahead and asked for them to accommodate her.

She lets out a quick shriek before wrapping her arms around me too tightly. "It feels like it's been forever!"

I step back and tilt my head to look at her. "Lauren, it's been less than a week."

"Which is basically forever for us." She swings her hands forward while speaking. Exaggerated hand gestures are her specialty. She can make the most boring story much more gripping because she tells it with her entire body. "When you accepted my offer of friendship twenty years ago, you signed away your rights to go longer than a few days without seeing me. Didn't you read that clause in the friendship contract?"

She doesn't need a reply from me before she shoots off into another conversational direction. I descend back into the side of the booth I was seated in before she arrived.

"Don't you love this place? It's so cute," she says while sliding into the booth opposite from me. She leans forward and grabs a piece of bread from the center of the table. She shoves a piece in her mouth but continues speaking. "So, why are you acting like you're in witness protection all of a sudden?"

Of course, she wastes no time in getting straight to the point. I don't even have a second to get her liquored up. "Let's get you a drink first," I reply, offering a small smile.

She stops chewing abruptly and her eyes widen. She knows this is something serious. Her neck cranes as she leans closer. She shoves her pointer finger into the tabletop as she says, "You better tell me right the fuck now."

Her direct nature can be off-putting for a lot of people. She and Richard can't stand each other, which isn't a surprise. They're two alphas in a constant battle to own the room and be the primary object of my affection.

I let out a long sigh and my shoulders deflate. I brace myself for what will happen next, hoping she's at least creative with her method of torture. "Richard has been cheating on me with his secretary."

I swear her eyes turn red and I can almost see steam coming out of her ears like in an old cartoon.

"He's fucking dead," she says through her teeth while she slams her fist on the table, earning us annoyed glances from people nearby. "Why didn't you tell me as soon as you found out?"

"I knew what your reaction would be." I pause, tilting my head slightly in an acknowledging way. "And I needed time to think about everything myself. But there's more."

The attractive waiter who brought me my cocktail approaches our table. But he's met with Lauren pushing him away with a single finger extended in the air.

You know she is pissed when she turns down alcohol.

Her hazel eyes roll underneath her eyebrows. Raising her right hand, she crooks her right finger and wags it toward herself: A silent request to let her have the rest of the story and she'll keep quiet.

"I found text messages on his phone, so I had no choice but to confront him the moment he got home. I couldn't just sit on that information." I let out a breath before continuing. She's going to adore this next part, and this is exactly what I'm dreading the most. "I'm really going to need you to stay seated during this part," I say.

Her head turns, and her eyes cut to me. Her lips tighten and I see her chest rise and fall with a deep exhale. She's expecting me to deliver the final blow.

"He wants me to have my own affair to even the score," I say before shutting my eyes momentarily to let the words wash over me.

Then my eyes shoot open as something that could be categorized as a squeal fills the air around us. Her mouth has fallen open, with a small smile blooming on her lips. "No. Fucking. Way." She claps between each word. "We have to go out after this—oh my God, why didn't you wear something hotter? I'm just kidding. You look perfect. Seriously, you do." She's frantically waving her hands around while she's talking, her voice becoming shriller the longer she speaks.

I shake my head and smile. It's impossible to be upset whenever I'm around Lauren. I met her when I was five years old. Even then, she was exactly the way she is now. She was the cool kid everyone wanted to be friends with. She had a pair of hot-pink sneakers that I envied so much. I remember begging my mom to please get me a pair. When the day finally came and I got those shoes, I knew it was a sign that Lauren and I would become best friends.

Just like I predicted, one day at recess, she pranced up to me, put her hands on her hips, and said, "I have too many boyfriends. Can you take one or two to help me out? Oh, and nice shoes. They're like mine."

Even then, Lauren was the center of attention. As the years went by, she stuck with her routine of having more than one boyfriend. Then one day in high school, she told me she also liked girls. She's always emphasized that she has too much love to give, it would be rude to not share it with everyone. I adore that about her. Someone who is so confident in themselves that they don't need a label. She can be herself and it's enough.

I've watched people come and go from her life, but she has always been the most incredible person I know. Her unwavering loyalty and kindness have always been a constant source of strength and sanity for me. It's true, she does have a big heart and a lot of love to give. Plus, I don't think just one person could keep up with her sexual appetite.

She reaches across the table to place her hand on top of mine. "Are you okay?"

"Yeah, yeah," I sputter out. "I'm fine—it's just a lot, and I'm honestly kind of offended by what he proposed."

"*Offended?*" she gasps, pressing her palm to her chest as if I've wounded her. "You should be honored. He knew a good dicking might work in his favor to not lose you." With this, she waves over the hesitant server before pointing at my drink, then throws her hair over her shoulder and turns back to face me.

"Well, he wants to organize the dates," I finally admit.

Good thing she doesn't have her drink yet. This would be a fantastic opportunity for her to demonstrate her famous spit-take. "No fucking way," she heaves.

"Unfortunately, yeah." I sigh. "I actually went on a date last night. It was horrible. This twenty-two-year-old kid showed up, basically admitting that his father owed Richard a favor. You can't even imagine how mortified I was."

Her facial expression twists into rage, and her hands begin to tremble.

"It's no big deal," I tell her. "I put my big-girl pants on and walked out on him."

"I'm proud of you," she announces. "Fuck him and fuck Richard, too."

As the seconds tick by, her fury begins to wane, clearly replaced by the sinking feeling of realization. She pauses momentarily to consider the fragility of the situation. There are so many things she knows that no one else does.

Her right eyebrow shoots up her forehead, and she looks at me inquisitively. "But what about every—"

I wave my hand to cut her off, signaling that this is not the time nor the place to discuss it. She accepts my dismissal with a quick nod of her head while she presses her lips together.

The exterior Lauren shows to the public is bold and brash, but she does have a soft interior. She's wildly protective and will do anything for those she cares about. I'm at the top of that list and she's the only person in this universe who knows my full story.

She was the only person who really helped me get over my parents' sudden deaths. I felt like my world had collapsed, but Lauren was my lifeline. She was there for me every single day, offering a shoulder to cry on. She helped me navigate the darkest days of my life and for that, I'm eternally grateful to her.

She raises her cocktail glass in my direction and gives me that sly smile I've come to dread. It can mean only one thing when coming from Lauren…mischief.

"With that, cheers to us and fuck everybody else."

I laugh as I press my drink to hers, feeling even more thankful for her friendship than usual.

"Richard won't know what hit him, will he?" Her smile sharpens while her teeth sink into her bottom lip and her nose scrunches.

I'm standing in the middle of a local dive bar that is packed with sweaty bodies, wondering how the hell Lauren convinced me to come here. There is live music tonight, and it's almost impossible to find a place at the bar to order a drink. Lucky for me, Lauren loves a challenge. She returns to our stationed spot with two shots in hand.

She hands me one before raising the other in the air. "To my best friend and all the lucky men who are now able to get into her panties." She giggles.

I shake my head and clink my glass to hers before throwing back the clear liquid.

"With her shitty husband's permission, of course," she jokingly adds before taking her own shot.

I squeeze my eyes and fight back the urge to retch. The smell of vodka pools in my nostrils as it coats the back of my throat. "Gross, Lauren. That was your idea of a celebratory drink?" I sputter, coughing into my palm.

She giggles as she scans the bar, "looking for her next victim," as she calls it. She makes eye contact with a tall Korean man in a business suit across the bar. Her spine straightens, and she gently nibbles on her bottom lip. She wiggles her fingers in his direction before turning to me. "I bet this hottie has some friends for you." She offers me an innocent smile before scurrying away.

I sigh before huffing an awkward laugh. It's not surprising it took her all of two minutes to become preoccupied. I'll hang around just long enough for her to not scold me for leaving early and then head back to the hotel to get a good night's sleep.

Maybe if I'm lucky, the incredibly sexy man will be at the hotel bar again tonight. That shot wasn't such a bad idea when I envision spotting him and prancing over to plop right into his lap, like I wish I had last night. I wonder what floor he is staying on.

I'm nodding along with the music and deep in my thoughts when I feel a hand on my shoulder. I turn to see Lauren, followed by three guys.

"V, this is Liam, Shawn, and Lucas," Lauren says in her singsong voice. "Everybody, meet my best friend, Veronica." She waves her hands in my direction, looking like Vanna White.

I turn to offer a smile to her companions. The one closest to me—Lucas—is tall and broad-shouldered with dark, neatly combed hair. His suit is impeccably tailored, and it is a deep navy that complements his crispy white shirt. The second man—Shawn—is next to him. Shawn is slightly shorter, but equally well dressed. He has sandy blond hair styled with a casual flair and a warm, easy smile. His gray suit has a more modern cut, and he wears a pale-blue shirt that matches his eyes. The third man—Liam—already has his arm wrapped around Lauren and whispers something in her ear, which makes her chuckle in my direction. He has striking hazel eyes and sports a sleek black suit with a subtle pinstripe.

"I'll go get us some drinks," Lauren's man calls out to the group before turning toward the bar.

I glance after him for a moment, trying to place him. He looks familiar but from where?

"Veronica, where are you from?" the blond guy asks, his smile deepening.

I'm pulled from my thought and focus on the rest of the group. Before I have the chance to answer, recognition flashes across the other's face. "Wait a minute, I recognize you," he says, his brow furrowing as he tries to recall where he knows me from. "Oh shit, aren't you the district attorney's wife?"

Fuck.

Lauren's face looks equally uncomfortable.

"I interned at his office two years ago before I graduated," he adds. "I remember seeing you there."

I offer a weak smile before saying, "Small world. Unfortunately, I was just heading home. You guys have a good night." I don't give Lauren a chance to try to recover from the situation before I spin on my heels and quickly walk toward the exit.

Feeling a hand tightly grip the back of my arm, I whip around, preparing to give one of Lauren's guys more excuses about why I'm running at the first mention of my husband. But I'm shocked when I see who has gotten my attention.

Jacob. The prepubescent boy my husband wanted me to fuck. It's impossible to hide my shock and disdain.

"Hi, Jacob." I clear my throat. "What are you doing here?"

"What am I doing here? What are you doing here?" He snorts and I can smell the liquor coming off him. "I was hoping I might run into you." A sly smile plasters across his face, intended to be charming, but it comes off as sleazy. He has a group of friends behind him who seem just as drunk as he is.

I jerk my arm from his grip and fold my arms across my chest. "I'm not interested," I scoff, taking a step backward to walk away.

He narrows his eyes. Any hint of a smile has completely fallen from his face. I see his jaw clench as he grits his teeth. Again, I'm stopped mid step. This time, he grabs my wrist, yanking me back to face him. His grip is tight and unyielding. His fingers press painfully into my skin, sending a sharp jolt of discomfort. I wince, trying to pull away from him, but he only deepens his grip.

"Stop acting like you're fucking better than me," he huffs. His eyes look almost black in the bar's dim lighting and there is a small crease between his brows. I tug my arm again, trying to release myself from his grasp, but it's no use.

"Richard didn't warn me that you were such a cunt," he says with a small laugh.

His words ignite a fire in me. With my free hand, I rear back and slap him across the face as hard as I can. "Don't you ever lay another hand on me," I bite out, spittle accidentally flying from my mouth. "You're a fucking nobody and you always will be."

He cups his cheek with one hand, finally letting go of my wrist.

I see the rage deepen in his eyes as his face reddens with embarrassment. He leans in so close that I can feel his breath on my face.

"Same to you, sweetheart." His smile is sadistic, the picture-perfect definition of a wolf in sheep's clothing. "Your own husband doesn't want you. You were simply a pity fuck and a foot in the door for me." He leans closer and whispers in my ear, "I'd never touch you with a fifty-foot pole."

Then he moves back and goes to brush a strand of my hair behind my ear. I swat away his hand before it makes contact. Fighting back the tears welling in my eyes, I hold his gaze and refuse to let him see how much he's upset me. In the next second, I storm out of the bar, desperate to get as far away from him as possible.

18

Ronan

I t takes every muscle in my body to keep myself from rearranging the bones in his face after what he said to Veronica. No, he deserves so much worse than that and I need to be careful. This setting is too public, and I can't risk it.

My driving urge to see Veronica again overpowered any common sense I have left. I feel like I need to protect her from people like her husband and Mark.

From people like me.

She's too beautiful to be caught up in this shitty situation. I need to make sure she stays away from it all and in this, I'm the only who can keep her safe.

I had to lie to Sylvie about why I needed the DA's wife's location but at this point, she knows something is up. She knows this is different from any of my earlier targets. She's not stupid.

When Veronica's eyes caught mine the other night at the hotel bar, it was the first time someone looked at me like that.

She wasn't scared of me.

Her eyes were filled with intrigue, like she wanted my attention on her. Since that night, I haven't been able to stop thinking about her.

I came here tonight just to see her again, unsure if I would even make a move. Now I know there was a reason driving me here tonight.

This asshole again.

I bide my time until he's alone on the street, drunk and swaying on his unsteady legs, waiting for his car. His hands are shoved deep into his coat pockets, and I see the huffs of his breath against the chilled early-morning air.

The streets have died down in the late hours and his friends have disappeared into the city. He made a mistake being alone right now. A mistake that may cost him his life.

He glances at his phone a few times before looking up to scan the road for any sign of an approaching car. With each passing moment, his anticipation grows, his foot tapping impatiently against the pavement.

When I'm sure the street is clear, I come up behind him silently. He doesn't notice me until it's too late. With one hand covering his mouth, my other closes around his neck with enough force to drag him into the unlit alley that awaits us.

He fights me, grabbing at my arms, trying to unwrap the one around his throat. He lands a few weak blows to my ribs and legs with his elbows. He's too drunk to do any real damage. I'm sober and steady on my feet.

His breath becomes haggard, and I can feel saliva hitting my hand as he tries to rasp out words. Every word he said to Veronica replays in my mind. A piece of shit like this does not deserve to breathe the same air as her.

I don't know exactly what it is, but I am overwhelmed with this need to protect her. This need to shield her from any harm. I'd do anything to ensure her safety.

And it's not like hurting people is new to me.

I feel his body go slack in my grip. His knees buckle, and he starts to sink to the ground, but I still don't let up. I lower myself down with him, keeping my arm wrapped around his neck and my palm pressed tightly against his mouth.

I deny him the satisfaction of knowing why his worthless life is ending. Let him think this was a chance interaction, that there was no true reason behind it.

Fate, if you will.

If I let up now, he'd probably survive. He'll wake up on the street in a few hours, unsure of what exactly happened to him. But a small voice in my head tells me that I shouldn't let him leave here alive. If I let him walk away now, would he continue to be a threat to Veronica?

I'm not going to take a chance on letting anything happen to her.

I tighten my arm even further until I no longer feel the dull throb of his pulse.

19

Veronica

I blink my eyelids at the harshness of my phone's illuminated screen, reading the texts Lauren sent me first thing this morning.

Lauren: Where the fuck did you go last night?

Lauren: I'm sorry that fuck boy brought up Richard. I cussed him out as soon as you left. He couldn't leave the bar fast enough with how badly I embarrassed him.

I ignored her phone calls after I left the bar but assured her by text that I was fine and heading back to the hotel. I don't want to tell her about Jacob. She's already angry enough with what's going on.

I shake my head when my phone vibrates again in my hand.

Lauren: By the way, I got laid.

Lauren: Please tell me your night ended the same way.

Luckily, I haven't heard a word from Richard about my encounter with Jacob.

I hope it stays that way.

I have a rotten feeling Jacob immediately ran to him to tattle on me. Surely Richard wouldn't expect us to still hang out after last night. Maybe he's already moved on to the next pawn in his game.

Or worse—maybe I was never more than a temporary distraction, a convenient player that could be discarded the moment I stopped being useful. The thought settles like acid in my stomach. I force myself to swallow the bitterness and straighten my spine, pushing the thoughts of Richard and his mind games to the back of my mind.

There's work to be done—real, tangible things I can control—and I won't let his manipulation derail me any more than it already has.

I type out a short text to Lauren to keep her from giving me a full-on play-by-play of her night as I collapse back into my pillow.

Veronica: I'm okay, I promise. I hope your night was good despite his shitty friends.

An almost immediate reply pops up on the screen.

Lauren: Seeing him again tonight. Could he possibly be the one to tame the beast?

I snort out a laugh before quickly slapping my hand to my face to contain it. Leave it to Lauren to try to be my wing woman for one night and somehow find the man of her dreams.

Lauren: And I told him if he wants to keep seeing me, he needs to keep better company.

I lay my cell phone face down on the comforter and turn to my side, nestling my cheek deeper into the pillow. Maybe I should take a page out of Lauren's book. Go out, drink too much, and see what happens.

Maybe if I go back to the hotel bar tonight, I'll spot the mystery man with the baby-blue eyes. After last night, I've earned the right to blow off some steam.

I think back to the other night right before it all went to shit. Something in the stranger's eyes made me feel safe, untouchable. Desired. Even though more than twenty-four hours have passed, I can still feel his eyes on me, and my skin prickles with excitement.

My phone rings and I grab it, hoping it's not who I expect it to be. But luck is not on my side, and I know I cannot avoid my husband forever. He's likely calling about last night, and I need to just get this conversation over with.

Letting my shoulders sag, I click the screen to accept the call.

"Hello, Richard," I say flatly.

"Veronica." His tone is cold. "I'm glad you finally decided to answer. I thought I was going to have to show up at the hotel to get you to talk to me."

I can hear a tinge of annoyance in his voice.

"Silly me, I was hoping you'd finally catch a hint, but I should've known better," I retort with a smile creeping over my face.

There is a small pause. I know he's deciding whether to play into my comments or move on. He settles on the latter. Smart choice.

"Have you spoken with Jacob?"

"Yeah, actually, I have," I reply sharply.

"Great—when are you guys seeing each other again?" He sounds pleased with this information.

"Never, Richard," I bite out the words. "You'll be thrilled to know your guy grabbed me in public last night and I slapped him across the face."

I can hear the exhale leave Richard's nose.

"Veronica," he starts. "Jacob's father is a very important donor to my campaign—"

I don't let him finish spewing whatever bullshit was about to pour from his mouth. "Richard, just leave me alone. I don't want to play this game of yours. I'm not a pawn in your campaign." I hang up the phone before throwing it across the room.

My brow furrows in irritation as I rub a hand over my face. My phone begins ringing in the corner of the room and I can't shake the frustration that courses through me, the tension coiled tight in my muscles.

Enough is enough.

I leave my phone where it is and quickly get ready. I apply a subtle eye shadow that shimmers in the light and brush my hair until it cascades down my shoulders in soft, silky waves. Then I finish off my look with a bold red lip. I walk into my closet and grab a low-cut black shirt and a pair of tight jeans that hug my curves.

I slip my feet into my familiar black heels to complete my outfit. I stand in front of the mirror, my fingertips tracing the edges of the red lipstick I applied. As I glance at my reflection, a surge of confidence builds deep within me.

I may have been hurt, but I am not broken.

I shoot a text to Lauren to let her know I'll be getting stupid drunk tonight if her guy cancels, and she wants to join.

Then I grab my coat from the back of the hotel's armchair and let out a breath. My steps are purposeful as I make my way out of the room.

20

Ronan

I 've been here for a few hours before the elevator doors part, and I spot familiar blond hair.

Funny how I came here to get intel on her husband and ended up finding her instead. She wears a low-cut top that shows off her tits. Her jeans look painted on, and she wears the same heels from the other night.

Fuck, she somehow looks even hotter than before.

I'd crawl on my knees to see her in those heels and nothing else.

She sits down at the bar, and I watch her from my usual booth. She immediately orders two shots of clear liquor. Miranda, the bartender who was here two nights ago, sets them in front of her, and Veronica takes them in succession before rolling her head from side to side.

Impressive.

She taps her fingers on the bar while glancing over her shoulders. Again, it looks like she's looking for someone. Yesterday seemed a rough day for her, from what I saw. Her meeting at the coffee shop was tense, and then last night with Jacob was the cherry on top. That fucker got what he deserved.

I've done a lot of research on the people in her life to try to understand her better. This is, after all, my specialty—learning about my prey before I attack. I've got the basics. She's exactly who I thought she was, unfortunately. Veronica Sullivan. Second wife of District Attorney Richard Sullivan. The same one I've been hired to kill.

This complicates things.

Other than general information on her life with Richard and his career, Veronica is pretty much a ghost online. She has no real presence on social media, which is surprising nowadays. All I know about her is that she's been living comfortably since marrying Richard. If I'm going to learn all the things that I want to know about her, I'm going to have to learn directly from her.

I watch, intent on taking my time. She's worth it.

The woman from the coffee shop was none other than Claire Sullivan, Richard's daughter. And Veronica's stepdaughter, I guess.

Claire has an interesting history. There are a few instances of drunk and disorderly conduct on her records, which were swept under the rug quickly and efficiently by her father.

There was one incident that caught my eye—a domestic abuse charge. The police were called to an incident with Claire and her on-again, off-again girlfriend at the time. Her ex-girlfriend said they were fighting. She tried to walk away before Claire grabbed her and threw her to the floor, where Claire began striking her. Claire claimed she hadn't touched her, but the pictures taken by the police told a different story. I saw what her ex looked like after the fight, and it wasn't good. It appears Claire gets her temper from her dad. In the end, it was just another instance tidied up by her father.

Sylvie did some digging and found some transactions between Richard and the ex. She guessed that was a successful attempt to tie up all loose ends and ensure she wouldn't press charges. Now she is living on the opposite coast, as far away from the Sullivans as possible. Smart girl.

I didn't like the idea of Veronica meeting Claire. It's just someone else I need to keep my eye on to ensure Veronica's safety. Seems like the whole goddamn Sullivan family is going to need my attention.

I need to know about everyone in Veronica's life. Lauren is her best friend, and that's who she was out with last night. Lauren is the only person who Veronica regularly communicates with outside of Richard. She seems to be a good friend, except when she bailed on Veronica last night to hook up with some guy. Better than her playing matchmaker, like she tried to. Then again, if she hadn't brought Veronica out, I would never have been able to take care of Jacob.

I have no idea who the fuck Jacob was or what role he played in her life. But that's not something I need to worry about anymore.

I watch as she orders another drink from Miranda, now switching to her usual glass of red wine. The bartender gives her a once-over while setting the glass of red wine in front of her. She says something quickly, to which Veronica nods her head.

The overwhelming need to know more about her engulfs me. I'm desperate and starving, like I've never been able to taste anything until I found her. I need to know who she is. In less than forty-eight hours, this woman has taken over my mind. She's all I think about.

She continues to drink and casually chats with Miranda, whose eyes are softer. She looks at Veronica with kindness. She likely caught the tail end of Veronica's evening the other night and has been worried about her. Miranda has been the lead bartender here for years. I don't know how much she knows about me, but we're civil and she mostly keeps her distance.

As I'm watching them interact, Veronica throws back her head and lets out a laugh. The sound is delicious. It's the first time I've seen her with a genuine smile on her face. Her facial expressions are laced with the effects of the alcohol she's already consumed.

She's drinking too much, way too fast. It won't be long before she's a sloppy mess. I tense at the thought of her being vulnerable to other men. Men trying to get what's mine.

My eyes stay trained on her, recognizing that tonight is not the night for me to approach her. She needs to get some things out of her system, apparently.

The first time I touch her won't be when she's this drunk. I'll make sure she remembers everything I do to her.

Over the next hour, the bar steadily fills. People funnel over after checking in. Like always, hotel bars are unpredictable. I use my peripherals to assess every attendee, but my eyes never falter from their primary target. Miranda often catches my eye and stares at me in defiance.

She stays close to Veronica, never realizing I'm not the predator she should be watching out for.

Not too long after, Veronica's swaying in her seat and her skin is flushed from the alcohol, I spot movement to my left. Two men slither toward her, their predatory eyes fixed on the stunning lone woman seated at the bar. Their movements remind me of vultures closing in. They separate and sit on either side of her.

It takes her a moment to register their presence, but she offers them a welcoming smile. They quickly introduce themselves before settling into more authentic conversation. Their twisted grins hint at their sinister intentions for approaching. The buzz of their chatting and laughter derails me.

The two men are likely in their twenties. One is blond and the other brunette. The lighter-haired one has a more muscular build, while his friend is leaner. The blond male places his hand on

Veronica's lower back as he leans in to say something in her ear. My jaw clenches in frustration, and my teeth grind unintentionally.

I'll break every single one of that motherfucker's fingers for touching her.

The other male leans in closer to her, swiping the hair off her shoulder to get a better look at her chest. He raises his hand to signal to the bartender to bring three more shots filled with gold liquid.

Shit.

They cheer before tossing back the shots. The two men glance over her shoulders at one another, devious smiles on their faces. She shakes her head playfully while coughing at the aftertaste of the liquor.

Miranda rushes over to say something directly to Veronica, and Veronica replies, placing her hand on Miranda's shoulder affectionately, likely trying to reassure her about the situation. Miranda gives a subtle nod and purses her lips as she watches the two men help Veronica from her seat. She's wobbly in her high heels, so the blond man hoists her up from underneath her arms, then helps her to the elevator. Miranda's eyes stay trained on the group. There's a hesitant look on her face. She ignores the customers waiting for service at the bar and doesn't peel her eyes away from Veronica.

I'm not going to let these pieces of shit go anywhere with her. Let them try to take what they think they are entitled to. I'm going to get her away from them.

Right. Fucking. Now.

I act quickly before they disappear. Miranda meets my eyes eagerly, and I give her a quick nod of reassurance as I rush over to the elevator. I know the two men won't notice, they're so focused on their conquest.

I shove a hand through the closing elevator door, catching it before it shuts completely. I offer a smirk at the two men, whose eyes trace me as I step in.

"She okay?" I nod to the mostly limp Veronica between their arms.

"She's fine," the man with chin-length brown hair snaps at me. A snarl crosses his lips before he scans me, assessing the situation.

"What floor?" His voice drops, trying to ensure I have difficulty overhearing their conversation. They both look down at Veronica, who slowly holds up two fingers on her right hand and one finger on her left.

The blond male presses the button for the twelfth floor.

"Floor twelve, right?"

"N—no, that's two, then one," she slurs, shoving her fingers out to emphasize what she is trying to communicate.

Jesus, she's drunk.

The douchebag quickly corrects himself. The button showing the number twenty-one is now illuminated, along with floor twelve. Both men quickly draw their eyes to me to see where I'm going.

I press the button for the eighteenth floor.

They all reek of tequila and sweat. The only sound in this elevator is Veronica's labored breathing and occasional drunken giggles.

The elevator dings at my supposed floor, and I step off. I turn back to lock eyes with Veronica, who looks at me sheepishly. As the door is about to shut, slight recognition shines in her eyes. I hold her gaze, and it's my silent way of telling her she's safe.

The door closes, and I sprint up the narrow hotel stairs, my feet barely touching the concrete steps. The dim light casts long shadows, making the staircase feel like it's closing in. I push up the three flights of stairs with ease while my heavy footsteps echo loudly.

When I reach the twenty-first floor, I creak open the door and hear them whispering in hushed tones.

"Sweetheart, where is your room?"

Silence. Then a loud hiccup.

"Yeah, baby. Come on. Just tell us which number your room is."

I see them approaching from the other end of the hallway. The blond male slides a hand around her waist, brushing her ass in the movement.

She's shaking her head, aggressively, realizing this has gone too far, and she's too drunk. More hiccups exit her body.

Reaching into her back pocket, the handsy blond pulls her key card from her jeans.

"Don't make me try this card on every room on this floor," he snaps at her, waving the key card in her face. They're not going to take no for an answer.

"C'mon, we just want to make you feel good." The brunette male slides a hand along the curve of her ass, squeezing when he reaches his destination.

I stiffen with anger. Visions of how I'm going to make them pay for this roll through my mind.

"P—please, just leave me alone," she stutters out, followed by another series of hiccups. "This was—is a mistake." Her eyes widen as the two men move closer to her. "I think I'm going to be sick," she pleads.

Her hiccups turn to gags.

I can't stomach this situation any longer. Realizing they are not going to take a hint, I step out of the shadows that enclose me. "You heard her. Get the fuck out of here."

The two men snap their gaze up to me. "You again?" The brown-haired man pulls his hand from her ass. "What—is she your bitch or something?"

"You can either walk out of here right now and never come back," I say quietly as I pull a knife from the inside of my jacket pocket, "or you can never walk again."

Their eyes widen. The smell of fear is palpable in the air. They drop her slack body between them and approach me slowly.

Before they have a moment to register it, I'm moving. My fist that is not holding the knife swings and connects with the blond's jaw, easily dropping him to the floor in front of Veronica.

He looks up at me, blood spilling from his split lip. "What the fuck, man?" he says.

The other guy flails and tries to land a punch, but I quickly dodge it, then grab his hand and twist his arm behind his back.

"One more move and I'll rip this arm out of its socket," I bark in his ear before shoving him away.

The one on the floor rises unsteadily to his feet, and they both sprint away toward the opposite stairwell, not wanting to get any closer to me.

"Crazy son of a bitch," one of them yells before they disappear into the stairwell.

I rush over to Veronica, who is still on the floor, hunched over her knees. Her face is still flushed and yet pale at the same time.

"You okay?"

Her green eyes, shaking and heavy, look up at me. Her pupils are small, and her eyes look glazed and vacant.

"I've seen you..." Her eyes flutter as she speaks. "You're the beautiful stranger."

She blinks and is slow to open her eyes. Her chest rises and falls. Then, without warning, she turns her head and projectile vomits all over the hotel's carpeted hallway.

21

Veronica

T he first thing I notice when I wake up is the pounding in my head. My mouth is dry, and it tastes like something died inside it. I try to open my eyes, but the glaring sun makes me hiss.

Holy hell, I'm hungover. I glance around to see where I am, and it takes a moment for everything to come into focus.

The sight of my familiar hotel room allows me to settle down for a moment. The hotel's soft, white sheets are tangled around my legs.

Oh, thank fuck, I think I'm alone. I groan as I try to sit up. My head is spinning, and the last memory I have is of talking to two guys at the bar. I remember the bartender making sure that I was okay, but then everything gets fuzzy. I massage my temples with my fingers, trying to piece together the rest of the night.

Then a surge of distant memories flashes through my jumbled brain. It hits me—the tequila shots, the red wine, the two guys from the bar. Fuck. They tried to take me back to my room...

Wait, something else happened. It's all fuzzy after we got off the elevator, but I remember the blue-eyed man from the bar, dressed in all black. He was here.

Why was he here?

Oh fuck, no wonder my mouth tastes disgusting. I puked all over the carpet right in front of him. I bolt upright, ignoring the dizziness that threatens to overwhelm me.

There is no way I could've gotten in here on my own. I don't even know who he is. I pause to listen for any noises that might give away someone's presence. No shower running. The coffee machine is off. I'm alone. I'm surprised to find that I'm a bit disappointed at the realization.

I glance over at my nightstand. Next to my head is a glass of water with two red pills. I pick up the pills and read the writing scrawled across them: Tylenol.

Accompanying the items is a message on a hotel napkin that reads, *See you at the hotel bar tonight at 9 p.m.*

At least my vomiting escapades didn't completely scare him away.

My heart flutters. I should throw the napkin out and barricade myself in my room tonight. This is probably a bad idea. Look at everything that has happened in the last week. As excited as I feel about seeing the blue-eyed stranger again, a sense of dread also looms in the back of my mind.

I flop back down on my pillow and blush at the effort he put in last night after seeing me at my absolute worst. But I have no idea how I'm supposed to drag myself out of bed and go back to a bar for the fourth night in a row. I don't think my stomach could handle anything other than a saltine cracker.

I might still be drunk. My mouth even tastes of tequila.

I glance at the alarm clock beside my bed.

12:01 p.m.

Sighing, I tug the pillow over my face and huff as I hear my phone buzzing next to me. I groan at the intrusive noise, so loud I can feel it in my queasy stomach.

I pull the pillow from my face, then roll over and reach for my phone. There are four missed calls from Richard and one from Lauren, but no new text messages.

I was desperately hoping I had somehow given my number to the blue-eyed stranger who made sure I got back safe last night. Who am I kidding? I was throwing up on the floor. Of course, I wasn't coherent enough to give him my phone number. I probably would've given him the wrong one. Oh shit, did I give him the wrong number? I drop my face into the heels of my hands and press into my eye sockets, hoping the pressure will alleviate my headache and embarrassment.

Sitting up, I bring the glass of water to my lips after swallowing the painkillers. I finish all the water in one swig.

I stand from the bed and slowly walk into the bathroom. I gasp as I approach the bathroom sink and catch my reflection. I look like I'm dying. My unsteady hands wash my face and brush my teeth, careful not to trigger any retching. Sluggishly, I strip off my clothes from last night and hop into the shower. Turning the water up hot enough to steam the entire bathroom, I let the heat scald my skin. Images and memories from last night continue to flood my mind.

My skin prickles under the hot water as I think about meeting up with him tonight. Maybe with him, things will progress along the path Richard has been so desperate for me to take.

Who can blame me for being curious about this man? I mean, I'm only human. And he is the most attractive man I've ever seen.

My hands roam over my body as I lather on some lavender-scented body soap.

A smile plays across my lips as I think about the retaliation that I'm now looking forward to having.

22

Ronan

I push on each knuckle with my opposite hand while sitting cross-legged in a lounge chair as I think about how Veronica must be feeling this morning. The cracking noise each finger makes releases a little bit of my tension. I decided to take a quick detour after continuing down Mark's list earlier. That's how I ended up in what could only be described as a frat boy's house.

My phone dings and I glance at the notification. A new payment has successfully been wired to my bank account from Mark. I stuff my phone back into my jacket pocket and place my hands in my lap. Another one of those assholes gone. I'm over halfway through the list, and the closer I get to the bottom, the more uneasy I feel.

The latest victim on his list proved to be rather interesting. Mark had no interest in using these men to obtain information, but that doesn't mean I can't use their predicaments to my advantage.

"If you want to find the rat, you need to go higher up the food chain," he said before spitting a glob of blood onto the floor. His breathing was heavy, and he looked up at me from all fours.

Pathetic.

"So, where does that put you on the food chain?" I asked, cracking my neck.

"You and I both know where I'm at on the food chain." His voice was low under his breath. "You're wasting your time."

I clicked my tongue. He was right—I was wasting my time.

"You know, you're not wrong," I finally replied.

For a moment, his eyes brightened in a hopeful glaze.

Unsheathing my knife, I told him, "I don't have time to waste because I have a date tonight." And without giving him a second to process my words, I gripped the hair at the back of his skull and dragged my blade across his throat.

Even after that kill, my itch still wasn't scratched. My mind kept going back to the two assholes from last night. I decided to take the guy's advice from earlier; I wasn't going waste any more time giving my targets what they deserve. I want them to remember my face and I want them to remember why I did this to them.

It wasn't hard to find out who they are. Matthew Hunt and Nicholas Jones. Two twenty-four-year-old roommates living in an expensive condo in an old building funded by Daddy's money.

That's the problem with this city: too much money and power in the hands of the wrong people.

Matthew's father is the CEO of a tech conglomerate, while Nicholas comes from a family of high-profile defense attorneys who help keep the trash on the street if they can pay enough.

Both have a history of assault and disorderly conduct. It's a trend among children of the powerful, I'm realizing. Sylvie was a little suspicious when I asked for her help in finding these two.

"Who are these shitheads?" she asked. A familiar crunching noise sounds through the speaker. "I mean, yeah, they suck, but why them? Why not their dads?"

"I'm not going to take them out entirely," I let her know. "I just need to take care of some things."

Her fingers continued clicking on her keyboard, and there was a moment of silence.

"Does this have anything to do with the fact that one of their black cards was used at the Addingham Hotel bar last night?" She continued typing. "Or perhaps with the security footage I just saw, where they were escorting a very drunk Mrs. District Attorney out of sight?"

That was one of those moments where Sylvie is *too* good.

"Don't ask questions you don't want the answer to, Syl," I responded.

She took a quick inhale before letting me know the information had been sent over to me. "Be careful, Ro," she said before hanging up abruptly.

The foot on my crossed leg begins bouncing in impatience.

I showed up to their shittily decorated apartment around three this afternoon. I knew neither one of them was home, so I've been waiting patiently ever since. The place stinks of stale beer and a lingering scent of weed. Finally, I hear the familiar jingle of a key entering the lock on the front door. Nicholas stands still with his mouth open, staring at me with wide eyes. With three quick strides, my hands are gripped around his shirt collar, holding him steady.

I take my time bloodying up his face, letting the rage drip from my body each time my fist connects with his bones. The crunching noises are somewhat cathartic. Because I am a man of my word, I break each finger on the hand that wouldn't stop touching Veronica last night. And I pay close attention to each joint that grazed her perfect skin.

Through his ragged breaths, laced with his own blood, I hear the door open for a second time, and Matthew comes trekking through it. He stops suddenly, realizing he is not alone. The twelve-pack of beer in his fist drops to the floor and shatters.

Recognition flashes through his eyes. Good, he remembers who I am. I want him to know exactly why I'm doing this to them.

"What the fuck are you doing here?" His eyes dart around the room, and his nostrils flare.

I rise to my full height, my expression unwavering as I stare him down. A small smile breaks across my face.

This is the moment I live for. The moment my prey realizes it has nowhere to run. Nowhere to hide. The predator is closing in.

God, I love what I fucking do.

I'm a few minutes early to the hotel bar, clad in my all-black tailored suit and new boots—without any drops of blood, despite the extracurricular activities that took place this afternoon.

My lips curl upward as I press my stinging knuckles against the cold glass of my drink, waiting for Veronica to show up. I don't know how much she remembers from last night. For a second, I think about whether she'll even show up at all. Trouble does follow her everywhere and I've been preoccupied all day.

But then there she is. Her eyes are more tired than usual, but they have a spark in them that hasn't been there these last few days. It's like she is revitalized. Gone is the hesitation and uncertainty I read in her eyes on previous nights. Now she emits this confidence that pulses through the entire room.

She's so fucking perfect, even more so with the new fire in her gaze. In a leather skirt, she's all legs, just like the first night I saw her. Her white shirt shows off her tanned skin, and her long blonde hair is pulled back into a sleek ponytail, showing off her neck. I want so badly to wrap my fingers around her delicate throat as I bury myself between those thighs.

The second she spots me, she smiles.

And for fuck's sake, my heart skips a beat.

Jesus, what am I getting myself into?

I slide over to make more space for her in the booth, positioning myself close enough to touch her. "I wasn't sure you'd show up after last night," I say mildly, cocking an eyebrow in question as she slides into the booth.

Her skirt lifts to expose more of her thigh, and I'm desperate to know what she's wearing underneath. I know she has to notice how I'm looking at her. She lets out a small wince, and I chuckle at her reaction.

"Do I get to know the name of my knight in shining armor?" she asks, leaning forward to rest her chin on her hand.

I wait to respond, taking in this moment completely. Savoring that her attention is on only me.

"Ronan," I finally say.

A genuine smile stretches across her face, and she extends her hand.

"Nice to meet you, Ronan. I'm Veronica." She tightly squeezes my outstretched hand.

"Veronica." Her name tastes delicious in my mouth. "I'm glad you're more—" I clear my throat before continuing. "Coherent," I say, then lift the glass to my lips.

"I can definitely say I've had better days. But, uh—from what I can remember, thank you."

She smiles shyly and glances down at her fidgeting hands in her lap before placing one on the table. I watch as she raps one of her fingers against the table, almost in a planned rhythm.

"No problem," I say softly. "Those guys were assholes." Men taking advantage of women is something I'll never put up with. I should've done much worse to those two, but they won't forget the lesson they learned.

She glances up at me, appreciation in her eyes. Once again, not an ounce of fear can be found. She seems...comfortable, like she's at ease. She notices me watching the way she taps her fingers and quickly closes her fist.

I know what intentions she came here with. I recognized them the first night I laid eyes on her. Another thing we have in common. I smirk again, knowing she's finally here with me.

23

Veronica

The next words out of his mouth are almost comical, but I'm too busy drowning in secondhand embarrassment.

"At least you puked all over the carpet and not me."

A loud groan escapes my throat, and I wish I could curl up in a hole and die right now. This beautiful stranger saw me hurl up my guts in the middle of a hotel hallway on all fours. I manage a strained smile and quickly steer the conversation to anything other than my upchuck reflex.

"You were here on Tuesday night too, right?" I ask.

"Yeah," he says, and I suddenly regret acknowledging that. I hope he doesn't think that's creepy. Despite my inner conflict, his lips turn up in a small smile at my recognition.

"I often meet clients here," he adds, and that damned smirk is still hanging on his gorgeous mouth.

I'm lost in the desire to press mine against his, to stop this need from pounding in my body.

"I thought you looked familiar," I manage to say.

My eyes are glued to his lips as my thoughts focus only on how soft they look. He must notice because he runs his tongue over his bottom lip before sliding his teeth across it. My core tightens as I raise my eyes to look back into his and realize I'm no safer up here, either. As if I could ever forget his piercing stare with those blue eyes, heavily contrasted by the rest of his dark features. I'm not sure how the hell I'm supposed to have a normal conversation with this man.

"When you were here on Tuesday, who were you with?" He tilts his head slightly, and his gaze darkens.

A shiver runs down my spine in response. I had forgotten all about who I was with when he first saw me. I drop my face as it reddens with embarrassment.

"It's a long story." My voice breaks.

He glances at his watch before returning his gaze to me.

His eyes flicker with that intensity. "Lucky for you, I've got all night, love." A small smile crosses his flawless lips, and once again, everything else in my mind vanishes.

He waves over a server before ordering another old-fashioned for him and a glass of pinot noir for me. "Eight-ounce, please," he adds.

I grin at the recognition before tensing slightly at the thought he knows that's my go-to drink here. "How—"

"You'll find I'm very observant." He bounces both eyebrows up his forehead quickly as his eyes roam the full length of my body. Then he waves his hand at me to continue with my story.

Nausea rolls in my stomach as I think about pouring my soul out to this perfect man that I hardly know. I don't want to scare him away before I even have the chance to really get to know him. I don't want to go back to the hollowness I felt before he came around. But at the same time, he watched me throw up last night, and he knows something is going on.

So, against my better judgment, I tell him everything. My husband. The affair. The busty brunette who would blow Richard in his office. How we married after only three months when I was twenty years old. How he insists on setting up dates for me. His ruthlessness and need to be in control. It all comes pouring out so easily, I feel as though the weight has finally been lifted off my chest. I pause only to take breaths or sips of my wine after it arrives.

I let out a deep exhale as my chest feels lighter. I haven't given myself the opportunity to grapple with all I've been through in the last few weeks. Tilting my head to the side, I finish with, "In his man logic, he thinks the best way for us to reconcile is for me to have sex with someone else."

Ronan's breathtaking blue eyes widen in surprise.

I let out a soft chuckle at his response, but his stare doesn't soften. His eyes remain trained on me. My face burns beneath the heat of his gaze.

At this moment, I've never wanted someone so badly. There's something undeniably captivating about him. He exudes this ominous aura, like a storm lurking beneath calm waters. I can sense he's harboring his fair share of secrets, and that's an intriguing challenge. After all, we all have secrets hidden beneath the surface.

I close my eyes and let my head fall back as I realize how pathetic he must find me. Here I am, salivating over him like a hormonal teenager.

A silent pause fills the air around us. I wouldn't be surprised if I looked back at the booth and he was gone. Hell, I'd run too if someone had just told me my absurd story.

I glance down to find him cracking into a grin. He covers his mouth, mutters an apology, then bursts into a fit of laughter. His laugh is deep and sensual.

I realize I haven't truly laughed in weeks. The sound of his laugh is infectious, and I find myself joining him.

He stretches his neck and calms himself. "I'm sorry. That's not funny." He coughs. "But fuck, what a pompous asshole your husband is."

"We agree on something," I say, raising my glass to meet his.

"I have a feeling there are a lot of things we'd agree on." His perpetually heavy eyelids drop a bit lower as he scans my body. Then his eyes spark with fascination as they rise to meet mine. "Is an affair something you want?" he asks, his tone almost a purr.

I'm not sure if it's because of the question he asked or the way he asked it, but I'm at a loss for words.

He takes my silence as his answer. "Your husband is an idiot." His tongue swipes over his bottom lip as he looks at me. "If you were mine, I'd never let anyone else touch you."

I can't help the sudden intake of air while my body tenses.

If you were mine...

His phone vibrates next to his elbow. It takes him a long time to peel his eyes off me, but when he finally does, he doesn't pick up the phone. He just glances at the name. His shoulders deflate in defeat, and a noise like a small growl escapes his throat.

"You have to go?" I ask, feeling sadness wash over me, that our night is being cut short.

"Unfortunately, it's work." He brings his eyes back to mine. "If you're free tomorrow night, I'd love to take you out for dinner."

He shuffles from the booth and extends a hand to help me to my feet. He places his arm protectively around my waist as we walk to the elevator. I can't help but feel safe in his arms.

The elevator dings with its arrival, and he turns to face me. He gently takes my face between his hands. He leans in and presses his lips to mine in a soft, tender kiss. It's sudden, but my body responds instantly, and I melt under his touch. A moan escapes my lips at the impact.

He pulls back and whispers, "Tomorrow night."

And just like that, he's gone.

I'm frozen in place as the elevator comes and goes. The only movement my body can handle is when I reach up to lightly graze my fingers across my lips. The absence of his has already taken a toll.

I shake my head and take a few steps away from the doors and lean against the lobby's wall, feeling dazed and elated at the same time. I've never felt a connection like this before. It terrifies me, but in the best way possible.

If you were mine...

I don't think I've ever wanted something so badly in my life.

My eyes are pinched shut until something deep within me begs me to open them. It feels like the temperature in the room has dropped forty degrees when I see who is walking quickly toward me. His gray eyes are bloodshot, and his face is red with fury. His shoulders are slightly hunched forward, and his footsteps are heavy.

My eyes widen with fear. How much did Richard see?

As he closes the distance between us, I see that his eyes are wild. I realize just how unpredictable he is in this moment. I can't let him get me alone. Because here in public, his image is too precious to make a scene.

I steady myself and plant my feet on the floor firmly. Let him try.

"Veronica," he spits through his teeth. "What the fuck do you think you're doing?" He grabs my forearm and yanks me over to him.

I stand taller and look him dead in the eyes. "Exactly what you told me to, Richard," I say, my voice low. "I'm seeing other people."

His jaw trembles, and I know he's biting his tongue, but only because we are in a public place.

I lean closer to his face before whispering a reply. "Get the hell out of here, Richard. Follow me and you'll fucking regret it."

Shock projects across his face—he's never known me to be so brazen. But as always, his image and reputation come first. "At least do it in private," he grumbles. "That's what we agreed to."

"*We* agreed to nothing," I say before swiftly turning and strutting to the staircase. Over my shoulder, I call out to him, "You made this decision for us, now live with it."

My feet pound against the concrete steps as I walk up to the second floor. I slow to catch my breath only when I'm sure there is no one behind me and the stairwell is silent. I enter the hallway and take the elevator up the remaining flights.

I'm pissed off but not pissed off enough to climb twenty-one flights of stairs.

24
Ronan

My frustration boils over as I struggle to keep my temper in check. The timing couldn't have been worse. If Mark is asking to meet in person, it has to be something serious. I can't afford to ignore it.

While I was off playing lover boy, shit went down.

The tires squeal as I pull into a small parking lot off the Interstate. A cheap motel looms in the distance, its neon sign flickering erratically. I shift my car into park and step out onto the black concrete.

Taking the stairs two at a time, I dismiss the grimy room entrances and any people who loiter outside. The stale smell of cigarette smoke is suffocating. No matter how many times I tried to smoke when I was younger, it never stuck, and I'm grateful for that.

The paint peels off the walls and the air hums with the buzz of pulsing lights. Room 204 is weakly lit, and there are long shadows threatening to swallow what little light there is. A sense of dread hangs over me; I know it's going to be a long night. I can't shake the feeling that it's about to get worse. I push open the worn door and quickly shut it behind me, never turning my back to face the room.

In the corner of the room, I see a red circle burn and then fade as a cigarette is inhaled. Smoke clouds and then creeps further into the room when a voice speaks in an urgent growl. "What the fuck is going on?"

It's not quite the opening I expected. I let my silence hang in the air to show my annoyance at the demand to turn up here at the last minute.

"I should be asking you that. You're the one who called me here."

"Have you seen it?" Mark says. Rising to stand, he places his cigarette back between his lips.

"Seen what?" I ask, puzzled.

Keeping the cigarette dangling from his mouth, he reaches into his pants pocket and tosses his phone over to me. There's a page pulled up on the screen, an article on the Channel 7 News website with a *Breaking News* banner plastered all over it. My eyes skim the information on the screen, unsure of why Mark is ruining my night by making sure I'm up to date on the city's current events.

Two More Bodies Found; Possible Connection to Previous Disappearances reads the headline. My eyes quickly scan the rest of the article, unsure why he felt the need to pull me from my night for this. I look up at him, my mood darkening. "What does this have to do with me?" I bark; the impatience in my tone is thick.

Mark's jaw clenches as he flexes his fingers down at his side. Rising to stand, he paces over to me while taking a deep inhale of his cigarette, then pulls it from his mouth. "It's not my mess, it's your fucking mess," he spits. "Those bodies are two of *your* kills from *my* list."

I glance down at the article and keep reading, understanding more of what I'm looking at. Further down the page, there are pictures of the victims found. I recognize them, but they look different from the last time I saw them.

More alive.

"Fuck," I yell as I slam my fist into the nearest wall, watching the weak plaster crack under my knuckles, which sting with overuse in the last twelve hours. Blood creeps through the broken skin and reopened scabs. "There's no fucking way."

I pace, thinking of a way to get this situation under control. I can't afford to get caught now. I've got too much on the line and too much at stake. There would be no worse time, in my opinion—not when I've finally found something I want.

"You better hope you're as good as you think you are," Mark grunts, crossing his arms over his chest. "If they find any fingerprints or trace a bullet back to your gun, you're fucked."

I look at him, glaring hard and seething with rage. This is my fucking city. No one interferes with me. No one.

"Don't worry," I growl, turning away from him to exit. "I'll take care of this."

"You're getting sloppy," he announces. The tension hangs between us. "No one wants a sloppy hit man."

With that, I storm out of the hotel room, feeling the anger boiling inside me.

I've left behind dozens of corpses in the past, and none have ever been found. My patterns and procedures haven't changed, so how is it possible they've found the bodies of my victims now? This is the most important aspect of doing what I do. You need to make sure someone stays gone when they're gone. No evidence and no trace. I rack my brain with possibilities, and only one makes sense.

Someone is setting me up.

25

Taylor

Six Years Earlier

O n the day our new patient is set to check in, my stomach is twisted up with anxiety. I have an irrational fear that she may recognize me. But how could she? It's been years, and I'm completely different now.

She walks into the building slowly, with an older man glued to her side. I take a moment to really look at her. It's been a while, and though she has changed, there aren't too many differences. Not a single strand of her hair is out of place, and large designer sunglasses are propped across the bridge of her nose.

Her clothes are impeccable, and her high heels delicately clack against the floor as she walks through the entrance. It looks like she's going on vacation instead of checking into a rehabilitation center.

The man, who I know is her husband, grips her arm tightly while carrying her beige duffel bag on his other shoulder. His skin is bronzed, like he's spent the last few weeks in the sun. He's dressed in a full suit, which is much too formal an outfit for today's agenda. They are every bit the rich couple you'd expect them to be, and it's almost as if they're just on a casual stroll to a local brunch restaurant in the city.

I rise to my feet and clasp my hands together as they approach. Her husband's face is stern and unforgiving. Smile lines are nowhere to be found. My eyes zero in on his companion specifically. Her steps are clumsy, but not from hesitation. I grit my teeth at this callout before exhaling a deep breath and putting my mask back on.

"Hello there, welcome," I say calmly, trying not to draw too much attention to myself or let my aggravation become noticeable. "My name is Taylor and I'll be assisting you today."

I let a warm, deceiving smile spread across my face.

I've waited too long for this moment. I won't mess it up now.

26

Veronica

S ipping on my third cup of bland hotel coffee from a paper
cup, I try to fight the exhaustion overtaking my body. Sleep
did not come easy last night. I was slightly shaken up after my
encounter with Richard, especially since the intensity of my high
with Ronan was followed by a low with my husband. Even with
the door dead-bolted and a chair placed strategically to disable the
handle, I was still fearful he would find his way into my room.

Lowering the paper cup, I rest my arms across my thighs. I
have to get out of here. I don't think I can stay in this room any
longer. I've been anxiously waiting to hear from Ronan about our
next date. There's something about how comfortable and safe I
feel with him. I know that I won't have to worry about Richard
whenever he's around. And our brief time together last night
wasn't long enough.

Leaning forward, I place my cup on the coffee table and then rest my elbows on my knees. I catch myself tapping my fingers against the table in front of me as the thoughts rattle inside my head.

A loud ring from my phone pulls my attention back to reality. To my disappointment, it's not Ronan—but luckily, it's not Richard, either.

It's his daughter.

"Hey Claire," I say into the phone. "Is everything—"

My words are halted by the noises I hear in the background. Someone is yelling, and the sounds seem panicked. I listen closely, trying to discern what I might be hearing. A moment of silence comes, and I tense.

"Claire, what's going on?"

The second I finish speaking, a bloodcurdling scream rips through the phone. It belongs to a female, and it sounds familiar.

My phone goes crashing to the floor, and I'm frantic to snatch it.

Pinning my phone closely to my ear, desperate for any sound, I find only silence, then what sounds like footsteps boom through the speaker. They're heavy and quick across the floor. There is a noise like the phone being picked up, the faint rustle of fingertips wrapping clumsily around the metal. The ragged, labored breaths echo through the phone, and each exhale is like a needle that stabs the silence.

"Claire?"

There's a pause.

"Veronica." Her breath still sounds short, irregular, and filled with emotion.

"Are you okay?" I say, panicked.

"Yeah...yeah," she says quickly before clearing her throat. "I'm okay, I'm sorry. It was just a butt-dial."

She lets out a very unconvincing laugh.

It's possibly the worst excuse she could've given me after all of that.

"Who is over there with you?" It feels like the right question to ask at this moment.

"Uh..." She hesitates before answering. "No one. I'm at Dad's."

A cold knot tightens in my stomach. She's with Richard.

"Claire," I say cautiously. I need to tread lightly here. I know what Richard is capable of, but I also need to be careful. "Did your dad hurt you?"

She pauses again before I hear a sniffle.

"No, of course not." I swear I hear tears in her voice. "I've got to go."

I hear the beep, signaling she's hung up before I have a chance to respond.

I know firsthand Richard can be a violent man. Claire mentioned he didn't know she was back, and that she didn't want him to know. Maybe he found out we met up earlier this week. There is always some kind of ongoing argument between them, but I've never seen Richard lay a hand on her, at least not since we've been married.

My stomach drops as I think of their altercations and how much worse they might be behind closed doors. Maybe this is why Claire has always been so disconnected from the world. I need to find a way to protect her while I save myself from the exact same situation.

I finally hear from Ronan a few hours after my unsettling interaction with Claire. I haven't been able to calm down, and I almost consider rescheduling with him, but after these last twenty-four hours, a distraction is more than welcome. Besides, I need to get out of this hotel room. He also sounds a bit stressed, so maybe it's a good time for both of us.

We agree to meet at a nearby sushi restaurant after I mention that I've been craving it over the last few days.

My thoughts are jumbled inside my head, and I remind myself to relax. Ronan is just a person—there is nothing to be nervous about. But my convincing is pointless. Everything about this man sets me on edge. I spend the entire time getting ready, reminiscing on the feel of his lips against mine. I think about how badly I want them all over the rest of my body and how much I want to run my own fingers through his hair.

I groan, dropping my face into my hands. I have an insatiable thirst for this man. I have no idea how I'm going to sit across the table from him and ignore my desire to pounce on him.

I show up at the restaurant five minutes early, and I'm pleasantly surprised to see him already seated, waiting for me. His blue eyes pierce me. I'm not sure I'll ever get used to the way they look at me. He has such an intensity in his eyes that my body tightens under his gaze.

He looks ridiculously handsome. He's wearing a black shirt that hangs perfectly on his broad chest and shoulders, and I see the tops of his black jeans, which look like they were made for him. And he has those eyes. They're practically shining against the dark backdrop of his attire.

Is his entire wardrobe only black?

He's already ordered a bottle of pinot noir for the table and poured me a glass.

One side of his mouth tilts up as he takes me in, eyes roving over me.

"Hey," I say weakly, forcing myself to ignore the flutter I feel in my stomach at the sight of him.

"First things first," he says, and I freeze, slightly panicked at what he's about to say.

He picks up his cell phone and holds down the side button until I see the "slide to power off" option. His fingers swipe across the screen effortlessly, and he returns it to his pocket without breaking eye contact.

"No distractions or early departures tonight, I promise."

We smile at each other, and a sudden wave of dizziness descends over me. He makes my knees weak, and I'm sitting down. Everything that has happened over the last week simply disappears when I'm around him. The crackling sensation remains and burns between us.

"I know you said you were starving," he says, placing his forearms on the table. His sleeves are folded up, and I'm already gawking at his arms. "So, I got here a little early to order some wine and appetizers."

"Thank you." I smile. Jesus, everything about this man is perfect. I'm completely out of my league. I take a big sip of the glass of red wine already poured for me.

He cocks his head slightly and his eyes narrow. "You seem a bit tense," he says.

My body shrinks in disappointment. I had hoped I was concealing all my stress better, since the last thing I want him to think is that I don't want to be here. I want to shove everything into a mental closet and lock the door for the next few hours. There is nowhere else I want to be, physically or mentally. "Yeah, I'm sorry, it's been a really weird day." I let out a sigh. I can't stop thinking about that horrible phone call from Claire.

Ronan reaches across the table and places his hand on top of mine. The contact startles me before I relax into it. The skin on his hand is rough and soft at the same time, and I could've sworn I felt a spark like electricity course through my body when he touched me. Glancing up, I look into his eyes and see sympathy, and my breath hitches in my lungs.

"My day hasn't been so great, either," he says. "How about we both put everything to the side and appreciate this time together?"

Butterflies glide in my stomach at these words. He seems to be a tall, dark, and handsome stranger with a kind heart, but there is still a cloud of darkness that encircles him. Clearing my throat, I offer him a small smile and nod. If he's willing to put everything aside for me tonight, then I can absolutely do the same.

I straighten in the booth and pick up my chopsticks to grab a dumpling before dipping it in soy sauce and plopping it into my mouth. He follows suit, never taking his eyes off me for more than a few seconds. Groaning in appreciation, I close my eyes and enjoy the deliciousness. Then I open them again to find him watching me intently.

"So, tell me a little more about yourself?" My cheeks instantly redden at how silly the words feel coming from my mouth. It's been too long since I've been on a first date.

He snorts a laugh. "Oh no, don't tell me I've already bored you enough that you have to resort to small talk?"

I smile and glance down at my hands. It must be obvious to him that I'm feeling nervous. "I just want to know everything about you."

His eyes widen slightly at the mention of "everything."

"What do you do for work?" I ask, placing my chin in my open palm as my elbow rests on the table. "I was wondering about it, since you had to rush out last night."

He clears his throat and adjusts slightly in his seat. "It's complicated," he says.

This makes my eyebrows rise in question. "It's complicated, huh?"

He braces his elbows on the table and leans forward. Before speaking again, he takes a few quick glances around the table. "Let's just say I take care of people for other people."

I tilt my head slightly to the side in question. "So, you're like, what? A hit man?"

I burst out laughing until I notice his face remains statue-like.

He doesn't crack a smile.

"Oh, shit. I'm—um, I'm sorry."

His face still doesn't change until a huff of laughter falls out of his mouth.

"Let's say that I'm more of a fixer."

A smile pulls at the corners of his mouth.

"Fixer? Like Olivia Pope?"

His jaw clamps shut, his eyes widen, and he sits up straighter. "You're comparing me to *Scandal*?"

My mouth drops open at the fact that he knows who Olivia Pope is. It's hard to imagine him relaxing on a couch and bingeing TV. I find my composure and, grinning, say, "Yeah, and it's obviously a compliment to be called Olivia Pope. She's a bad bitch. But you're telling me that you watch *Scandal*?"

He scoffs and looks up at me through his eyelashes. "Are you shocked I have hobbies that include TV shows?"

"I mean, I can't lie and say I'm not surprised. I just didn't think it was your speed."

His facial expression is amused. "But yeah, I deal with some heavy shit, and some fucked-up people."

There is a casual flicker in his eyes as he dissects my reaction to his words. He wants to see how I respond. His smile, though disarmingly charming, holds an unsettling edge. I purse my lips, not really knowing what to say. What is he telling me? A chilling thought creeps over me like a shroud of dread—what if my joke wasn't a joke?

I had a feeling Ronan was dangerous, but I have no idea how dangerous.

It's not just in his piercing gaze—I knew there was something a little more sinister lurking beneath the surface.

We fall silent for a moment, and the air seems to thicken with ominous tension, as if warning of the danger lying between the two of us. Now I suspect that I'm on a date with someone who could be truly dangerous.

So why am I so turned on?

And why do I want to know if my suspicions are true?

"I've always been fascinated with death," I say, and for a moment, I can't believe I said it aloud—this thing I've never admitted to someone else—but I want him to know he can trust me with his truth.

"Seems we have more in common than I thought." He smirks at me, and his eyelids grow heavier.

He is right about that.

I know what I'm about to say is risky. Normally, I might stay quiet, let the moment pass and pretend that my curiosity isn't eating me alive. But not this time. This time, I want the truth, not just for answers, but to show him that he is safe with me. That his darkness doesn't scare me. I can carry his secrets.

I just need to know if he can carry mine too.

"Ronan," I say, my voice is low but steady. "You can be honest with me. You can trust me."

He doesn't look away from my stare. "Is that right?"

Ronan sighs and something unreadable passes between us—something sharp and flickering just under the surface. An understanding between two people who have too much to hide.

"You want honesty?" he asks.

I take a breath, then swallow, hoping it hides the shake in my voice.

"I want *you*, Ronan. But not if you keep making me guess who I'm sitting across from."

If I'm asking for honesty, it's only fair I offer it in return.

He looks down at his hands before answering.

"I don't... do normal things. For work," he said slowly. "Not anymore."

"What does that mean?" He's still not being completely honest with me.

"It means I don't sit in meetings. I don't wear a tie. And when someone calls, I go where I'm told. I don't ask questions. I just finish what I started."

I study him as I try to understand the puzzle pieces he hopes I'll put together.

"Are you a—" I clear my throat before dropping my voice to a whisper. "A *killer*?"

He is silent for a beat too long.

"I don't like that word."

"But it fits?"

He doesn't answer. He only reaches for his wine glass before taking a long, slow sip. When he sets it down, he says, "If you walk away now, I'll understand."

I don't move.

Instead, I whisper, "I'm still here."

And that was the scariest part.

For a moment, neither of us speaks. The weight of our discussion sits between us like a third guest. Just as I'm afraid I've pushed him too far, he cracks a smile, and I know I've done the right thing.

"I should probably also warn you," he says, finally breaking the silence. "I'm also terrible at sharing food."

I let out a surprised laugh, the pressure in my chest cracking open just enough to breathe. "Oh really? Now that one might actually be a deal-breaker."

"Guess we'll have to negotiate," he says, nudging his plate towards me.

I pick up my chopsticks and pluck a piece of sushi from his plate, popping it into my mouth with a grin, playful and unbothered. A bit of avocado lingers on my lip, and I swipe it away with my tongue.

I see it and I can *feel* it. The way his gaze intensifies on my mouth, like his brain short-circuits just looking at me. His fingers tighten around his glass, and he gives a quick, breathy laugh. Ronan clears his throat and tries to recover. But I saw the flush rising along his neck, just under the collar of his shirt.

"Sorry, what were you saying?" he asks, even though I haven't spoken.

I smile, letting the silence stretch a little, just to watch him squirm.

He is flustered.

And it is kind of adorable.

"Do you have any exes I should be worried about?" I tease, happy to keep things lighter between us.

To my surprise, he doesn't return my smile. "There is absolutely no one who could compare to you."

Now his tongue dances along his bottom lip.

I shift slightly in my seat and blink frantically, dropping my eyes to my lap.

He cocks his head to the side as if he's studying me, unaware of the effect his words have on me. "Why do you do that?" he asks. His voice is stern and jarring.

"Do what?" I manage to squeeze it out. His stare is suffocating, and I can't catch my breath when he's looking at me like that.

"When I compliment you, it's like you're trying to disappear."

"I'm not used to it, I guess," I respond sheepishly, dropping my eyes to my lap. I'm even more embarrassed by the fact that I'm stumbling over my words.

Grow the fuck up, Veronica. You're embarrassing yourself.

"Look at me." His voice is rough and low.

My face jolts back up to face him, attentively.

"When did you see him last?"

"Um—what?"

"Richard. When did you see him last?"

The mention of Richard catches me off guard.

Ronan's chest rises and falls with a deep inhale. "When you're around him, I can tell that it throws you off. You're not quite like yourself. You said you had a bad day. Does that mean you saw him?"

My throat bobs with a swallow. How can this man already read me so completely?

"He was at the hotel last night," I say quietly.

Ronan's nostrils flare, and his eyes widen. The lights in the restaurant reflect off his onyx pupils. "Last night?" His tone makes me flinch. "After we saw each other?"

"I'm not sure how much he saw, but he approached me right after you left. I barely gave him the chance to speak, but I know he was mad. He must have seen us together."

Ronan's hands, previously flat on the table, curl into tight fists.

"He wants me to go on dates—that was the whole purpose of this setup," I say, trying to de-escalate the situation.

"But I'm not someone he chose for you?"

I shake my head, and my hair falls over my shoulders. The change in my appearance has a visceral effect on him. He tilts his head down, and he peers up through his eyebrows at me. I see his throat bob with a sudden swallow. My lips part and I suck in a breath of air.

"What if I told you that I don't give a shit about him and what he wants?" he says through his teeth.

The air seems to evaporate entirely, and I can't pull in enough air to catch my breath again. I'm barely holding it together at this point, and I all but fall apart when he speaks again.

"Veronica, I only want you."

27

Ronan

Luck is not something I usually care to think about, but this moment makes me reconsider. The woman I haven't been able to get off my mind has a piece-of-shit husband who cheated on her, and now he's basically shoving her into my arms.

I'm torn between wanting to beat the shit out of him or give him a hug. But after he approached her last night, I'm inclined to go for the former.

She audibly swallows before looking down, not even daring to look at me after what I just said. Emotions play across her face. I reach across the table and grip her hand again. She looks up at my touch, and I resist the urge to lean across the table and press my lips against hers again. The skin on my hand has been tingling since I touched it earlier. I'm aching to touch her more, to touch her everywhere.

I'm tired of waiting around. I need her to know how I feel about her.

"The only person I'm concerned about is you," I say, keeping my eyes locked on hers, "and what you want."

She parts her lips again with a sudden inhale. "I don't know. This all feels ridiculous, and I feel pathetic."

I place my elbows on the table and lean closer to her. "I'll ask you again, what do you want?" My tone is harsher than I intend, but I feel like I'm going to have to rip honesty out of her. I can't sit here and deny any longer how badly I want her. I can't play games with this woman, and I won't let her husband continue to get in my way.

The silence hangs heavy. There it is again, that sadness in her eyes. It makes sense now. She's losing herself and needs someone to help her find her way back.

Beyond that, her eyes still hold on to something else. Something cold and dark. It's something familiar, almost like it's calling out to me.

I narrow my eyes at her, and she keeps her eyes down on her fingers, wrapped around her wine glass. She raps her fingers again in a deliberate pattern.

She turns to look at me slowly. Her eyebrows lower slightly in question.

I clear my throat before speaking again. She's not much of a talker. We'll have to work on that.

"I have no idea who your husband is and, quite frankly, I couldn't give a fuck less who he is."

I know exactly who Richard Sullivan is, but I don't intend to let her know that. I know it's shitty of me to lie to her, but it's true that he means nothing to me. I can't run the risk of her thinking this was all a setup. I can't be just another person who is trying to get to Richard through her.

No, I found her by chance before I knew who she was, and now she's all that matters.

A slight smile of defiance curls on her red lips. The overwhelming need to crash into those full lips returns. I want to make a mess of her lipstick and see my cock moving in and out of her mouth. I crave the sight of the red lipstick she loves to wear, marking my skin.

"So, tell me, Veronica...What. Do. You. Want?" I pause between each word.

Her throat bobs again with the motion of a sudden swallow, drawing my eyes there. I think about sinking my teeth into the shallow area between her neck and her shoulder and marking what's mine.

"You," she says faintly, her voice barely above a whisper.

She said it. She finally admitted what I've been waiting for her to say. Every doubt I've been harboring dissolves in an instant with only one word from her lips.

She jumps at the deep groan that escapes my throat. My jaw clenches as a dark, possessive thrill surges through my veins. I've craved this moment with an intensity that borders on madness. Now that she's confessed her desire for me, I feel the primal need to claim and protect her.

Every fiber of my being wants to ensure she'll always belong to me, that no one else will ever come close to touching what is now undeniably mine. A fire burns in me, and I make a silent vow to guard her with everything I have, no matter the cost.

She chose me.

I straighten swiftly, offering her a reassuring smile before rolling my tongue over my lower lip.

Her eyes shine with curiosity, and she lets out the breath that was expanding her chest.

"Good. Then it's settled. Let's go," I say.

28
Veronica

My body vibrates with nervous anticipation, and excitement buzzes beneath my skin. Everything is push-and-pull with this man. Parts of me are screaming that I should keep my distance, but the rest of me is chasing after him. He's like a drug I haven't even tried yet.

I haven't even known him for long, but I know I'm not making up that there is something between us, an undeniable magnetic pull. My heart races at the connection that has been building since we locked eyes on Tuesday, and the thought of us finally seeing what this means.

I wet my lips as he waits for my response about leaving. His perpetually hazy blue eyes stay trained on me. The truth is, I've never wanted anything more in my entire life. I'm hyperaware of

NICOLE J. OWENS

the way he's watching my mouth. My mind is swirling with the possibilities.

This may be a bad idea...

Unable to find my voice, I give a quick nod, letting him know I agree.

But I really, really don't care. The only thing that matters now is Ronan.

We stare into each other's eyes, and the world around us blurs. He raises his hand to signal our server for the check, his eyes never leaving mine, and my body shivers underneath their intensity. He pulls out his wallet and hands a black card to the server without glancing at the receipt.

I guess being a fixer can be quite lucrative.

He slides out of the booth with ease and approaches my side of the table. He reaches for my hand, and I take his without hesitation. The fiery sensation as our skin collides is even more intense than earlier this evening. His grip is tight and strong.

He glances down at me before speaking, taking his time to let his eyes climb back up to mine. He's drinking me in, and my thighs instinctively clench together as the spot between them aches for his touch.

"My place, though. I don't want you back at the hotel if he is showing up unannounced." The side of his lip curves upward, and he tugs me to stand.

We walk out of the restaurant in silence. The only sounds permeating through the parking lot are my heels clicking and the

184

soft thud of his steps. My legs are weak, but against all odds, I'm moving confidently, matching his stride.

I follow him as he leads us to his car. It's all black, and I can't say I'm surprised. Everything about this man is dark and ominous. Sexy. Everything about him is breathtakingly sexy. He opens the passenger door for me, and I slide into the seat. The cool leather licks the back of my thighs, and I tremble slightly. The slightly chilled seat is a stark contrast to the heat radiating from my body.

The air inside his car is crackling with unspoken desire, and I steal glances at him as my heart pounds in rhythm with the soft hum of his engine. After pressing the button to start his car and shifting the car into drive, he reaches out and grips my thigh tightly.

The quick journey feels like an eternity with him touching me; the impact of our flesh burns, and my leg twitches involuntarily. I long to have his hands press into the skin of my hips, down my thighs, and over my ass.

He slows before parking on the street in front of a row of contemporary brick buildings. He steps out of the car quickly and opens the passenger door for me. When he extends a hand to help me from the seat, I rise to meet him.

He towers above me, his blue eyes continuing their relentless pursuit, searching for something in mine. I suck in a quick breath as his eyes dip to watch my lips. The desire swirls low in my stomach, and at this point, I'm afraid I might explode with lust.

He cups my face with both hands and tilts my chin up to him before pulling me in for a kiss. It starts slowly, like we're getting to know each other. He runs his tongue along mine in an invitation, and I respond by massaging his tongue with my own. He releases a groan against my mouth as one hand slips down to my lower back to press me deeper into him. I raise up onto the toes of my shoes, desperately trying to get closer to him.

I can feel him smiling on my lips before he pulls back.

"I've wanted to do that since you walked into the restaurant tonight. I couldn't help myself anymore."

I chuckle into my hand, trying to hide the blush in my cheeks. From the outside, this man seems so dangerous, closed off to the rest of the world. How is it that he makes me feel so safe?

He grabs my hand and turns to lead me to a welcoming house with large windows. He pulls his keys swiftly from his pocket and it takes only a second before a key fits the lock and the front door swings open.

The ground level boasts an open floor plan with high ceilings and walnut hardwood floors. The interior design is minimal and chic. Most surprising of all, it's spotless.

I wasn't expecting a "hit man fixer" to live in a townhouse, especially one this clean and chic.

Walking farther into his house, we end up in the kitchen. It's all white and pristine. Functional, yet stylish; kitchen appliances adorn the counter tops. On the walls are open shelves that hold pots, pans, and glasses. He drops his keys on the counter and walks to his bar to pour us both a glass of red wine.

After handing me a glass, he leans against the counter with his arms across his chest, his gaze still burrowing into me. He takes a sip from his glass before returning both arms to his chest. His eyes darken as his fingers press hard enough into his biceps to leave an indentation.

I take a large gulp of the wine and let the burning sensation travel through my body. I look back at Ronan, our eyes meeting again for what feels like the billionth time this evening.

No matter how many times it happens, I still feel my knees get weak.

The air is thick with anticipation. Pure hunger radiates between the two of us.

"Do you do a lot of cooking in this kitchen?"

He lets out a small laugh. "I think you'd be surprised what a good cook I am."

"Oh, really?" I ask, playfully. "Care to show some of your skills?"

He straightens suddenly, putting the glass of wine on the counter behind him before dropping his hands. He stalks toward me, placing his hands on either side of my hips. He leans in, and his breath is warm against my cheek as he crowds me against the kitchen countertop. His eyes pin me with a smoldering intensity, a hungry gaze that seems to devour me.

"Veronica, there is only one meal I'm interested in tonight."

29

Ronan

My lips crash down onto hers again, and, unlike our kiss outside the house, this one is less timid. It's more teeth. More primal. More need. We press our bodies into one another as our kisses deepen. Our breaths are heavy and intertwined, and I inhale her sweet scent.

More. I need more of her.

I pull away, and my eyes comb over every inch of her, pausing on the places I'm aching to touch. I grab her hand and lead her in the direction of my living room, where I guide her to the couch. She sits down nervously while I stand before her, taking her in.

"The moment I saw you at the bar on Tuesday, I knew I had to have you."

Her eyes jump up to meet mine, and I raise an eyebrow before dragging my eyes back down her body. She audibly swallows and adjusts on the couch as I kneel before her. Placing my hands on her calves, I slowly palm my way to her thighs, her hips, her waist, and her rib cage.

"I'm going to worship every single inch of you."

A gasp leaves her lips as I rise to my feet and look down at her. What a pretty sight she is, looking up at me, eyes wide and pleading. Sliding next to her, I see her breasts rise and fall against her tight white shirt. I rub my palm down her arm before pushing it back up and into her hair at the base of her scalp. Her skin prickles beneath my touch, and she trembles. She nods slightly, her way of giving silent approval to keep going.

Tucking her blonde hair behind her ear, I lean forward to kiss her again. I run my hands down her back and under her. Cupping her ass, I pull her up in a swift motion to straddle me. She lets out a light gasp at the sudden movement but makes no move to pull away. She settles into my lap, spreading her knees wider to lower herself onto me.

I lick the space between her neck and her collarbone, the same spot I envisioned sinking my teeth into so many times. I use my tongue to trace my way back up to her ear; my teeth graze across her neck before biting down gently. She lets out a breathy moan and wraps her arms around my neck, tugging me closer to her.

I glance down, looking at the light teeth marks I left on her, and smile at the sight. I'm marking my territory, claiming what belongs to me.

Mine.

My hands continue to grip her ass as I pulse her body up and down lightly, mimicking the motions of how it'd feel if she were riding my cock. The friction between us builds, and she groans again and bucks her hips before wrapping her arms more tightly around my throat. Tucking her face into my shoulder, she turns her head to kiss my neck. Subtle noises press against my throat along with her lips.

The noises escaping her mouth are making me feral. But I won't take it too far tonight; I'll ease her into this. Make her beg for more. I can't risk her regretting this or regretting me. But it's impossible to bat away the image of her spread wide open for me while I pound into her.

I pull her back to look at her face. She's panting, and there's a slight beg in her eyes. She needs more.

"Take off your shirt," I growl.

She nods eagerly as she grips the hem of her shirt before hoisting the white fabric over her head. A lacy white bra lies underneath, in stark contrast to my all-black attire.

An angel to my devil.

Her skin is flawless, an untouched canvas, and it radiates a slight glow from the anticipation and arousal. I reach behind her to unsnap the last piece of clothing that's concealing her chest from me.

I slide the straps off her shoulders one by one and then toss it to the floor.

Hesitation clouds her eyes, and I know she is feeling vulnerable. She's nervous to be this bare in front of someone she barely knows. Her chest folds slightly, as if she's trying to hide. It must be a habit for her to try to mask her naked body.

Not this bad habit again.

"No." My voice is stern. "I want to see you."

She straightens her back and locks eyes with mine. I watch as her breasts rise and fall with each breath she takes. They're supple and perfect. Her light pink nipples pebble underneath my gaze. I grip her shoulders and run my palms down the side of her body before resting on her waist as I look at this perfect fucking woman.

Her pupils dilate with lust, and I know she's not second-guessing what's happening anymore. I grab one of her breasts, and guide her nipple into my mouth. The collision causes a deep groan to escape her lips.

I lap and suck at her nipple, occasionally grazing my teeth down it. She writhes against me, pushing her hands through my hair, lowering herself even deeper onto my hard cock.

I pull away to look at her, and she hisses before I place my mouth back on its resting place, continuing the subtle movements with my tongue. She's craving more. Her arousal is building, and this single point of touch isn't enough for her.

That's the purpose of tonight. Give her only a fraction of pleasure and leave her begging for more of me. I want her to not be able to live without me, like I don't want to live without her.

I grin before biting her nipples, and she yelps with pleasure at the brief pain. I push her to stand in front of me. She looks confused and upset at the sudden loss of contact between my body and hers. I turn her around so that she's facing away from me. Spreading my legs, I pull her down between them. Her round ass presses against my straining dick. She turns her head over her shoulder, glancing back at me.

"Once you say yes to me, there is no one else," I tell her.

She nods and lifts her hips as I grab onto the waistband and peel her skirt down. She's wearing matching white-lace panties. This detail makes me smile as I realize she met me with the same intentions tonight.

She tries to reach for her underwear and pull it down, but I grab her wrists.

"Those stay on tonight."

She huffs out of frustration before settling back down on the couch. She's obedient and trusting, I'll give her that.

She keeps her eyes down, watching my hands as they rest on her bare legs. She hasn't yet noticed the full-length mirror I positioned us in front of. I'm going to watch every facial expression she makes while she comes.

"Say yes," I whisper into her ear. Sealing the statement with a kiss, I remind her of our agreement. I pry her legs open, and she arches her back into me. "Say it's only me."

"Yes," she moans. "Yes, it's only you."

My lips curl into a devious smile.

"Good girl. Now let's see how wet you are for me," I mutter into her neck as one hand smooths down her stomach to slip beneath her panties. My other hand finds one of her breasts.

She inhales sharply as my hand drops lower, inching closer to her center. I roll her nipple between my middle finger and thumb as I kiss and lick her shoulder.

My fingers sink lower until they find what they've been searching for. Just as I hoped, she's already drenched.

"Fuck, baby," I hiss. "You're soaked."

She spreads her legs further as I coat a finger in her arousal.

"So responsive for me." I chuckle. "Such a good girl."

Two of my fingers find her center and lightly trace circles there before increasing their speed. Her hips buck back into mine and I'm sure she can feel that I'm rock hard behind her. My cock is straining against my jeans. It's uncomfortable but she won't get that. Not tonight, at least.

My hand moves from her breast to her chin, lifting it slowly to meet my gaze in the mirror. She stiffens, shocked at the sight of her body on full display. I'm fully dressed and towering behind her, one hand cupping her chin to force her to look at herself. My other hand moves underneath her lace panties.

Her skin is flushed, and her green eyes are wild. Her long, lean legs are pressed wide open against my black jeans.

"Look at how perfect you are," I growl.

Her face reddens further as she stares at us. Her lips part and her breaths are raspy. She watches the mirror intently as my other hand continues to rub circles over her clit.

"Now be my good girl and watch yourself come."

My hand dips from her chin down to the outside of her panties. I slide the lace to the side while I keep massaging her clit with my other hand. I run my fingers up her, feeling just how wet she is. Seeing her spread wide for me in the mirror is almost enough for me to lose all control.

Unable to deny myself anymore, I quickly pull the fingers stroking her arousal and lick the wetness from my fingers. It's the only taste of her I'll get tonight.

She gasps as she watches, but she never lets her eyes leave mine. Her eyelids hang heavy from pleasure.

"You taste even sweeter than I imagined."

Her eyes widen slightly, still glued to me.

"Ronan, please," she breathes. "Please, I want to come."

Once I've licked her clean from my fingers, I trail my hand down her leg before it retreats back to her pussy, then I slide two fingers inside.

"So pretty when you beg."

Rhythmically, I rub her clit with one hand while I use my other to dip my fingers in and out of her, picking up the pace as I continue.

She grinds against me, pushing her backside into me further. I growl in her ear, and that seems to drive her wild. Lost in the feeling, she dips her head back and closes her eyes.

I pull my hands away from her and purr into her ear, "What did I say?"

She jerks up and returns her gaze to the mirror. She won't make that mistake again.

My hands find her again, and she starts gasping before I lean close to her ear.

"Don't come until I tell you to," I whisper.

She nods at these words, eyes wide and frantic. She's close and isn't sure how long she'll have to hold off.

She wiggles against me, holding her breath to calm herself. She's so obedient and I already want to give her everything.

I trail kisses across her shoulder until I'm closer to her ear. Picking up my pace, I let out a hot breath before whispering, "Come for me."

That's all it takes to send her shattering. She lets out a squeal while her clit throbs against my hand as I press my palm against her. My fingers inside her are slowing but not stopping. I ride out her orgasm with her, feeling her muscles contract around my fingers as she lets out continued sounds of ecstasy.

When she finally stills, I keep one hand palmed close against her pussy, applying pressure to her sensitive clit with the heel of my hand. I place my other hand across her throat, squeezing lightly.

She moans with her eyes closed and head tilted back; I let her linger and enjoy the aftermath, as she basks in her pleasure.

When she comes to, her eyes are still heavy with arousal. Who knows how long it's been since she's had an orgasm?

She looks at me in the mirror. For the first time, her eyes no longer hold that tight, guarded look. Instead, they seem relaxed, almost serene. A smile sits across her full lips.

I don't see an ounce of fear reflecting back at me in her eyes.

"Tonight is all about you," I mutter into her cheek as her brow furrows. "Seeing you get off is enough for me."

I smirk at her reflection.

She only looks at me in the mirror, panting and trying to catch her breath.

"Open your legs wider, love," I breathe into her ear. "I want to see you come again."

30

Veronica

A s I stroll down the street, the warm fall breeze blows across my face. I reveled in a slow morning at Ronan's place, all by myself. Shortly after I woke, the memories came darting to the front of my mind. My body was in a tangled mess of sheets, my bra still missing. My lips were chapped from the invasion of Ronan's stubble, leaving them raw.

I spent the majority of the morning looking at the other side of the bed with disappointment at the fact that it was empty, only a note on top of the pillow in place of the gorgeous man I had hoped to find sleeping peacefully next to me.

Had things to take care of. Stay as long as you like.

-R

I can't remember the last time I've felt that good, and all he used were his hands. I chew on my bottom lip, my skin tingling as I recount all the places he touched me. He was thorough and desperate for my release. My release only.

There's something about him, something drawing me to him like a moth to a flame. Maybe it's the supposed danger or the thrill of this chase. It's been years since I've felt desired. The feeling of someone like Ronan wanting me is intoxicating.

I took my time leaving in hopes that he would return, and we could continue where we left off last night. Unfortunately, that didn't happen. I sent him a quick text message to let him know I was heading out, but I haven't heard anything since.

After one night, I'm already feeling desperate. I wonder how many other women feel this way about Ronan. It's unhealthy, really. I barely know him.

Knowing that his place isn't too terribly far from the hotel, I opted to walk back instead of calling for a car. It's a nice day and I know I'll appreciate the breath of fresh air. Lucky for me, the outfit I wore last night seems to fit in among the other strollers today, plus Ronan's scent lingers on me, and I can't get enough of it. It reminds me that last night was real.

There is a small farmer's market out on the street today, with dozens of different vendors. The air is saturated with scents of blooming jasmine and freshly baked bread. The stands are lined with trinkets and handmade crafts, the sellers standing proudly behind them with large grins on their faces. There are distant murmurs of laughter and people speaking in hushed tones. My footsteps are light, and the feeling of peace consumes me. I act half interested in the items being sold; my mind keeps going back to Ronan and last night.

I'm pulled from my daydream when a familiar face comes into view. Standing about twenty feet away from me among the busy crowd is Claire. Her eyes focus on something straight ahead of her while she stands on the sidewalk, motionless. All the things I put away last night to focus only on Ronan come crashing back: The horrible phone call with Claire and the confrontation with Richard from the night before.

"Claire!" I call out, hoping she can hear me. I desperately need to talk to her and make sure she's all right after that call.

She doesn't seem to hear my voice as her eyes remain trained on something, like an animal watching its prey. I call her name again, but it still doesn't rattle her focus. The crowd parts around her and continues scattering.

It doesn't take me long to catch up to her. My hand falls on her arm to grab her attention. She jerks in my direction, ripping her arm away from my touch. It's then I get a full glimpse of her face instead of only her side profile. The eye previously hidden from my view is bruised and swollen, a colorful detail among her otherwise darkened features. The purple shades near her gray eye look like an impending storm overhead. Her gray eyes dart back and forth as if she's surprised to see me here and looking for a way to quickly exit.

"Claire, what happened?" I say, breathlessly. Her eyes drop to her feet, and her cheeks redden. "Oh my God, are you okay? What happened?"

Her throat bobs with a sudden swallow as her eyes rise back up to meet mine.

"Yeah, I'm okay. Really, it's nothing."

She reaches into her purse to grab a pair of large sunglasses to place on her face.

"Claire, please be honest with me," I plead. "Did Richard do that to you?"

Her mouth drops open slightly, no doubt shocked at my direct question.

"Veronica, please," she rasps. "Just let it go, please."

I stare at her as tears begin to pool in my eyes. I can't help her if she won't let me.

"I promise, I'm okay," she adds.

My stomach flips at her indirect answer to my question. My hands vibrate against my sides as my anger starts bubbling over at the realization that I'm not the only one who is a victim of his. A tear slips from my eye and rolls down my cheek as her eyes behind her sunglasses track it.

I grip her wrist tightly and pull her closer to me. I speak in a hushed tone: "Claire, you need to talk to me. I can help you."

She rips her wrist away from me and takes a few quick steps backward. "I don't *need* your help, Veronica." Turning to walk away in the opposite direction, she quickly disappears into the crowd.

"Claire!"

I hurry in the same direction she goes, shouting her name. My head anxiously spins in different directions as I attempt to keep my eyes pinned on her before I lose sight of her.

Shit, shit, shit.

I try to close the distance between us, frantically chasing after her. I continue shouting her name, but I only grab the attention of onlookers. I've almost reached her when someone's shoulder strikes mine, and the intensity of our collision makes me lose my breath. I watch over the person's shoulder as Claire discreetly disappears from my line of sight.

I exhale a breath of frustration, knowing I may never get another opportunity to speak so openly with Claire again. My shoulders sag with disappointment.

Reverting my attention to the other person I collided with, I see that she is fumbling with items that fell to the ground. I bend down to help collect her things from the sidewalk, and both of our faces drop toward the small pile.

"I'm so sorry."

Then I pause as she looks up to face me. I take in the familiar face and blink my eyes rapidly to try to focus.

"Oh, Miranda," I say.

It's the bartender from the hotel.

She furrows her brow in question, and I remember how many faces she must see on any given day.

I lightly shake my head with embarrassment, shifting my weight between my two feet, and remain kneeling to match her view. "I'm staying at the Addingham Hotel and have been down at the bar the last few nights."

She narrows her eyes as she analyzes my face and stands up slowly. She nods her head just as she's about to step away, but then freezes suddenly.

"Oh, yeah," she says. "I do remember you."

I huff a laugh. "Sorry, I know you probably see people come and go every day. I shouldn't have expected you to immediately recognize me."

She looks uncomfortable, so I try to offer her a small smile. She steps closer to me before speaking in a tone so low, I can hardly make out her words.

Her eyes dance around like she's looking for someone behind me. She leans in closer, and her voice is hushed. "Listen, I can't right now, but I need to talk to you."

"You need to talk to me?" My face flushes with embarrassment, assuming she wants to talk to me about the things she's seen at the bar the last few nights. Miranda was there each night I was at the bar. The first time with Jacob. The next, I was hammered and left the bar with two guys. Then, the next, I was with Ronan.

Probably not a very good look for me.

"I saw who you were with the other night."

"I'm so embarrassed," I say, trying to keep my voice steady and relaxed. "Those two guys tried to take advantage of me in my drunken stupor—I won't be seeing them again."

She shakes her head and then looks over both of my shoulders.

"No," she says sharply. "Not those two guys."

I tilt my head in question, and a shiver runs down my spine when I realize who she might be referring to.

Ronan?

"Miranda, what do you mean—"

"But seriously, not here." Her voice lowers even further. "Come by the bar tonight and I'll explain. I get off at midnight. Be careful."

These are Miranda's parting words as she heads in the direction of the hotel. My heart sinks in my chest as I watch her walk away from me. Feeling numb, I stand there, hoping my thoughts will sort themselves out.

Is she talking about Ronan?

I know this man is dangerous to those around him, but he would never hurt me. Would he? Has her obsession truly made her blind to her own safety?

My heartbeat quickens as I sense the overwhelming feeling of someone's eyes glued to me. I pull my cardigan a bit tighter on my shoulders as a chill runs through my body, despite the warm weather.

31

Ronan

I watch Veronica disappear, and my eyes flip to Miranda, trying to decipher the tense look on her face. The way she spoke to Veronica seemed so rushed, like she was afraid someone might spot them together.

Miranda's pace quickens as she crosses the street, narrowly missing a red Porsche cruising by. The driver slams on the brakes and blows their horn in response. Miranda does not even hesitate and begins to move at a slight jog.

It's easy for me to catch up to her. After about seven blocks, she anxiously checks over both shoulders before slowing her pace. She stops, resting a hand on a brick wall while trying to catch her breath. I quietly approach her and grab her wrist, pinning her hand to the wall.

She sucks in a sharp intake of breath. "Please," she lets out, tears filling the bottom of her eyes. "I didn't do anything."

"What did you say to her?" I bite.

"Leave her alone," she pants, still unable to catch her breath. "Seriously, leave her out of this."

"Leave her out of what?" I ask as I step in front of her, my eyes boring into hers.

Her face is flushed, and her eyes are wide while beads of sweat prick her hairline. When she recognizes me, she relaxes and leans against the wall further.

"Jesus, Ronan," she says. "You scared the shit out of me."

"Who did you think I was?"

"I thought—" She pauses and snaps her mouth shut, realizing she is saying too much.

My face tilts down in question, quietly urging her to continue.

She shakes her head lightly, and I realize she will not budge on finishing that sentence. "Trust me, Ronan. I'm doing you both a favor. Stay away from her."

She rips her wrist from my grasp and turns to walk away.

She turns her head over her shoulder to look back at me before saying, "You should've never gotten involved."

I stand still, my feet glued to the concrete. I should chase after her, but I have enough sense to know she won't say anything else—nothing beyond what she's already said. I've known Miranda for years, but only because of my frequent visits to the hotel bar to do business.

I'm nervous about what she said to Veronica, and I don't know why she was talking about doing me a favor. Miranda and I were never close, but I expect she knows more about me than she's willing to let on.

I try calling Veronica, but it goes straight to voicemail. "Fuck," I yell as I punch my fist into the brick wall before shoving my hands deep into my pockets and walking away.

I finished early and was hoping to get back to Veronica when I got her text that she was heading back to the hotel. I decided to keep an eye on her and see how she was doing after last night. I saw her weird interaction with Claire, followed by another hurried conversation with Miranda. Maybe I've used up the luck I thought I had.

I rush back to my car and drop into the driver's seat, revving the engine before heading to Sylvie's. I need to figure out what the fuck is going on here.

Typically, I arrive without warning or a heads-up—Sylvie expects that. I nudge open her front door and walk in before slamming it behind me.

In her main room, I find her facing her computer screens. Even though I know she heard me enter, she doesn't turn around.

"Sylvie—" I rasp as I continue approaching her.

She holds up a hand to silence me. Surprised, I stop. Slowly, she turns around to face me, and I can tell she's been crying.

"Ronan, listen to me."

She sounds breathless.

"What happened?" I ask, a slight hesitancy in my voice at her urgency.

She hesitates and looks down at her hands in her lap. She sucks in a deep breath before her eyes return to mine. My breathing quickens, and I can feel my heart rate climb.

"Please promise me you won't do anything—"

"Spit it out, Sylv." I'm growing impatient, and I can handle only so much in one day.

She winces before saying in a muffled voice, "Ronan, he's up for parole."

32

Taylor

Six Years Earlier

S he has been at the facility for almost a month now. Per her records, her stints are normally about three months before she's allowed to return home.

From what I've been able to gather, this is a regular part of their routine. She goes off on a major binge, does something that crosses the line, and in order to restore their marriage and public image, her husband checks her in here, all expenses paid. She stays for three months, becomes a changed woman, and returns home to continue living her fucked-up life.

It's always been the same ol' routine—until now.

This time, it'll be different.

One day, as I'm trying to gather my composure to follow through with my plan, I do some administrative work at the office to take my mind off everything. Repetition always seems to bring me peace.

A teenage girl comes striding through the front door. She has the kind of eyes that bore into your soul. Her light brown hair is styled intricately, and her clothes give the idea that she comes from money, even if I didn't already know she's likely a family member of a patient here.

"Hi, sweetheart." I smile. "What can I do for you today?" I stand from behind the desk with a folder full of paperwork in both hands.

She doesn't return my smile. Instead, her eyes dance around, catching on everything except my face. She stands tall with her arms hidden behind her back.

"Um, I'm here to see my mom," she says quietly, barely moving her lips while she speaks.

"Of course. What's your mom's name?" I ask.

My face drops as I take in her response. My throat is dry, and I force myself to swallow as best as I can.

She has a daughter, and here she is, in the flesh.

I inhale in a breath and purse my lips into a tight line. I try to offer a small smile, but she registers the change in expression on my face. Her eyes narrow slightly.

"Sure thing," I say as optimistically as I can. "I'll just need to confirm your identity and have you sign in first. I'm sure you're familiar with the process."

I realize the sting in my words a moment too late. She adjusts her posture slightly, recognizing the words for what they are: *Your mom is a fuck-up and I know you've been here enough to know how this works*. I wish I could suck those words back into my mouth.

She approaches my desk slowly.

I work as quickly as I can, but at this point, I wish she were lying about who she said she was. I wish I could crawl under this desk and hide from her.

Her right arm retracts gradually from behind her, keeping her left pinned in place. At her peculiar behavior, I glance down as she signs in. My teeth bite down hard into my bottom lip. The skin on her hand is heavily bruised and swollen.

Her signature is about as legible as I expected it to be. I check her profile on our computer, and yep, there she is: The somber picture on my screen confirms her identity.

I glance up at her face and see the same grave look in her eyes. "Do you know where her room is?"

She nods slightly before accepting the visitor badge I hand her. She turns on her heels and walks away briskly.

How did I not know she had children? I consider this new information and wonder if, perhaps, I'm doing them a favor.

I lose myself in my busywork and almost forget about that young girl in the building. I glance at the watch on my left wrist and see that it is getting closer to the end of visiting hours. I place my wrist back down on the desk and continue clicking through my project on my computer screen. That's when I hear a scuffle in the hallway, followed by shouting.

I pause for a moment to see if the sounds continue. The yelling gets louder, and I jump to my feet to run toward the noise. It's likely just the result of a difficult interaction with a patient, but it's in my nature to see what's going on. Besides, if I don't, I'll probably be scolded.

I freeze when I see a security guard gripping a girl's arms and dragging her away. Turning my attention to the name on the wall in front of the room she's being dragged from, my breath catches in my throat.

"You little bitch!" her mother shouts, her face burning red. Tears leak down her face. "You ungrateful little fucking bitch!" Spit flies from her mouth, and she looks like a rabid animal.

I run over to insert myself between the two women. I look at the daughter before stepping over to her mother to see if she's injured.

I glance at the teenage girl being held in the security guard's arms. She looks...amused. Like she's happy about what's taking place. She is proud of whatever she did to get this rise out of her mother. She clenches and unclenches her fist, and I notice blood dripping down her forearms. I pull in a sharp rasp of breath while the security guard continues to drag her away.

I look back at my main priority, our patient. I'm shocked that I don't find any fear on her face, only pure rage etched into her features.

"Please," I say, placing my hand lightly on her shoulder.

She jumps back as if I've struck her, and her eyes are wild with fury.

"That little bitch tried to kill me," she snaps at me before storming back into her room and slamming the door in my face.

33

Veronica

It takes me walking a full mile before I realize I'm heading in the direction of the condominium I share with Richard. Abruptly stopping in the middle of the sidewalk, I earn a few sour looks from people passing by.

The familiarity of our street, lined with tall Norway maples, calms me down. The glossy green leaves sway in the breeze while a hint of orange dangles amid the bundles of greenery.

I close my eyes and lift my face to the sun, soaking up the warmth on my face. Pulling in a deep inhale, I slowly blow the breath through my lips. As I try to make sense of the situation that just unfolded, the anxious pit in my stomach does not lessen.

I push my interaction with Miranda to the back of my mind because I need to focus on Claire. If her father is hurting her, I have to find a way to get her to talk to me. I'm the only person who might be able to help her. I think back to the memory of how nervous she seemed when I had seen her, and her black eye. The phone call yesterday. Everything points in the direction that Richard is abusing her.

I turn on my phone to call her, but she sends it straight to voicemail.

I'm letting emotions cloud my judgment, and I can't lose focus. I consider calling for a cab, but ultimately give in to my need to walk off these uneasy feelings.

I whip around to face the direction that will guide me back to the hotel. Home. My home for however long it needs to be. This familiar place I was walking toward is no longer my home.

At least, not with Richard.

As I hurry back to the hotel, the world around me feels distorted. The sounds of the city—blaring horns, snippets of conversations, and the buzz of traffic—seem amplified, heightening my anxiety. My heart races and my thoughts are chaotic; I replay the unsettling events of the last twenty-four hours. I keep my head down, focusing only on where my feet will fall next, avoiding eye contact with each oncoming passerby.

Entering the familiar hotel lobby, I'm surprised by the change in atmosphere hanging over me. The space normally feels lively, but today, there's something stiff and heavy in the air. Curiosity leads my eyes toward a small group of patrons huddled together in the bar area, their eyes fixed on the television screen mounted on the wall, as if they're in a trance.

Approaching the bar, I see that Miranda hasn't started her shift yet, and my throat constricts.

The low murmur of conversation ceases as the news reporter's somber voice fills the space. The reporter speaks quickly, and his eyes are sad. The caption flies past the bottom of the screen: *Three More Bodies Found; Possible Connection to Continued Disappearances and Murders Throughout the City.*

I step closer to hear what the reporter is saying.

"Three bodies were found, and the police believe they may be connected to the earlier disappearances of young women in the area. The only major difference is that two of the bodies found were men in their late forties. The third is another woman, whose victimology matches those of the previous victims." He takes a brief pause while keeping intense eye contact with the camera. "The two male victims were found a few days ago, while the female victim was found this morning, and the time of death was yesterday afternoon. It appears no one is safe from this killer."

An audible gasp comes from a woman a few feet away from me. There are whispers of uncertainty alongside uneasy glances. We listen to the reporter continue.

"We will leave out some of the more gruesome details, but residents are encouraged to be vigilant and go out in groups. The police are discussing the implementation of a curfew until this deranged individual can be brought to justice."

My heart sinks, absorbing the gravity of the news. Three more victims. That makes four total in the last week. The disappearances had slowed down these last few months. It seemed as if the culprit had been brought to justice, or perhaps they'd died at the hands of someone else.

"I heard the two men were difficult to identify because of the condition of their bodies. Instead of being strangled, they were shot," a man next to me whispers to no one in particular.

My hand flies to my mouth as an older woman begins to cry quietly.

The air grows heavy with collective concern as the reporter continues speaking about the police investigation, mentioning earlier victims. These victims still haunt the city and now, no one is safe.

This must be the case that has been stressing Richard out, alongside the election. Why haven't they been able to find the killer? The fact that this person is still parading around free on our streets, and has completely changed their modus operandi, is unsettling.

My chest tightens, and each breath becomes increasingly shallow. A cold sweat breaks across my forehead, and my hands begin to tremble uncontrollably. A wave of nausea rises in my throat, and I realize I'm on the brink of an anxiety attack. It's all too much, everything I've been through these last few days.

I wait for the pit in my stomach to soften slightly before I turn around to exit the bar. I need some fresh air. I need to get to my room. I turn to see a familiar face staring back at me from the same booth Ronan and I sat in the other night.

Never peeling his eyes from mine, Richard reaches his right hand down to the seat and pats it gently.

It's not an invitation, but a command.

34

Ronan

The rest of Sylvie's words seem distant as I slowly back out of her apartment. My heart pounds against my chest; fury claws at my throat, and my vision tunnels. My breaths are hard and fast as I clench my teeth.

Closing my eyes, I feel myself slip back into the darkness. I fought and scraped my way out of this miserable shadow, and yet, it consumes me once more.

My mind is rushing with memories I tried to forget. Bloodied handprints. The dull *thump* of fists connecting with flesh. The sharper *crack* when knuckles hit bone. Empty eyes staring back at me. Eyes that are identical to my own.

I turn without saying a word to Sylvie and sprint toward my car with my phone clutched in my trembling hand. Fumbling with my keys, I finally unlock my car and collapse into the driver's seat.

I take a deep breath and start the engine, knowing where I need to go next. A small smile curls on my lips, and I'm rushed with a feeling of adrenaline and terror at the thought of maybe finally coming face to face with the man who ruined my life. I've been waiting for this possibility for twenty years. I wasn't sure I'd ever get the opportunity in my lifetime.

Trying to ease my hands from their violent shaking, I grip the steering wheel. My knuckles go white with tension.

Everything is distorted as I speed down the highway. I'm heading to a place that was once my home—a place that made me who I am today. It holds memories I'll never be able to shake. Good and bad.

Mostly bad.

Weaving in and out of traffic at a dangerously high speed, I take Exit 43. Even though I haven't been here in years, I'm on autopilot, knowing I could make it here with my eyes closed.

As I move deeper into the neighborhood, older houses come into view. They are all messes of peeling paint, boarded-up windows, and overgrown yards.

I turn into the driveway of the seventh house on the left. The yard is covered in dead leaves. After parking, I beat my fists against my steering wheel, trying to release some tension. The rhythmic pounding matches my pulse. I keep punching the steering wheel until the familiar sting in my knuckles calms me.

Taking a few deep breaths, I clench and unclench my fingers. I rise out of the car and slam the door shut with enough force to rattle the exterior. Staring at the house over the hood of my car, I'm met with another wave of anxiety. It's familiar and unfamiliar at the same time.

An entire lifetime stands between the boy who lived here before and the cold-blooded killer who stands in the driveway now.

Rage boils inside me as I remember the abuse that happened in this house—to my mother and to me. I have memories of her telling me to go hide in my room for a few hours and not to open the door for anyone who didn't know our special knock.

I tap the familiar sequence on the hood of the car.

Approaching the front door of the house, I see that the deck is falling apart. It creaks with old age against the wind, and I'm not surprised to find the front door slightly ajar.

It wouldn't be a surprise to find some people using in this vacant house.

When I step through the door, the first thing that hits me is the musty smell. So similar to all the places where I do business. Every window is shattered, and the floor is covered with broken glass. The pieces of furniture that are still here are covered in tattered cloths, with layers of dust blanketing every inch of them.

This house has been in my mom's family for generations. It was the only thing she had left to her name before she passed. The only thing she had left to give me.

She was a good woman at times, and I know she loved me. Since the house became mine, I haven't touched it. I wanted it to rot like my insides. After all, it's the last physical item of what created a monster like me.

I'll never pretend my childhood was anything pretty. What do you expect from someone who grew up to be a killer?

I never knew my father. When I was younger, my mom would tell me stories about him, and I'd always ask for more. I never admitted to her that I knew she was lying about him because every story was always different. Now that I'm older, I wonder if she even knew who my father was. I knew she wanted me to feel proud that I was an important man's son.

In some stories, my father was a war hero who lost his life fighting for our freedom. In others, he was a world-renowned astronaut who was sought out for lengthy missions. He was also a member of Congress, a tiger handler, an archaeologist, a fire-fighter, a lawyer, a pilot, and a contender to be the next President of the United States of America. I think she used these stories as a way to daydream about her and me having another life. A better life. What our life might have looked like if different decisions had been made.

My favorite story was that he was a crime fighter and would do anything to defend those who needed his protection. I became attached to the idea that my father was a man who took care of the bad people in this world. The people who hurt people who didn't deserve it, like my mom and I. When bad things happened to us, I'd close my eyes and wish with everything I had that he would show up and save us.

My wishes never came true.

My mom was a complex woman. She dabbled in alcohol, drugs, and sex. She had her vices, but she did love me. She did her best to take care of me, despite her addictions. In moments of clarity, she would hold me close, her blue eyes filled with a protective love for me. This is how I'll always remember her.

With my mom's lifestyle, people filtered in and out of our lives quickly, and they were mostly men. Mostly bad men who only made my mother worse. I remember one night my mom stumbled through the front door, her eyes glassy and her speech slurred. She wasn't alone. The man behind her had a menacing grin and a rough demeanor. His eyes were so dark, they almost looked black.

This was the beginning of the end.

My mind is flooded with memories of my mother's pleading cries that still send shivers down my spine. That final night marked the end of her life, but also mine as I knew it. Police lights flashing through the window, the coldness of the officer's words, and the emptiness that followed.

With no living relatives willing to claim me and no will for them to consult, I went into foster care at the age of eight. Let's be honest, no one wants to adopt a troubled eight-year-old whose drug-addicted mother was murdered. I lived up to the stereotype, getting into trouble and sabotaging any opportunity that came my way to be adopted. I started getting into more fights, and most ended in me getting my ass handed to me. Then life went full circle when I started selling drugs.

But what I learned from my experiences is that violence is the real gateway drug. Once you feel the power of hurting someone, you'll spend the rest of your life looking for a more intense high.

There are so many people to blame for why I became who I am today. But the one person who had the biggest impact has been untouchable, only because he spent the last twenty years in a maximum-security prison.

The early dreams I held onto of my dad being a crime fighter also led me down this path. I wanted to stop those bad people and keep them from hurting others.

My rage and sorrow flow through me like electricity. I take out my frustration on everything I can touch inside the house. I smash the walls and break the furniture. Exhausted, I drop onto the floor of what used to be my bedroom. This is the room where I would lock the door and hide from the abuse that was happening downstairs. It still feels so real. I swear I can hear my mother screaming from the level below.

I cradle my head in my hands, and for the first time in years, I let myself cry as I think back to being that scared little boy who lived within these walls. I'm unsure if my tears are fueled by exhaustion, frustration, or relief. To my own surprise, a maniacal laugh tears through my throat.

I may finally get the chance to repay that piece of shit for what he's done.

35

Veronica

I walk over uneasily to where Richard sits with impatience painted across his face. I'm not even walking fast enough for him, that's how much my existence annoys him at this very moment.

"Hello, Veronica." His voice is low and cold. "Sit."

My movements are hesitant and slow, though I know I need to tackle this situation head-on. If I avoid him now, he'll only keep coming around.

"Wow, Richard," I say, annoyance lacing my tone. "You really can't take a hint, can you?"

"As you can see on that television everyone is gawking over, I have my hands full right now, so you can imagine how annoyed I am to have to step away from work and the election to come to reprimand you." His face is filled with arrogance.

Reprimand. Like I'm a child who needs to learn the difference between right and wrong. My jaw clenches as I tilt my vision slightly upward, looking at his forehead in a small act of dominance. I will not let him belittle me.

He adjusts in his seat, straightening his spine like we're in a standoff.

"Veronica, I have eyes everywhere. I know what you've been up to." His tone is cold and emotionless.

This is what I expected. That he would already know what I've been doing behind closed doors.

"This was not what we agreed to," he snaps.

I know there's nothing more irritating to him than disobedience. In his eyes, it's the exact opposite of what a wife should be.

He scoffs. "You think your little affair would go unnoticed? I've turned a blind eye these last few days because I've had too much going on, but now it's gone too far."

A laugh comes bursting from my chest. Oh, the irony.

"Gone too far?" I shout. "Are you kidding me?"

His eyes narrow at me. "This isn't some game, Veronica. This is our marriage. This is our life."

"Is it?" I respond. "Because you've been the one cheating on me for who knows how long."

He flinches at my words but quickly stiffens his spine, sitting up straighter.

"That's *different*."

His words are like poison on his tongue, dripping with deception.

"Is it different?" I ask. "How much time have you been spending with Olivia since I've been staying at the hotel?"

He purses his lips and his nostrils flare. I struck a nerve at mentioning Olivia. His silence is very telling.

"I know you think I'm stupid, but I'm not. I know you didn't fire her."

He clears his throat quickly. "That is true, I didn't fire her. She has a background in PR, and she's been helpful in preparing for the campaign."

"For fuck's sake, Richard," I sputter. "Do you seriously think you're not the stupid one here?"

His face reddens, and he clenches his teeth together, biting back the insults he'd like to hurl in my direction.

"We're not doing this here, Veronica. I mean it. I also wanted to ask you in person if you've spoken to or seen Jacob since the night you said you ran into him?"

"What?" I rear back in surprise. "Of course I haven't spoken to him," I scoff. "I don't want anything to do with him."

Discontent creases his mouth into a tight line.

"Why?" I ask.

"His father hasn't seen him in a few days, and it seems no one has spoken to him since that night you said you saw him last."

I bite my tongue, and my gut turns with nausea as a thought claws its way to the front of my mind.

"He couldn't have been one of those victims…"

I trail off, gesturing toward the TV that's still gripping everyone else's attention. Bile rises in my throat as I take in this turn of events. The man's voice from earlier sounds in my ear.

The two men were difficult to identify.

Richard would likely know the identities before it's released to the public. Of course, he would come straight here since I could have been one of the last people to see Jacob alive.

Richard shakes his head, and my tension lessens a little bit. He takes a deep breath before bringing his eyes back up to meet mine. Whatever he knows about the murders, he's not sharing any information.

For once, he's doing something right. Perhaps he knows something that the rest of the public doesn't.

"Because I'm being courteous, I'll give you one week to get everything out of your system," he says with his lip curled up in disgust. "Then I want you home. Do you understand me?"

I don't reply. I know it's a rhetorical question, and he doesn't intend for me to answer.

"Once you return home, we will never speak of this again. Ever." He rises to stand and adjusts his jacket before turning to leave. Glancing back at me from over his shoulder, he adds, "Don't make me regret this, Veronica."

His threat hangs in the air long after he's disappeared.

"What a piece of shit," Lauren says with her mouth full of her food. "He better hope I never see him again."

She continues chomping.

After the last twenty-four hours, I desperately needed someone to bring me back down to earth. I'm still unsure about my interaction with Miranda and what it means about Ronan. Plus, Jacob is missing. Who else would have a reason for wanting him gone?

I try to recall that night at the bar where I last saw Jacob before our altercation.

Surprisingly, Lauren was with Liam again when I called her, on the edge of tears after speaking with Richard. But she rushed away from Liam to make sure I was okay. When she showed up, her hair was slightly disheveled, and there was a gleam in her eye. Is this bitch falling in love?

"Am I crazy?" I say, rubbing my hands up my forehead.

Her eyebrows shoot up. "For hooking up with this hot motherfucker you were just telling me about?" She scoffs. "No fucking way. You're the best kind of crazy there is. You're a realist."

"But isn't it odd that I am sleeping with this man who I really know nothing about? Could there be something up with him?" I place my chin on top of my balled-up fists. "Since I've met him, so many terrible things have happened. It can't be a coincidence."

One eyebrow rises as she looks up to meet my gaze. "You have always had a thing for complicated men, haven't you?"

I shake my head, and she takes another bite before adding more validation. "As I see it, you're doing exactly what he told you to do. No one can fault you for that."

My shoulders deflate. I should just cut ties with Ronan, but I can't. There is something about him that I can't get enough of. Even now, I'm fighting the urge to call him and beg him to come see me, to wrap me in his arms and make me feel safe.

"Yeah, you're right." I sigh. "I'm just making an already complicated situation even more complicated."

"What are you doing about..." She pauses, and her eyes dart around. She lowers her voice. "About everything else?"

I bite down on my bottom lip and let out a deep exhale from my nose. "I made a call the other day. That should give Richard something else to worry about instead of me."

She nods quickly. "What did you give them this time?"

I shake my head again, looking down at my hands resting on the table. "Some tangible information on a botched case that he oversaw. Once the heat dies down over the two most recent bodies that were found, it'll no doubt be all over the news."

Richard doesn't have a clue that the anonymous person giving the news information on his corrupt character is his wife. With Lauren's connections, I've been able to remain anonymous, supplying information that will help them ruin his reputation. He has an idea it's someone close to him, but he doesn't know it's me.

Or at least, I don't think he knows.

A small smirk curves on Lauren's lips. "Anything you need from me?"

"Things are just expedited a tad now," I say, swallowing the lump in my throat.

"That's a good thing, right?" Lauren says, cocking her head to the side.

But at this point, I'm not so sure if it is a good thing.

36
Ronan

The familiar scent of leather and sweat greets me as the thud of fists sounds against punching bags. The gym is buzzing with activity. With my bag slung over my shoulder, I make my way across the worn-out mats to the center of the room. My eyes are fixed on the boxing ring, standing in the corner.

I needed to go somewhere where I could release some of this pent-up energy after Sylvie delivered the final punch that almost knocked me out. I climb through the ropes and onto the canvas.

I can sense I'm not alone before this fact is confirmed.

"Shadow," a faint voice says from the dark corner at the edge of the ring.

I don't let the surprise show on my face. "Mark, what a pleasure," I say. I am not a fan of being easy to find. Ever since our last interaction, I've been quick to avoid Mark as much as possible. I'm not convinced he's innocent in all of this.

He pushes through the ropes and climbs up to the boxing ring. "I wanted to check in on our conversation from the other day," he says, stepping into the light. He huffs a ring of smoke from his lips before dropping his cigarette on the ground and stomping it out.

My eyes drop to the place where he put out his cigarette. Mark offers me a smile and toes the remnants off the ring and onto the floor.

"Yeah," I reply, warming up my arms by throwing quick combos. With each swing, I visualize an opponent and predict their moves. I think about how much I'd love to knock out Mark and how much I regret taking this job from him. "It's under control," I add.

Mark grunts before taking a few steps closer to me. "Better be," he says. "And I also wanted to give you an in-person message to forget about the last name on my list."

This catches me off guard, and I stop abruptly, standing up straight.

"Why?" I ask immediately.

His eyebrows lower, and his eyes darken. "I don't need to explain myself to you," he spits. "There is enough heat on us right now. Just fucking cool it."

Of course, he's talking about letting Richard go. Fuck. I was really looking forward to that one. I clench my fists tightly, my jaw set in frustration. His smirk is the only tell that he caught onto my frustration. Why the sudden change of heart on his last target?

"Be careful, Shadow." He laughs. "Looks like you and I are at the top of someone else's list."

With that, he disappears as quickly as he came. I continue slamming my bare fists against the heavy bag. It reverberates like thunder.

Man, fuck that guy. At least that means I'm almost done with him.

Raw fury drives me, and sweat pours down my brow as I push my body beyond its limits. I ignore the burning ache in my muscles.

When I hear a noise from outside the ring, I glance up to find that Mark is still watching me. His gaze bores into me, and my irritation causes my skin to prickle. It's like he's studying me.

Our eyes connect briefly in a standoff before he spins on his heels to exit.

After the gym, I head back to Sylvie's. I left abruptly after she delivered the news. She's obviously scared for me and is wondering how I plan to retaliate if he gets out of prison. My feelings are caught between nerves and excitement, reveling in how I will make him pay for what he's done.

She doesn't even look surprised when I burst through the door, like she already knew I'd come straight here, desperate for a direction. The only thing that keeps me from unraveling. I assure her that I'm fine and ask her to do some digging on our dear friend, Mark. She raises an eyebrow but doesn't question me, just nods and turns back to her computer. While she types, I pace the room, running through every possible scenario in my head. This isn't just about revenge anymore; it's about control. And for the first time in a long time, I feel like I finally have some.

"See!" she shouts excitedly. "Told you it was all fishy. You should've listened to me from the beginning."

"Yeah, yeah, sure," I groan. "You were right, like always. Is that what you want to hear?"

She beams a smile at me, pride in her face. Then she taps away on her keyboard, and I step back, pulling my phone from my pocket.

Veronica.

Veronica: What are you doing? Do you want to come over?

I smile before typing out my reply:

Ronan: I do want to come over. As soon as I'm done with work. Why don't you send a preview for what's to come?

"That's not good," Sylvie's voice interrupts my thoughts.

I can see she's watching me, but I don't look up from my phone. "What isn't good?" I ask flatly.

"You smiling at your phone like a fucking dumbass."

I scoff and raise my eyes to meet hers. "Ouch, Sylv. You should be nicer to your boss."

"Oh, shut up, Mom." She huffs out a laugh. "But really, that is a bad idea, you know?"

"What is a bad idea?"

She turns to stare at me intensely. The worry in her eyes is obvious, and she tilts her head slightly. "Anything or anyone that has you cheesing from ear to ear like that. It'll make you put your guard down. Like I said, bad idea."

I roll my eyes before glancing back down at my phone. Right on time, another text message from Veronica has arrived.

Even better, it's a picture.

She stands in front of the bathroom mirror in her hotel room. She's topless, but she has her arm pressed across her chest, covering her nipples. She's cut off most of her face, but I can see a cocky little smile curling at her lips at the top of the photo.

Veronica:

"You do remember who you are, right?" Sylvie's tone is more serious. "Because people would pay good money to find a way to get to you after everything you've done. Whoever has you smiling like that has a big, gigantic target right in the middle of their fucking forehead."

Her words set my nerves on edge. And more than that, it's the truth behind them that gets me.

Seeing Veronica is a welcome distraction from the fucked day I had. I'm not ready to share any of this information about me. She still doesn't know she was right about me being a hit man. I know I don't deserve her, but I have to have her. There's no way I'll be able to hold myself back from her tonight.

As I stride through the hotel lobby, I can't stop the thoughts of last night replaying in my mind. It was more intense than I expected. I can't deny the pull I feel toward her, a feeling that is foreign and comforting for the first time in my life.

I pause momentarily as Miranda meets my eyes from across the bar. She narrows her eyes at me, and I can see annoyance on her face that I didn't heed her warning from earlier.

Shit, in everything else that's happened today, I forgot all about Miranda.

I'll chat with her later. Right now, I need to see Veronica. I need to drink her in like the first sip of water I've had in weeks.

I rap my knuckles on her door and wait for her to open it. When she does, my heart pounds in my chest. She's wearing a simple white sundress, but she looks absolutely stunning. Her hair cascades down her shoulders in loose waves, framing her face perfectly. Her smile is wide and dazzling. She looks genuinely happy.

As she leads me in, I take in the way her hips sway with each step. Everything about her is mesmerizing. She turns back to face me, and her cheeks blush as she notices the way I'm watching her intently. She lowers her eyes and shrugs her shoulders lightly.

It's as if time stands still when her eyes travel back up to meet mine. Her green eyes shine in the light, and I'm completely entranced. There is that slight darkness in her, hiding something. It's familiar and comforting.

There is nothing I wouldn't do for this woman, and I've known her for such a short period of time. My dick hardens in my jeans and I'm doing all I can to hold myself back from her. She pads off to the small kitchenette in her room and pours two glasses of red wine. She walks over to hand me one of the glasses and then gestures toward the couch. We sit opposite one another.

Sitting in a comfortable silence, she seems to simply enjoy my presence. Apparently, we both had some pretty fucked-up days. When we're together, it's like we're existing in our own little world. In our bubble, we're separated from reality.

Her cheeks flush further as she gazes at me. Her tongue darts out as she wets her bottom lip before sinking her teeth into it. She looks as desperate as I am. I can't wait any longer—I'm going to go crazy if I'm not touching her soon.

I move quickly, and my lips instantly find hers. She lets out a small gasp at the impact before she settles into me. My hands find her waist and the back of her head, and I press her body closer into me. My dick is already so hard, and this light foreplay isn't going to cut it. I pull back from her. She looks perfect. Her green eyes are hazy, and her lips are swollen, her lipstick already a mess.

"I'm sorry if this seems rushed," I say, running my tongue across my bottom lip. "But I had a bad day, and I've needed to see you."

She tilts her head slightly and stares back at me. "I..." she starts. Her throat bobs. "I had a rough day too, but I couldn't stop thinking about you."

I grip the hem of her dress and pull it over her head. To my surprise, she's not wearing anything underneath. I smile, realizing she's much more comfortable around me after the other night. She smiles back at me devilishly, confirming that her lack of lingerie was intentional.

A growl escapes my throat, and her lips part, knowing she's got me. I grit my teeth and push a hard breath out of my nose.

"Face the back of the couch and get up on your knees."

37

Veronica

He strips off his black T-shirt, and my breath hitches in my chest. I see his muscular chest and three rows of chiseled abs on display. He's gorgeous. It takes all my restraint to stop myself from running my fingers down his muscled flesh.

But I do as he says, and I turn around, poking my ass up in the air.

"Spread your legs and lean forward."

Placing my forearms on the back of the couch, I lean forward, further arching my back. I spread my legs, and the chilled air in the room nips at me.

I turn my gaze back to catch a glimpse of myself in the room's mirror. And there I am, on full display, already glistening with arousal.

He positions himself behind me as he caresses my ass, completing the sensation with a light slap across one of my cheeks. I let out a small yelp, and then he's pulling me wide open.

A growl erupts from the back of his throat. "Tonight, I want to taste you from more than just my fingers."

The harshness of his words makes my stomach twist. But with excitement, not fear.

He lowers to his knees on the floor in front of the couch and I feel his warm breath down my thighs. I tremble with anticipation.

Without warning, his flat tongue licks the full length of me at a desperately slow pace. I melt into his touch and bury my face in the top of the couch.

"Don't hide from me. I want to hear you," he whispers at my pussy.

I can feel every exhale from his words.

"Are you always this wet?" He slides his fingers up my slit before pressing one inside.

I groan at the sensation.

"Does that feel good?" He pulses his finger in and out, curling it at the top when he's deep inside me.

"Yes," I breathe out.

"Do you need more?" he asks between licks.

More. More. More.

"Yes."

"Then tell me. Tell me what you want from me."

I gasp at his request.

His voice is low, almost angry. It's rough like gravel, but it makes me hot.

"Use your words," he growls. "Tell me exactly what you want."

I inhale deeply before answering, trying to steady myself before tucking every inhibition away. "I want you to lick me from top to bottom. Lick my pussy while you fuck me with your fingers."

The words feel foreign to me. I've never had a man ask me what I want them to do to me. And my own vulgar honesty turns me on even more.

As soon as the words leave my lips, he attacks with a newfound ferocity. He uses his tongue with the perfect amount of pressure, alternating between swirling his tongue in circles and delivering short flicks on my clit. He inserts another finger inside me while using his other hand to spread me open further. It's like he can't get enough of me. He needs me to be wider, more open, so that he can take all of me.

The rolling sensation builds as my hips flex more to give him full access to every inch of me. I'm close when he abruptly pulls away. The loss is almost unbearable.

"I want you to come all over my face," he says breathlessly while turning his back to me.

He sits down on the floor underneath me with his back against the couch. He drops his head so that the back of it is resting on the couch. He grips my hips and lowers me onto his face.

My eyes roll into the back of my head with this new position. He leaves no inch of my pussy untouched. He picks up his speed with both his hands and his tongue. He sucks on me as I continue building, starting right where he left off.

His fingers and tongue seamlessly switch duties between plunging inside me to paying close attention to my clit. My stomach clenches and my thighs tighten. I keep grinding on his face, his touch too much for me to handle.

"I'm...I'm..." I rasp out.

With the promise of my impending release, he grips me harder and pulls me down even further to him. He holds me in place by the crease between my hips and my thighs, not letting me move an inch. My pussy is pulsing with sensation, and I'm overcome with the explosion that takes me so hard that my vision goes black for a moment. My walls clench as he continues to lick me and push his fingers in and out. It's clear he likes riding out my orgasm with me, which only makes me come harder.

I'm gasping to catch my breath between my moans. As I give him every inch of my orgasm, I allow myself to enjoy this euphoric feeling. I continue grinding on his face until I'm completely spent, slowing my hips, and pressing more of my weight into my forearms, which are still resting on the back of the couch.

I slowly lift up further, but he lingers underneath, his fingers running along my curves. My skin prickles with his touch. How can I already be craving more of him?

"You're so fucking perfect."

My eyes roll back at the sound of his voice.

He places a soft kiss to my sensitive clit, which makes me shudder before he slips out from underneath me and rises to his feet. He goes to grab his shirt, and then I realize it's the same scenario as last night. He got me off, and now he's going to leave. I'm not ready for him to leave—I'm still desperate for him. And craving more. I don't want him to move this slowly.

"Wait," I nearly shout, much louder than I intended.

He looks at me inquisitively.

"I don't want you to leave yet."

A single brow rises. He's hanging on to my every word.

"I want to see you," I say, my voice sounding shyer than I hoped.

He flashes that seductive smirk that has my stomach tightening all over again. And then he drops his T-shirt to the floor. He stalks over toward me, reminding me just how much bigger he is than I am.

"Do you now?"

He places his hands on the back of the couch with his arms beside my face.

"Yes, please stay." My voice is barely above a whisper. I've never needed to beg before.

We stare into each other's eyes for a moment before I look down and reach between us. My hands are shaking, whether it's from the orgasm or my nerves, I don't know, and I don't care. His gorgeous ice-blue eyes are heavy with desire, and I see a flicker dance within them.

Never breaking eye contact, I slowly unbutton and unzip his black jeans. His eyes have darkened, and his lips are still curled in that deadly smirk. He looks at me through his thick, dark lashes, hunger painted all over his wicked face.

His lips part, and then he bites the bottom one.

I slide his jeans down and let them drop to the floor. His legs are just as muscular as the rest of his body—thick and strong. I inhale a deep breath as I think about how powerful he is. The thought of those legs working while he pounds into me from behind makes my thighs clench instinctively. I hinge my fingers into the waistband of his briefs before pulling them down slowly.

His cock springs loose and pops up to meet my gaze while his briefs sink to the floor, meeting his jeans. I gasp at the size of him. He's thick and long, and his balls are tight underneath. Veins cascade throughout his rock-hard dick.

Every ounce of confidence I had before is melting away.

He must be able to sense my faltering. "Don't tell me you're hesitant now, baby," he chuckles lightly while fisting his cock and pumping slowly with one hand. "You've got me hard as fuck."

He smirks at me again, his blue eyes burning as he curls his finger underneath my chin and lifts my face to his. "So, what are you going to do about it, love?"

38

Ronan

I knew she wouldn't let me walk away that easily. Not after what I've already given her.

Mine.

The word beats in my mind like my heartbeat.

I can tell she's nervous at the sight of my cock. I continue stroking while she gathers herself. She looks up at me, green eyes shining through her long-painted lashes and perfectly sculpted eyebrows. I hate seeing fear in her eyes. She's always looked at me so confidently, like she knows exactly what she wants. She finally looks at me like I've always wanted...like a normal person. Not for the fucked-up man I've become. She makes me feel normal and like I could live an everyday life.

She leans forward and replaces my hand with her own. She strokes softly, and I groan. I've been dreaming about this moment since I laid eyes on her. She doesn't know the effect she has on me.

"Harder," I grunt, and she obeys.

She squeezes me tighter and pumps her hand faster.

"Put me in your mouth."

Her large doe eyes return, an expression of shock and fear. But then she leans forward and wraps her pink lips around my cock. She takes me as deep as she can and uses her hand to cover the rest of my length. She never lets her eyes leave mine.

She learned her lesson the first night.

"Oh, fuck," I bite my lower lip. "That's a good girl. Eyes on me."

I play with her nipples as she takes me into her mouth, letting out a deep breath from her nose as she works me further back into her throat.

She pulls back and swirls her tongue over the head of my cock while pumping her hand at my base. She licks up the centerline of my dick before plunging me deeper into her throat. Her other hand cups my balls and pulses lightly as she moves me in and out of her mouth.

God, she feels so fucking good. Her mouth is warm and wet—an appetizer to how her pussy will feel. My cock twitches at the thought. The mental buildup is almost too much.

She knows I'm close and keeps stroking, licking, and sucking until my body shakes. I grab the back of her head and push her a little deeper, holding her there, as I spill into her throat. The sounds of her gagging fill the air as I dip my head back in my release. When I'm finished, I soften my grip on her head and look back down at her.

She swallows every drop and pulls her mouth off me, tantalizingly slow. When she sits up, she keeps her eyes focused on me, smiles, and then licks her lips.

She's fucking playing with me.

"I'm not done with you yet," I snarl.

Her smile reaches her eyes, and they light up. "Good," she whispers.

She pulls my face down to her by my neck. Within seconds, our mouths are tasting each other. Her kiss is hungry and feral. Our teeth clank as our tongues swirl around one another. I reach down and hoist her naked body up to me. She wraps her legs around my waist and locks them behind my back. I step out of my pooled jeans on the floor and stride to the bed, never breaking our kiss.

I drop her on the bed before stepping back to admire the scene before me.

She's lying where I dropped her, legs slightly open, knees drawn up. She's touching herself, drawing small circles with her pointer finger on her clit. I'm salivating at the sight of her, readying herself for me.

"Good girl," I praise as I walk toward her slowly, keeping my eyes trained on her moving fingers.

I start kissing her neck and reintroduce the bite mark I left last night.

She yelps at the pain but presses her naked body into mine.

I trail down the rest of her body, marking her. Pausing at her breasts, I squeeze one in my hand while nipping at the other. Her skin is burning hot to my touch.

I swirl my tongue around her nipple before biting it.

I reach down to feel in between her legs and discover that she's beyond ready for me. I slip two fingers inside as I pulse them. I pull out and swirl her wetness around her clit.

"Ronan, please," she rasps.

"I love it when you beg."

She closes her eyes as her chest rises and falls. She lets out a cry as I pick up my pace. "Please, I want you so bad."

I continue my teasing as I wait for her to continue. She looks at me. Her pupils are wide with desire.

"Remember, use your words," I growl.

There is something so arousing about demanding she tells me what she wants from me. I crave the sound of those filthy words that spill from her gorgeous lips.

"Please fuck me."

I pull my hand back from her. "Yeah?" I fist my cock as I stare at her.

"Fuck me hard, Ronan. Fuck me until I'm screaming your name and exhausted from coming."

I growl with approval before asking, "Who do you belong to?"

"You—I'm yours," she pants.

With that, I rise up to meet her face, locking my gaze with hers.

I line my cock up at her entrance and slide it through her slickness. She moans, wrapping her legs around me and hooking them behind my hips.

I gently work my way into her, filling her up. She tenses, and her thighs and pussy clench around me, begging me to go deeper. But her face gives away the slight pain she feels from my size.

"Baby, breathe," I say into her skin.

I pull out before pushing back in, a little bit deeper this time as her pussy works to take me in. I slide back out and glance down at my cock, shining with her arousal. When I look back up at her eyes, she's staring at me with impatience.

With that look, I slam into her, giving her every inch of me. She cries out and bucks against me, raising her hips to give me a better angle of her center.

"Look at you, taking me so well," I purr into her ear.

She moans my name, and that's all it takes to send me into a frenzy.

I pound into her, feeling our slick bodies pressed up against one another. I bite the sensitive flesh of her exposed arms.

Her walls tighten around me as we both build. I press my mouth to hers as we breathe into one another. And finally, this.

This is what I've been dreaming of since I saw her, being completely buried in her. My name is like a prayer on her lips.

"Fuck, baby. How long has it been since you were fucked like you deserve?"

She's drenched, so I pick up my pace as I beat into her, harder and faster. Her eyes roll back as she cries out again. I feel her pussy pulse from her orgasm and it's not long before I'm spilling into her.

I fall beside her before placing my cupped hand on her cheek. Her eyelids are heavy and she's struggling to keep them open.

"You did so good for me," I tell her. And at that moment, I'm not sure I'll ever be able to get enough of her.

39

Veronica

My body buzzes, and my skin tingles. I lie on my back with my eyes closed, taking in this moment. I feel Ronan's body collapse next to me on the bed, his weight tilting my body toward his. His warmth is so comforting, and his presence makes me feel at ease. To think that earlier today, I was thinking I was wrong about him. Surely Miranda needs to talk to me about something else, not Ronan.

I'm staring at him, and the words leave my mouth before I have a second to consider what I'm doing. What I'm asking. "Will you stay with me tonight?"

I know it's a bad idea, a horrible idea. But I'm desperate for more of him, and I feel so much safer when he's around. I'd love to see Richard try to demand things of me with Ronan at my side. He'd probably piss his pants.

And besides, if he does stay, a little more sex couldn't hurt, either.

I finally open my eyes as I roll over to face him. I'm surprised to find he isn't mortified; he's smiling up at the ceiling. It's the most genuine smile I've seen from him. He turns on his side to face me and settles into the bed. I do see a glimmer of disappointment in his eyes.

"I would love to stay with you tonight," he says, "but I have to be somewhere around midnight for work."

"Midnight?" I bark. "Why couldn't I have found myself entranced by a man who works a standard nine-to-five?"

"Oh, already getting sick of me, are you?" he asks before letting out a small laugh.

I melt into his chest. His body heat burns against my flesh, and it's everything. I rub a finger down the middle line of his chest. We're both still completely naked, and I don't know if I'll ever get used to the sight of him.

Every ounce of uncertainty I had about him earlier has been completely erased. What is it about him? When I'm around him, I'm unable to feel anything but sheer desire. I'm completely blind to every bad thing this man could've done. He's good to me, and that's more than I can say about most people who've come and gone from my life.

"I do have some time to kill before that." His right eyebrow shoots upward momentarily. "What did you have in mind?"

I let everything else in my life fade away. All that matters right now is Ronan and how he makes me feel. He makes me feel safe. I know he'd never hurt me.

And I'd never hurt him.

This feeling between the two of us is so strong. When we're apart, it feels weakened, almost like the bond between us is injured, but when we're together, it's all-consuming.

I just need to come clean about my past. But that—that can wait, at least until after tonight. I have some time to do that.

I feel bold in the moment, as the desire in his eyes ignites me. The effect he has on me is everything. I crawl on top of him and spread my thighs as I press my still-wet pussy against his hardening cock.

"I have a few ideas," I whisper as I begin to slowly roll my body. His hands shoot out to grip my hips before a groan escapes his throat.

For once, I'm ignoring everything else that is happening in the world. No Richard, no Claire, no Miranda. It's just us two. For just a few more moments, I want to live in this moment with Ronan. We'll have it be just him and me.

I smile at him, and he tips his head back in pleasure as I slide down on top of his length.

And then I say, "I think I'd like to be in control this time."

———

I'm awakened suddenly by a slight shifting on the bed. I'm disappointed at the heat leaving my body but I don't open my eyes yet. I roll to the newly vacant spot on the bed and reach my hand out, one last desperate attempt to get him to stay.

He grabs my hand and kisses each one of my fingertips.

"I'll see you again soon, baby," he promises, before placing my hand back down on the mattress.

My stomach tightens and I realize there is no way to get him to stay. I let out a deep sigh and nestle further into the sheets, which now smell of him.

Once I hear the familiar click of the bedroom door, I open my eyes and glance at the clock on the nightstand. It's 11:33 p.m. My eyes widen at once as I remember Miranda asking me: *Come by the bar tonight and I'll explain. I get off at midnight.*

In my haze of my obsession with Ronan, I forgot all about her plea to come meet her. At least I've been able to pass the time, and now I can finally get some clarity about what she was talking about.

I jump from the bed and rush to get dressed, throwing on some jeans from earlier with a dark colored T-shirt. I clip my hair up on the back of my head, knowing it looks like an absolute mess from the last few hours.

I rush downstairs. The elevator doors part, and I am walking toward the bar when I see Miranda and Ronan chatting.

What the fuck.

Their conversation seems heated, and I'm confused as to why he said he had things to take care of for work when he meant he'd be downstairs talking to the bartender—the same bartender who said she needed to talk to me.

I take a few steps to the side to ensure I'm concealed from their view.

Throwing up his hands out of frustration, Ronan eventually turns away from Miranda and stalks out of the hotel lobby. I feel a sob build in my chest, and I cup my hand over my mouth. The dishonesty hurts but what hurts more is his inability to notice me. The bond between us that previously had felt so strong is now weakened enough that he doesn't even sense me nearby.

I'm always made to look like a fool in every situation. I try to bury my emotions and compose myself long enough to talk with Miranda. I'm too upset to talk to Ronan right now.

Approaching the bar, I see the shock go across Miranda's face when she notices me.

"Hey, Miranda," I say quietly. "You, uh—you know Ronan?" I can feel my cheeks heat.

"Oh yeah, he's been a regular here for a while." She jerks her head to the same door he just exited. She looks back at me and sees my pained expression. Her eyes widen before the realization settles in, and she puts two and two together. "Oh gosh, no. No, it's nothing like that. Never."

"Oh my God," I say, dropping into an empty barstool. "I'm so fucking pathetic."

"If anything, I was trying to protect you both," she says.

My breath catches in my throat. "P-protect us?" I stammer. "What do you mean, protect us?"

A cold chill runs down my spine, and my skin prickles with disbelief.

"Listen, let me close down the bar and clock out. Then we can go somewhere better to chat. Okay?"

I nod quickly and adjust myself on the barstool, feeling like the air has been knocked out of me.

Miranda disappears behind a closed door, and I find myself glancing at my phone's clock every few seconds. My impatience seems to grow with each passing minute, a relentless reminder that time is slipping away. I wring my hands together. They feel cold and clammy.

After an hour has passed and she has still not returned, my anxiety twists into a knot of fear. I continue staring forward at the empty bar. Not a single person is around me.

I stand from my seat and begin to pace, waiting just a little bit longer to see if she returns. After a while, my legs become weak, and tears blur my vision.

Miranda never returns for our promised conversation.

40

Ronan

My mind is still reeling from my conversation with Miranda. She was dodging my questions and speaking in riddles, never giving me any clear information. It was a waste of time.

It did pain me to leave a naked Veronica lying in her hotel bed, with her hair tousled across her pillow and her full lips slightly parted as she let out slow, deep breaths.

I did actually have work to take care of last night. The last person on the list, outside of the newly removed Richard, has been taken care of and disposed of in a way that means he will never be found again. He didn't seem surprised by my arrival, like he had been waiting for me. It's less exciting when they aren't begging for their lives.

It's risky for me to continue taking out people on Mark's list but once this contract is done, maybe I'll take some time off to sort my shit out. Give myself more time to be with Veronica. I can't risk being caught after everything I've been through. Plus, if Shitbag is granted parole, I'll especially need my time to pay him back for the hell he put me through.

Driving back to my house, all I can think about is how badly I want to drop into my bed and sleep for days. Last night with Veronica was exhausting but I need to see her again.

Pulling up, I am greeted by a terribly unpleasant sight.

Police officers on my front porch.

Fuck.

I step out of my car and approach them. One is a heavyset older man, and the other is a taller younger man. They each have a stern face and eye me from my head to my feet.

"Ronan Cole?" the older man asks.

It's a rhetorical question, I'm sure. They know exactly who I am.

I nod slightly. "What can I do for you, officers?"

The older one clears his throat and nudges his younger accomplice in the ribs. "We have a few questions to ask you about your whereabouts a few days ago," the younger one sputters.

I'm trying to decipher who is playing bad cop and who's the good cop in this situation. But perhaps with my reputation, I'll be getting bad cop, bad cop.

"Sure," I say, lifting my keys in my hand before stepping toward the door. "Just let me open the door and you can come in."

This surprises them. They were expecting to be met with apprehension, but I know how to play their games. It would only make me look more suspicious if I didn't do as they say. I have no doubt they're here about those bodies that turned up. I knew it wouldn't be long before they came looking for me. Someone has done a damn good job at those crime scenes, pointing in my direction.

"Do you know a man named Jacob Kiernan?"

This question causes my eyebrow to rise. It's not what I was expecting.

Jacob. Maybe this *is* about something I did.

"Nope, can't say I do," I say as I sit down on the couch adjacent to them and cross my arms over my chest. "What does he have to do with me?"

The older cop is doing his best to memorize every inch of my house. His eyes dart around the room and pause momentarily before moving along to the next item. But if they're looking for something to convict me with, they're going to need to do a hell of a lot better than this.

"Seems he's been missing for a few days," the younger cop says. "He was last seen at a bar where you were also spotted."

"Interesting. Yeah, I was there momentarily to meet a friend," I say, keeping my face stoic. "Lots of people were there, though, so why the interest in just me? Or are you visiting the homes of every single person who was at the bar that night?"

The younger cop's face reddens with embarrassment. "Uh, no. We have other reasons to want to speak with you. We also heard Jacob had a heated interaction with a woman you've been seen with." He glances down as if he has to read off the name. "Veronica Sullivan, the district attorney's wife."

I don't respond. I want to gauge how much they know about Veronica and me before I back myself into a lie.

"You guys have been spotted around town a little bit," he says. "That's certainly an interesting woman to entertain. Not exactly a low-key relationship, wouldn't you agree?"

They're baiting me, and I'm not going to give them the pleasure of getting under my skin.

"Veronica and I met at the hotel bar, and we've become friends," I say coolly. "She's having some problems with her husband, but she's never mentioned Jacob to me."

The older cop's eyes narrow at me, trying to act as if he's a human fucking lie detector.

"We obtained your gun license and tracked a few of the guns you own," the younger cop says, pulling a piece of paper from his pocket. He turns it around to show me.

I keep my face unamused. The form details my Mateba Autorevolver, a rare find among gun enthusiasts, as production was incredibly limited. It's different from others like it because the cylinder is positioned at the bottom of the gun, lowering the bore axis and reducing the muzzle flip and recoil. Basically, it enhances the user's control and accuracy. It's an easy gun for me to recognize.

"Not many guns like this one," the officer says, pausing for dramatic effect. "We uncovered that its bullets were used on those recently found bodies. They match the gun you own."

What the fuck?

Outside, I can't help but let the surprise engulf my features. Because on the inside, my wheels are spinning. That wasn't even the gun I used to kill those guys. I know better than to use such a traceable gun to kill anyone. I'd never be that stupid. Besides, I prefer more hands-on methods. My guns are mostly for show and intimidation if things get out of hand.

This confirms what I needed to know—that I'm being set up intentionally. And it's by someone who knows enough about me to strategically plant evidence.

So why me?

"I'm guessing you claim to not know those other two gentlemen who were found dead. Is that right, son?" The older cop chuckles at his own joke.

"That would be correct," I reply. "Weren't they just drug dealers who ran around in rough crowds? Surely you should be looking inside the drug ring and not at me."

"Okay, but what about some of the women who have been found dead? They weren't part of some drug ring. Maybe you know something about them."

"Yeah, maybe you could tell us. We've heard that you have quite a reputation around the city," the older cop adds, smirking. "Especially with the ladies."

"Sorry, boys. Wish I could be of more help, but I don't know any of these people. If you have any more questions, let me know."

"Oh, you'll definitely be hearing from us, Ronan," the older cop says. "Don't you worry about that."

I watch as the two police officers walk back to their cruiser, often looking back to give me sly glances. Only when they drive away do I finally retreat into my house.

How the hell could they tie Jacob back to me? They don't have a body, I'm certain of that. There is no body to find.

Sylvie's comments about me smiling too much yesterday were right. She is always fucking right. Veronica, the two bodies they found, and the cops sniffing around about Jacob, of all people—too much is happening for all this to be a coincidence.

I need to get to the fucking bottom of this.

41

Veronica

When I return to the lobby of the hotel the next day, my mind is still a blur. As I walk up to the bar, the dread continues to settle in my stomach. Miranda is still not there. Instead, a red-haired guy is working behind the bar.

I try to ease my discomfort by reminding myself that maybe I'm jumping to conclusions. I saw her last night and even though she did not return for our conversation, maybe she got caught up and forgot about me waiting to meet her. Or maybe she was exhausted and just wanted to go home. I can't blame her—she had a long night, I'm sure. The last thing she probably wanted was to talk to me at midnight.

The bartender approaches me with a smile splayed across his face. "What can I do for you?" His voice is deep and cheery.

"I was actually hoping to see Miranda," I say, my voice shaking.

He lightly shakes his head while tucking his tongue into his cheek. "She worked the late shift last night, but she's off today."

My phone pings and I pull out my phone to see it's Ronan. I need to talk to him about last night, but I need some time to make sure I'm thinking clearly.

The bartender looks at me with a concerned expression, clearly noticing my deep thoughts. I offer him a small smile with a quick "thank you" before distancing myself from the bar.

I'm overreacting and jumping to conclusions to punish myself. She probably went home and is relaxing on her day off. There is no way her heated conversation with Ronan had anything to do with why she abruptly left last night. She did say she was trying to protect us both. But protect us both from what? Even with the reassurances I'm trying to coax through my brain, the weight of my suspicions lingers, the worry clawing at my insides.

No matter what I try to tell myself, the fact remains that this is the second person who has interacted with me and then disappeared without a trace.

My stomach churns slightly, and I know I won't feel at ease until I have the opportunity to talk to Miranda. For my sake, I hope that it's sooner rather than later.

Knowing I can't be alone right now, I punch a familiar number into my phone and wait for a comforting voice to answer.

Lauren is at the coffee shop in record time. Her hair is disheveled again, and a little sweat beads on her brow. She's huffing by the time she makes her way over to the table where I'm seated. I peer up at her over my coffee cup.

"How many laws did you break trying to get here as fast as you could?"

Her smile is sinister. "No law too big that a blow job couldn't get me out of it."

I burst out laughing at her sheer ridiculousness. "Lauren, I can't with you." I push the plate of donut holes in her direction, knowing these are one of her many vices.

"Okay, enough about my sex life," she says, clasping her hands together in eagerness. "Which, if you *must* know, Liam and I are doing great. Thanks for asking. I left him naked in my bed to be here. So, chop chop." She flings her hand around with impatience. "Give me all the dirty details."

I tell her about the last few times with Ronan. Our conversation today. How I'm starting to feel about him. The encounters with Richard. How Ronan makes me feel. My mind is in chaos. If someone had told me everything I'd go through in these last few weeks—shit, in these last few years—I would've laughed at them.

"So let me get this straight." Lauren's hands emphasize each word in her sentence. "Not only did you find a deliciously gorgeous man who, apparently, fucks like a god, but you're now falling in love with him?" Her laugh drowns out everything else in the room before I can answer. "I'm sorry, love. Not funny, not

265

funny." She waves her hands in surrender. "I'm just so happy for you. Richard can truly eat shit." She tosses a donut hole in the air and expertly catches it between her teeth.

She has always been effortlessly and annoyingly smooth. She leans back casually in her seat and looks at me through her eyelashes, a smirk growing on her lips as she finishes chewing. She reaches for her coffee cup and takes a small sip.

"Lauren, this is serious." I drop my forehead into the palms of my hands. "It's like I'm in high school again, and I'm obsessed with a guy I've known for less than two weeks. This shit isn't normal."

"Normal?" She huffs. "Darling, normal is boring. Richard is boring. You, my beautiful friend, are anything but boring."

I stride back into the hotel after meeting with Lauren. She did little to nothing to calm my nerves. It's no secret she hates Richard. She has every reason to hate him, just as much as I do. I've never really been in love, I don't think. So, how do you know when you love someone if you have no experience to compare it to?

It seems so juvenile until you're in it yourself. Trying to describe my connection with Ronan is pointless to any outsider. They'll never know what it feels like when we're together. Obsession seems like the most honest word. But love. Could it really be love in such a short amount of time?

Walking down the hallway, I'm completely lost in my thoughts, trying to unravel them. Approaching the door to my room, I'm shocked to find that it is slightly ajar. I rattle through my warped mind. I'm fairly sure I shut it before I left. Although I guess I did leave in a hurry. Or maybe Ronan came back and kept it open for me. More likely, it's probably just housekeeping tidying up my room.

I wait for a moment before convincing myself that I'm overre-acting. I'm sure everything is all right, and it was just an accident. Trying to relax, I let my shoulders drop and my jaw unclench. The world is not always out to get me.

I push open the door and step inside. There, sitting with his right ankle atop his left knee with his elbows braced on the back of the couch, is Richard. His face is a mask of disappointment and anger. His gray eyes are trained on my every movement.

"I see you're not understanding what I'm saying."

42

Taylor

Six Years Earlier

The next time I see her, I'm as shocked as I was the first time. The sense of surprise is followed by curiosity. After the last visit with her mother, why would she be back so soon?

"Hello." A slight inflection of curiosity sounds in my tone.

"Here to see my mom," she says, never looking up from the floor.

"Sweetheart, I'm sorry." I stand up from my desk, wringing my hands together. "After the last time, I'm afraid I cannot allow you back there alone."

The tears fall down her cheeks and drip onto the polished floor.

Her voice is so quiet, I almost believe I imagine her next words. "I hate her so much," she whispers before sobs rack her body.

I rush over to her from behind the desk and grab onto her shoulders, my eyes staring at her lowered face.

"I'm sorry, I know this is so hard," I say. "We're doing all we can to make your mom better so she can come home for good."

She sniffs before responding. "There is no fixing her." Her voice comes out angry.

I'm not sure how to respond.

"She's so much meaner when she drinks. I wish she would just stay here and never come back."

I bite back my tears. She looks so much younger than the last time I saw her. My heart breaks as I take in her words. The woman who is supposed to love her unconditionally has no doubt made her life so much more difficult.

I grab her hands with mine, and my breath catches. She notices my reaction and quickly withdraws her hands, a shadow of discomfort and annoyance passing over her face.

On instinct, I wrap my arms around her and hold her tenderly. To hell if this is inappropriate. She desperately needs someone to comfort her.

With my cheek pressed against the side of her head, I pull my head slightly back so that my lips are in line with her ear. I speak as quietly as I can.

"Everything will be okay," I say. "It'll all be okay."

43

Veronica

"Richard, what the fuck are you doing in my room?" I stare at him in disbelief, and his face doesn't change as his gaze bores into me.

"It's under my credit card," he huffs as the door clicks shut behind me.

"I think it's best if you leave," I say as calmly as I can, tightening my fists down by my sides before crossing my arms over my chest. Protective armor.

"Nice try." His laugh is cold, and his eyes are flat. "Do you really think I'm going to allow you to keep running around like a slut?"

He rises from the couch and stalks over to me. The anger radiates off him. He wraps his fingers around my neck. Instead of recoiling, I lean my head back slightly to further expose my throat. I look down at him over my nose.

I shouldn't be afraid of this man, and I'm not going to let him bully me around anymore. I'm no longer going to cower from him. He'll have to look me in the eyes.

"Pretty ballsy of you to show up here," I say. "You plastered your face all over the security cameras and then left fingerprints on my throat."

He lowers his eyes in question.

I curl my lips up in a slight smile. "You lay another finger on me, and you just might lose that hand, Richard." I stare defiantly at him.

He rips his hand from my throat and steps back abruptly. "I'm not leaving here without you, Veronica. This ends now. You're coming home."

I clear my throat. "I'm not going anywhere with you," I spit. "You're out of your mind."

"Is this really how you want this to play out?" His eyes widen, and his nostrils flare.

"It is, Richard," I say. "I'm not going home with you. That's not my home anymore."

The tension hangs thick in the air. I stand firm, my gaze locked with Richard's—my husband's. A man whose cruelty has affected my life. His eyes, cold and calculating, mirror my own unwavering resolve. We now stand at opposite ends of the room. I refuse to yield to him any longer, this man who has plagued me for too long, poisoning my life. Richard, his arrogance bolstered by years of dominance, shows no signs of relenting, either. He's used to getting exactly what he wants.

In this silent standoff, neither of us will be the one to back down.

"You're going to regret this, Veronica," he promises. "Mark my words."

"Believe me, there is nothing I will regret when it comes to you," I say, smiling without teeth and tilting my head to the side. I drop my eyes and let them roam over the full length of his body. "Ever wonder how they've been able to gather some specific information about what you've been doing?"

Every step I take forward, he takes one step back. But I know he's nothing, but a caged animal preparing to attack after being cornered.

He struggles to keep his composure, his face reddening as his upper lip twitches. His anger surges so powerfully, it's almost tangible. Yet, beneath the fiery tempest, a flicker of sadness dances in his gaze, a fleeting glimpse at the trust that was shattered in an instant. He thought he could trust me. His loving wife.

"How does it taste, Richard?" I ask.

He squints his eyes at me, considering my question. "How does what taste?"

"Betrayal," I reply. "Is it sour? Or maybe acidic? I've always found that it tastes bitter. Like an unripe fruit that leaves an aftertaste. Like the sharp tang of vinegar."

I push my tongue behind my teeth and tilt one side of my mouth upward.

His gaze flickers with flashes of intensity, darting from one point to another as he struggles to avoid an outburst. With each breath he takes, there is a subtle tremor—a slight quiver that betrays the emotions roiling inside him. He stiffens slightly as he braces himself against the anger threatening to consume him.

He stalks toward the door and, before walking out, he turns to say, "This isn't over, Veronica."

I smile wickedly at him in defiance. "Not even close," I answer.

He holds my gaze before slamming the door so hard that the paintings on the wall rattle.

Adrenaline pumps through my veins long after Richard has disappeared through the door. The slam rings throughout the hotel.

I've been playing the submissive homemaker for so long. But now, the puzzle pieces are finally falling into place. I'm so close to being rid of this nightmare. I'm not his property anymore; he doesn't own me.

A realization settles over me, followed by a sense of disbelief. For so long, I've grown accustomed to the bitter taste of disappointment and the constant struggle of misfortune. But now, I'm watching as the pieces of my plans are falling into place. Are things truly aligning in my favor? My heart pounds with a mixture of excitement. A glimmer of hope flickers in me.

As if in answer to my thoughts, I hear a knock at the door and march over to it, fearful that it's Richard, returned to rehash everything again.

Nervously, I press my eyes to the peephole and am relieved to see a man dressed in all black with a baseball cap dipped down over his face. He's looking at his phone.

Ronan.

He probably saw my text message and rushed over here to make sure I was okay. My skin warms at the sight of them. His protective nature always makes me feel so adored. I long to wrap my arms around his neck and tell him that I can finally see it—I see a future so clearly with him. I told Richard that it's over.

I rip open the door and lunge in his direction for an embrace.

"You surprised m—"

I don't even have a chance to finish my sentence before a set of unfamiliar eyes looks up at me. I gasp and step back, but not in time to avoid the black bag that's dropped over my head as I'm tugged from my room.

44

Ronan

"**F**uck," Sylvie yells. "What the hell do you mean there were two cops on your front porch?" Shaking her head, she abruptly spins away from me in her chair.

I press my fingers so deeply into my eyes that I see stars when I rub. I'm fucking exhausted. "Someone is setting me up, and I need to figure out how and why."

Sylvie curses under her breath as she types on her keyboard. "This is bad."

"No shit, Syl. I don't need a reminder," I snap in response before letting out a tired groan. "I'm sorry, I'm out of patience here."

After everything I've done, there is no way I'm getting sloppy. I've only gotten more precise over the years. When you do what I do, there is no room for error. Ever.

"I'm not seeing anything in the police database that would correlate with why they visited you." A frown forms across her face, and her voice is tinged with frustration. She's not used to coming up empty-handed, a personal pet peeve of hers. She needs answers, especially when one of our lives depends on it.

"So, whatever is going on is off the record?"

I sigh, leaning back further in my chair. That makes this situation more difficult.

"That's what it's looking like," she says, never taking her eyes off the screen.

What's different now? Mark's entrance into my work is out of character, but he has as much to lose as I do. There is no fucking way he'd involve the cops in this shit. He'd rather die in a fiery blaze of glory than rot in a prison cell for what he's done. That fact, I'm willing to bet my life on.

The only answer I can come up with is Veronica. And where she is, there her husband is, too. It's likely he'd have a vendetta against the man fucking his wife. My fists tighten at my sides. It feels like a puzzle piece settles into place when I think about Richard. He has to be the one behind this.

I feel like a fucking idiot. I knew that getting involved with Veronica would have its consequences, but I had no idea they'd be this severe. I thought I would just need to keep her safe, but it looks like I'm not safe, either.

Christ, Ronan. Focus...

"Can you get me some more details on Richard Sullivan's latest movements?"

Sylvie sighs and her shoulders sink. "You know how hard that can be. He's a political ghost. All I can find on him is what he wants us to find. It's election time and his image is squeaky clean, especially with all the coverage on him recently."

"If Richard is behind this, why now? It's a risky time for him to be involved in some shady off-the-books shit." My brain pulses as I try to make things make sense. "How would he know about me killing Jacob? And why would he want to keep this off the books? It'd be better for him to keep this official. It'd look good for his reputation."

"Maybe it has something to do with the fact that he was trying to have Jacob sleep with his wife?" Sylvie asks. "I'm sure *that* wouldn't look very good for his reputation."

"It makes sense as much as it doesn't. We need something tangible on this before I can make any moves."

"Do you think there is any chance he could've found out about the hit?"

Now this is a possibility I haven't thought of. Richard has eyes everywhere. For fuck's sake, the man is the state's district attorney. It's not impossible, but it's still unlikely. Mark and I did our due diligence. Is there a rat somewhere, leaking information? It has to be someone in Mark's circle. Another reason why my circle is so small.

"Mark did withdraw Richard's name from the list. Coincidence?" I mumble.

Sylvie's eyes shoot to mine. "Excuse me? You didn't think this was something I should know about?"

"I—" Shit. I fucked up.

She waves her hand at me. "I get it, you wanted me to keep tailing him because of the wife. It's fine."

She's annoyed, and she has every right to be. How can she trust me when I'm leaving out important pieces of information? It's not just me who's involved in this. She's as guilty as I am.

"I'll keep digging until I find something," she says as she leans closer to look at her screens.

"Thanks, Syl. Really. Couldn't do it without you."

I feel guilty about not telling Sylvie something so important. In order for us to be a team, we need to work together. Another reminder that my head is not in the game.

"Yeah, yeah. I know." She laughs, the tension easing slightly. "Just shut up about it and give me a raise instead."

45

Veronica

Darkness surrounds me as the rough fabric of the black hood hangs over my face. Muffled sounds of the outside world come and go while I'm forcefully carried to an unknown destination. I'm thrown against metal, and the impact sends shock waves through my body. My heart pounds in my chest, the sound reverberating in my confined space. My hands are tied behind my back, and my ankles are tightly tied together. I hear only muffled echoes of distant voices and the low rumble of an engine firing up.

I shouldn't have pushed Richard so far. Why'd I tell him that I was the rat giving the journalist information on his doings? That was going too far. I should've made sure I had a plan in place to keep me safe before outing myself. I knew he would be upset with me, but his punishment is to have me kidnapped? What is he thinking?

Each bump and sway of the vehicle serves as a reminder of my helplessness. It's punishment for what I've done. Sweat beads on my brow, and I twist and fidget against my restraint, desperate for any shred of hope.

My breath is shallow and requires too much effort. I begin to feel dizzy as my consciousness fades out of reach. The darkness is now completely taking hold.

The hood is yanked from my head, and my eyelids blink rapidly, trying to adjust to the fluorescent lights beaming overhead. My heart pounds in my chest, and droplets of sweat travel down my skin. The edges of my vision are still black, and my eyes are unfocused, thanks to a skull-splitting headache that engulfs my head.

The space I find myself in resembles a basement, with its concrete walls and overpowering emptiness. The ceiling is supported by sturdy, exposed beams. The air is musty, carrying a faint scent of concrete and old construction materials.

A tall man comes into focus underneath the harsh lights and my eyes snap in his direction. He's not alone; I see two men behind him and another man standing back to guard the door.

"What do you want?" My voice quivers as I speak, my fear palpable.

As he walks across the floor, I see it's covered in a patchwork of worn-out tiles. Water stains mark the walls behind him; the only noticeable features are the various exposed pipes. Footsteps creak as they make their way over to me.

I huff a breath to blow the hair from my eyes, desperate to use whatever bargaining tips I can to get myself out of this situation as fast as possible.

"Please, tell Richard we can discuss this," I beg, softening my voice.

The first man who stands closest to me stares at me intently. A crease between his two brows deepens as they pinch together. His frustration is visible as the muscles in his jaw clench.

"Tell him I'm sorry for the stuff I said earlier. I was out of line," I cry, desperate to escape.

I didn't think Richard would take it this far. But I should've known better.

The man hesitates for a moment, then he spits onto the concrete floor before replying. The moment of silence can't prepare me for the words that come out of his mouth.

"Who the fuck is Richard?"

46

Ronan

Tailing two police officers is a lot easier than I thought it would be. Especially these two idiots—they're oblivious of everything around them, but right now, they are my biggest lead to figuring out what the hell is going on.

I take a picture of their license plate as they exit the car and send the image to Sylvie. Sitting in the parking lot of a local bar, I watch them as they disappear through the front door.

For a second, my annoyance gets the better of me, and I think about going inside. Drawing attention to myself will only make things worse. They'd probably try to provoke me, and it'd be impossible to keep myself from beating the shit out of them. That's one way to end up in a jail cell faster.

I need to wait them out and see where they go after this. That might give me a clue as to who they're working with.

I glance back at my phone and my annoyance peaks. No messages or calls from Veronica. I haven't heard from her since last night and it pisses me off. I click her name on my phone to call her.

You've reached Veronica Sullivan. Please leave a message after the beep.

I toss my phone into my passenger seat. Her phone must be off, and I wonder if she's avoiding me. All of this shit I'm going through is likely because of her and she's blowing me off. All I need is confirmation that Richard is involved in this, and I'll figure out where to go from there.

I had already been planning on killing him. Maybe I need to come clean to Veronica about everything and let her know I was hired to kill Richard. I need to make sure she understands that's not why I'm interested in her. She was never meant to be a part of this. It was by pure chance that I spotted her that night in the bar. With her involvement, she could help me take him out. Something a little less hands-off. It wouldn't be satisfying, but it would keep me out of prison in more ways than one.

My phone rings and I move quickly to grab it, anxious to talk to Veronica.

"Hey, Ronan," Sylvie says, her voice trailing off.

"Yeah?" I reply. "Did you find something?"

She pauses, and I can hear the hesitation in her voice.

"When was the last time you talked to Veronica?"

47

Veronica

His words echo in my ears as the first real tendril of panic winds its way through my chest. I'm in real danger. My breaths are uneven, and my lungs refuse to fill with air. A tightening sensation grips my throat, constricting it like an invisible hand. Each inhale is a desperate struggle. The world around me blurs, distorted by the haze of anxiety clouding my vision. My restricted palms are clammy. I'm trapped.

No one knows I'm here.

The unknown man steps closer before clearing his throat to speak again. "Your little boyfriend had the audacity to attack my son and his friend."

My mouth falls open momentarily before I snap it shut.

This is about Ronan.

I try to speak, but my voice croaks. I try to swallow, but my throat feels like it is coated in razor blades. I cough, trying to regain my composure.

"I don't know what you're talking about," I squeak.

He cocks his head slightly, but his gaze never falters. A sinister smirk that makes my skin crawl dances across his lips.

"Oh, don't you?" he purrs, taking a few steps closer to me. "You don't remember the two men you met one night? You almost took them both back to your hotel room."

He looks at me with true disgust on his face.

My mouth drops open. That's what this is about? Those two assholes from the hotel who tried to take advantage of me the night Ronan saved me?

He must see the gleam of recognition in my eye.

"Luckily, they decided you were too drunk and went home."

His smirk breaks into a devilish smile that sends a shudder down my spine. I'm going to be sick.

"That's not true," I spit out, then shout, "They didn't leave me—they were going to rape me."

His face burns in anger, and he shoots forward, wrapping a calloused hand around my throat. His smile has completely disappeared.

"Shut the fuck up," he spits in my face. "You were probably begging for it. Dumb sluts like you always do. Then you try to play it off like you didn't want it."

He pinches his lips together and looks down at me like he's the one who is going to be sick. All the while, his hand is still gripping my throat. Pressure pushes at my temples as my lungs struggle to take in air.

"You don't know what he did to them, do you?" he asks.

I shake my head aggressively. I don't have the slightest idea what he's referring to. For all I know, Ronan saved me and then we went on our first date that night.

"Your little boyfriend paid a visit to them the next day. Beat them both so badly that my son's friend will probably never walk again. He ruined my son's hand." He flares his nostrils. "Since then, we've traveled to many reconstructive surgeons, the best in the country, and nothing can be done to salvage the damage that was done."

I notice his other fist clenching by his side while his grip tightens on my throat. My eyes begin to bulge from the restraint. A single tear escapes from my eye and rolls down my face onto his hand.

"Your boyfriend broke his fingers at every joint. Do you want to know why he did what he did?"

His voice is unsteady with anger, his eyes twitching with un-kempt fury behind them. He finally lets go of my throat and pushes me back so that the chair scrapes across the floor.

I choke on coughs as spit sputters from my mouth. I drop my gaze and try to catch my breath. After a few moments, I look back up to him with tears coursing down my cheeks. I realize he wants me to answer him.

"No..." My voice is hoarse, and it hurts to speak.

"He said it was because that hand touched something that belonged to him. And since he'd touched something that was his, he would make sure my son could never use that hand again."

A sliver of pride churns in my stomach among the rolling nausea.

His.

I try to not convey the emotions on my face. What's wrong with me? Shouldn't I be horrified by what Ronan did to those men?

No, I'm not. They deserved it. Ronan gave them exactly what they deserved.

"Unfortunately for you, your boyfriend is not an easy person to get a hold of. But I bet he'll come running to save you. Won't he, princess?"

The man closest to him steps forward hesitantly, cracking his knuckles. He steps around me and goes to the back of the chair, grabbing hold of the pinky finger on my left hand.

"The longer he takes, the more time we have to dirty up his little toy. Perhaps we'll send you to him in pieces."

He twists my finger with a sickening crack.

48

Ronan

I hear a loud snap, and Veronica screams as I bite my tongue. My mouth pools with blood and saliva. This is because of what I did to those two fucks from the hotel bar.

They are hurting Veronica because of me. I've left a never-ending trail of enemies behind me. Sylvie was right—Veronica will always be a target when it comes to me. Thankfully, Sylvie saw some footage of Veronica being put into the back of the van in a dark part of the hotel's parking deck. Extra surveillance of the hotel has proven to be more than necessary over the last week. When I said I'd do anything to protect Veronica, I meant it.

And I'll kill anyone who tries to come between us.

I shove open the door with both hands. Every head whips in my direction. I see a brief wave of relief wash over Veronica's face before she tenses back up, her face contorted in pain.

She thinks we're both in danger. These men are unpredictable, and they have a score to settle.

But she doesn't know exactly who I am yet.

Unfortunately for her, she's about to find out.

I stop a few steps inside the room and tilt my head to take in Veronica's appearance.

"Hello, love," I say cheekily.

Her chest heaves in deep sobs as she leans forward, her face tilting down toward the floor.

The man standing behind her raises a knife to her throat.

I click my tongue. "I wouldn't do that, if I were you," I say.

The one holding the knife to her throat scoffs. "And why is that?" He smiles in my direction.

The other men shift in preparation throughout the room.

"If you hurt her," I say, as a smile spreads across my face, "then I have no reason to leave here alive."

"We don't intend to let either of you leave here alive," the man behind Veronica replies.

"Neither would any of you," I add. "You hurt her, and I have no problem setting this place on fire with all of us still inside."

One of the other men lowers his eyebrows in question. "You wouldn't..." he says, hoping to call my bluff.

The man's hand holding the knife at Veronica's throat twitches slightly as he assesses my threat.

"Want to find out?" I laugh, flicking open the lighter in my hand, finger atop the ignition. "Should've thought about where you were taking your hostage."

I've always hated the places where I do business, but it pays to have the knowledge I do. A lot of old warehouses store highly flammable materials, such as chemicals, paints, or oils, in their recesses. This one is no different. Older buildings always have outdated electrical systems or neglected maintenance that are obvious fire hazards, especially with faulty wiring or overloaded circuits.

The man behind Veronica retracts his knife from her throat and starts walking toward me.

"Then she'll watch you die."

His steps quicken, and I predict his first blow. He swings the knife at me, and I dodge at the last second, letting his blow slice through the air. He recovers quickly and spins to strike again. I catch it in a closed hand, letting the blade cut deep into my flesh. His eyes widen as he looks at my grip on his knife.

I smile at him as the blood drips down the handle of the knife onto his hand, showing him just how little the pain affects me. He tries to rip the knife from my hand at the same moment I knee him in his groin. He hunches over, dropping the knife and giving me the perfect opportunity.

I grab the knife from the floor, then pull him by the hair on his scalp to stand up straight. Cleanly, I drag the blade across his neck as I stand behind him.

Letting his body drop to the floor, I turn my focus back to Veronica to make sure she's unharmed. A large body collides with me from the side, and we crash to the ground as my breath heaves out of me.

I wrap my arms around his shoulders before turning him onto his back. I grab the pipe from his hands and strike him across the side of his head, knocking him unconscious.

I stand abruptly and brush off my shirt, looking at the only remaining person in the room besides Veronica and me.

"You must be the father."

I smirk, spitting blood onto the floor before wiping my mouth with the back of my arm.

"Pity. I should've killed your son and saved us both the fucking trouble."

His eyes glaze over as he lunges at me, wrapping his arms around my ribs and pushing me back into the wall. He grabs my shirt collar and lands a few jabs in my face. The next time he rears his fist back, I slip out of his grip and duck, letting his fist collide with the concrete wall. This gives me just enough time to twist his other arm and pin it behind his back.

"Ronan!" Veronica yells. "He has a gun!"

I see the man's free arm move as he points a barrel over his shoulder directly into my face. He pulls the trigger, and I drop to the floor to avoid the bullet. It ricochets off the wall, but I can't see where it hits. Veronica screams, and my heart stops.

Please, baby, please be okay. All of this can't be for nothing.

291

Focusing solely on getting the gun out of his hands, I yank him down by his legs. He fumbles with the gun momentarily, and I use that moment to slap it out of his hands. It skids across the floor, and he watches it move farther away.

I twist him onto his back and wrap my fingers around his throat. Pressing as hard as I can, I yell as my fingers squeeze tighter. His face is losing color. His mouth cracks open as he tries to pull in oxygen.

I hold tightly until I can see life leave his eyes, pausing for just a bit longer to ensure he's gone. I push up to my feet and drag my eyes slowly over to where the lone chair sits in the room. There, I glimpse Veronica and see her struggling against her restraints.

She's alive. She's okay.

I stand up and walk to the gun that's still resting on the floor. I pick it up and swiftly shoot the unconscious man right in between his two eyes—not taking any more chances.

Then I rush toward Veronica and drop to my knees to untie her feet. I crawl behind her to untie her hands and see her mangled pinky finger.

"You're about to be really mad at me," I say, breathlessly.

"What do you m—" She screams as I snap her finger back into place. "Holy fucking shit, Ronan. Was that supposed to be a heads-up?" She bursts into sobs.

"I'm sorry, I had to do it."

Untying her hands, I put one arm behind her back and the other behind her knees. I wrap her tightly in my arms, since shielding her from any more danger is more important than anything else right now. She collapses into my chest and lets out a sob. Her body trembles in my arms.

I pull back to look down at her and see her mascara streaking down her cheeks. Her eyes are red, and her expression is pinched. Overwhelmed with the idea that I almost lost her, I let the adrenaline drive me and my mouth crashes down onto hers. She kisses me back as she wraps her arms around my neck, slithering around my body until her legs are wrapped around my waist.

I step back until she's resting against a wall and allow her to lean back to support us. I push up against her. Our kiss is greedy and angry. It's packed full of every emotion we've both felt over the last twenty-four hours. It's a mess of tongues and teeth, as our hands grab at each other. She undoes my belt as I pull her shirt up to expose her breasts, tugging her bra down to cover her nipple with my mouth. With trembling fingers, she unbuttons and unzips her jeans before arching against me to tug them down.

I place her down gently, then put a hand on either side of her jeans and pull them to her feet as she steps out of them, one by one. Our eyes stay locked on one another. She drops her panties and I do the same with my pants and briefs. Wrapping her in my arms, I hoist her back up against the wall with her legs around my waist. With one arm cupped around her back, I use the other to brace against the wall.

I bury myself so deep in her as I push my face into her neck.

This woman. She's mine.

I beat into her until I feel her clenching down around me and hear her cry out. Her screams echo throughout the room. There's blood rubbing off on her, my bleeding hand leaving red handprints across her body and the wall. She drops down onto me and pants. Lifting her head slowly, she recognizes where we are and what has happened. She looks at the bodies littered across the floor.

"Ronan," she whispers. "What have you done?"

49

Taylor

Six Years Earlier

Her room is dark when I enter, and I hear the rhythmic breathing that lets me know she is asleep. I grab the door with both hands to ensure it closes without making any noise.

I quietly approach the center of the room, where her bed sits. It's easy to swiftly lift the comforter and sheet she has across her body, just at the corner, so her foot is visible. It twitches briefly, and I pause to make sure she is not waking up.

When she remains still, I act quickly. I pull the syringe from my pocket and exhale a deep breath. I slightly separate her big toe and her next one, knowing this will be an unlikely spot for them to notice a small syringe puncture. I pierce the skin and push the liquid from the vial into her body. My hands tremble as I press the plunger slowly, the solution disappearing beneath the skin as I hold my breath.

My chest tightens and yet, beneath the panic, a thrill buzzes in my veins like electricity. Sharp and addictive.

Once it is empty, I quickly cover her feet up again and stride out the door, back to my desk.

And, again, I wait.

50
Veronica

Sitting in the passenger seat of Ronan's car, my eyes focus on the blur moving past us. The throbbing in my head hasn't lightened, and I cradle my pinky finger delicately, the bruising already visible in an angry purple design.

My mind races with everything that has happened in the last twenty-four hours. I'm desperately looking for something, anything, to grasp onto that can anchor me back to reality. I haven't even told Ronan about Richard showing up in my hotel room yet.

My heart thunders in my chest like a beast trapped in a cage. The air feels thin, and I'm still struggling to breathe. I fold down the visor of Ronan's car and glance at my neck in the mirror. A necklace of fingerprints lines my flesh. I see him glance over at me uneasily.

I can't breathe. I can't think clearly. I can't comprehend what just happened. The bodies, the blood. It was all so messy, unlike anything I've ever done.

The undeniable truth of what has happened is like a relentless wave crashing over me.

I open my mouth to say something to Ronan, but only a croak escapes. I had known Ronan was dangerous, but to see it happen before my eyes is an entirely different experience. There's brutality in his actions and a swiftness in his movements. I was horrified and enraptured at the same time. To tie it all up with a bow, I had sex with him immediately after, while the bodies of my kidnappers were still warm.

I don't regret it. Not a single moment of anything. The fact that I feel no remorse is what scares me.

I don't know who I'm more scared of: Ronan or myself.

We are an explosive pair. One might say we are dangerous together. Is our addiction to one another healthy? Is this a path we should continue down?

Are we going to leave everything and everyone else to burn behind us?

"You hurt those men?" My voice is barely above a whisper, as if I'm afraid to disturb the dead. "For touching me?"

"Of course I did," he says like he's answering a simple question. "I promised to always protect you."

My lip trembles. Out of surprise? Or admiration? I don't know.

"Is there anything else you're keeping from me?"

He remains silent, staring ahead and not taking his eyes off the road. The silence is very telling. He is keeping secrets from me.

"Jacob has been missing," I say. "Did you have something to do with that?"

His jaw twitches, and his eyes narrow in a silent admission of guilt.

"But why would you do something to Jacob?" I ask. "He was nothing to me."

"I heard what he said to you that night at the bar," he says, his voice even lower. "No one will speak to you like that, not as long as I'm around."

"We hadn't even spoken, though!" My voice sounds shrill. "What did you do to the bartender? Miranda?"

His mouth opens and then immediately shuts, like he's not sure what to say.

"Did you kill her because she told me to stay away from you?"

His brow furrows. He looks confused and angry. "You think I hurt Miranda?" he asks. His voice is quiet, like he's struggling to speak. "She told you to stay away from me?"

"I saw you talking to her at the hotel the night after you left because you said you had to work," I add.

He pauses, and his eyes stay forward.

"Tell me what else you're hiding from me," I shout before he has a chance to continue with his admission of guilt.

For once, he looks like he's at a loss for words. His usually bronze skin has a slightly ashen tone to it. His eyes stay glued to the road.

"I lied to you about knowing who Richard was," he replies. "One of the targets I was following that night was your husband. At first, I didn't know who you were, I swear. I only knew that one of his credit cards was used for a reservation at the hotel." He glances over at me. His eyes are heavy and filled with sadness. "Meeting you was by chance. I never planned to use that against Richard."

"You lied to me?" My voice is hoarse, and I wrap my hand around my throat, trying to force the sob back down. "You were hired to kill Richard, but you decided to do something else, like fuck his wife?"

Even from a side view, I can see his eyes darken, and a growl escapes his throat.

"Don't you dare call yourself his wife. You know goddamn well you haven't belonged to him in a long time."

His eyes dart over to look into mine.

"You're right, Ronan," I say. "I don't belong to anyone. Especially not you."

I see his jaw muscle pulse as he tightens his grip on the steering wheel.

I thought I knew this man. But he's just been lying to me the whole time.

"I figured out who you were early on, and I'll forever regret not coming clean at that moment," he says. "Things were different with you. I didn't want to fuck it up and break your trust." His voice is sincere. His eyes gleam with sadness.

"You didn't want to fuck it up?" I can't stop the tears from falling now. They cascade down my cheeks. I feel defeated and heartbroken. This man promised he'd always take care of me. He made me think it would be different. I don't know what to believe anymore. "Well, what do you call this, then?"

He jerks the steering wheel to the right and pulls his car over suddenly, throwing it into park. He leans closer to me, and I back away out of instinct.

"You want me to be the villain in your story?" he asks, his eyes wild and searching mine. "Then I'll be your fucking villain, Veronica."

He presses his body closer to mine, his breath warm on my face.

"But let me tell you how this story ends. The villain gets the girl."

I stare deep into those blue eyes I've come to adore. I want nothing more than that to be the way this story ends. But how can you continue something that started based on a lie? I slump back into my seat and cross my arms across my chest.

"I want to go back to the hotel," I say.

"Great idea." He scoffs. "Walking through a public hotel covered in blood. No one will notice."

My eyes cut over to him as the car starts moving again.

"At least come back to my place and get cleaned up," he pleads. "I'll give you the space you need to digest everything that's happened."

We drive the rest of the way in silence before parking outside his house. He turns to face me, looking down through his full eyelashes, blue eyes blazing beneath. He grabs my chin and tilts my head up further to look at him. Even sitting, he towers over me. He lifts his thumb to rub it across my bottom lip while his teeth sink into his.

"I'd do anything to be with you, Veronica," he says, staring into my eyes. "Anything."

I feel myself unraveling, and it's so hard to feel anything but adoration for this man. I nod simply, the tears welling in my eyes again.

"I need to shower, and then I think I'll go spend some time with Lauren," I tell him. "I won't be alone, and I won't be at the hotel."

"Okay, I'll give you some space." His voice sounds somber. "I'll go out for a drive while you shower and get ready. Just let me know when you're leaving."

He plants a kiss on my forehead, and I feel my stomach tighten.

He nods and lets go of my chin. Pulling on the door handle, I step out of the car and toward his house. This house has felt more like home than anything has in years, and I'm not sure I'm ready to walk away. I feel the continued pull toward Ronan—my desire to be with him is stronger than my current frustration. He didn't tell me about Richard, but that probably would've ended our relationship before it even started. Can I blame him?

After all, I can't be this mad at him for secrets he's kept. Not when I'm still keeping my own.

"Ronan, please." I turn back to him before shutting the door.

His eyes are soft as he turns to face me.

"Don't leave."

51

Ronan

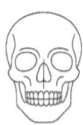

My shoulders sag in relief at her asking me to stay. I know she's not done with me yet. She came face to face with who I truly am, and it scared her. I don't blame her. My world isn't for the faint of heart, but I'm not giving up on her.

I thought she needed time to cool off and think about what's happened. It's been a hell of a week for her. I know how she feels about me—I can see it in her eyes every time she looks at me. I can feel it in her touch. I'm an obsession she craves, one she can't live without, and I refuse to live without her.

Never again. She's mine.

But I'm also hers.

I wasn't lying to her. I was going to give her the space she needed. I'd do anything for her, no matter how much it pained me.

I open the door and slide out of my car. Approaching my front door, I turn my shoulder to avoid running into Veronica. She is still holding onto her bruised pinky finger.

I unlock the door and push it open for her. "You can use the shower in my room upstairs. I'll shower down here, and then we can talk in the living room."

It feels like hours pass before she comes trudging down the stairs, hair still wet and pinned to the top of her head. She's opted to change into one of my T-shirts and a pair of gym shorts. Even when she doesn't try, she takes my breath away.

"Listen, Ronan. It's been a weird day. I'm sorr—"

I grab her hand from her lap and grip it between my two hands.

"There is no need to apologize. Today was a lot. I wouldn't be mad if you didn't want to see me anymore."

Her green eyes widen, and she looks up to meet mine. I notice they are lined in silver, and I reach out to grab the side of her face. I can't stomach seeing her cry anymore, especially over me.

"Ronan, are you crazy?"

I tilt my head to the side, unsure of what she's referencing. "I think after today, you could call me certifiably insane."

"No." She shakes her head aggressively. "I'm not so sure anything could make me not want to see you anymore."

A burst of hope explodes in my chest.

The next surprise is that she leans forward and kisses me. I press the back of her head to get her closer to me. I want to inhale the words she just said, hold them captive forever.

She pulls back suddenly, trying to catch her breath. "Ronan, I don't want to be without you."

We lock our eyes for a moment until we feel a buzz from one of our phones.

We glance down to see it's Veronica's. Her eyes fill with disappointment.

"He's calling again," she huffs.

"Then let me answer."

Anger pulses through my veins. Another thing Richard is fucking up for me.

She laughs and snatches her phone away. "No way. He'd send someone here to kill us both."

I raise an eyebrow before replying. "I'd like to see him try."

I plant a rough kiss on her lips as I'm still fuming with anger. Something deep in my gut tells me that Richard is behind a lot of these recent events.

"I can think of a million other things I'd rather do with you than have you talk to Richard," she says with a sly smile.

"Oh yeah?"

She climbs on top of me and begins grinding her hips against my already hard cock. I want to bury myself inside of her until she's screaming my name.

Her phone starts vibrating again, and before she can silence it, I roll over and pin her down on her back, holding her legs in place with mine. I reach down to grab her phone from her hands.

"Ronan, no—" She snaps her mouth shut as I click "accept" on her screen. Then I press the phone to her ear. "H—hey, Richard. What do you want?" She's flustered and trying to gain her composure.

"Why are you ignoring my calls again?" The voice is slightly muted but obviously angry.

Good.

I lower myself down on her body and stop between her legs. Her eyes widen as she stares down at me. I grip the waistband of my shorts she's wearing, tugging them slowly down her legs.

"I have nothing to say to you," she says into the phone, eyes still focused on me. She places her hand over the bottom of her phone before whispering, "Ronan, please."

After removing her shorts, my fingers slowly trace up her thighs, and her skin prickles beneath my fingertips. A smile breaks out across my face as I discover she's not wearing anything underneath. I press her thighs open wider. The last thing I hear is the angry tone of her stupid fucking husband buzzing as I bury my face in her pussy.

She yelps and pushes a hand to her mouth.

"N-no, I'm fine," she rasps, taking slow inhales and exhales to calm herself.

I circle her clit slowly with my tongue as she tries to hold it together. She closes her eyes, and I see her throat bob as she swallows.

I crawl up to her as she continues to listen to whatever rambling is happening on the other end of the phone. I hover over her face, and we keep our eyes locked as I slide my cock between her wet thighs. I shove myself in and can't help but groan at the soft warmth that fits me so perfectly.

She hisses in a deep breath and realizes her mistake a moment too late.

"Are you—are you with someone?"

Her eyes dart around, as if trying to decide whether to lie or be honest. After all, this was his dumbass idea.

"Uh..." she says, a combination between the word she tried to say and a moan that escapes her lips.

Slowly picking up the pace, the rambling from the speaker becomes louder and angrier.

"Who is there?" Richard screams. "What the fuck is this, Veronica?"

"I, uh—" she rasps. "I've got to go."

She hangs up and then throws her phone off the bed onto the floor.

I start pounding into her, and she squeals as she wraps her arms around my shoulders, burying her face into my chest. My selfishness and desire to have her sets my skin blazing. A stupid part of me hoped she'd come clean and tell him about me. And tell him it's over between the two of them.

Mine. She's mine.

As I feel her walls clench down around me, I let go and we ride out our orgasms at the same time.

Afterward, lying on my back, I put my hands behind my head in a casual posture with my eyes closing as I take deep breaths.

She rolls over to look at me.

"When will you tell him?" I ask through closed eyes.

She lays her head on my chest and strokes my arm.

And to me, her silence seems like a hesitation in her heart. Just like that, Richard has ruined yet another moment for us.

52

Ronan

Time passes slowly as we lie together on the couch in silence. I glance down at Veronica, who is tucked into my side.

She stayed over last night. She was afraid Richard might show up at the hotel after that phone call. I roll over to face her and wrap her in my arms. I could get used to this. She smells sweet, almost like flowers after a rainy day. I breathe in her scent.

Her green eyes flutter open, and she looks at me briefly before smiling. "I'm sorry about Richard," she says.

"No, I'm sorry I answered the phone. That was a shitty thing to do to you," I reply.

"It was." Her face cracks into a grin. "But it was pretty fun."

I chuckle at her response, and she sits up to gaze down at me. She stares at me in silence, her eyes searching mine for whatever answers she's hoping to find. "I don't know enough about you to feel the way I do," she finally says.

A triumphant grin spreads across my face.

"I'll tell you anything you want to know."

She adjusts uncomfortably, crossing her legs beneath her. I place a hand on her thigh over the sheet. I realize she's waiting for me to speak, not wanting to intrude.

I tell her about my upbringing, my voice shaking as I recall the painful memories I tried so hard to suppress. I tell her about my mother's long string of abusive boyfriends, each one more violent than the last. I talk about my mom's relentless struggle with addiction. My chest tightens as I speak of the love I had for my mother, a love that burned brightly in the otherwise suffocating darkness of my life.

I paint a vivid picture of the horror, giving her details of the abuse my mom and I both suffered. I tell Veronica about how my mom tried to shield me from their wrath, but how could she protect me when she was unconscious or too high to stand? Pinching my eyes shut, I can still see her bruised and battered body. I can still hear her sobs that she tried to stifle for my sake.

I open my eyes to see Veronica's filled with sympathy and horror. She listens intently, her expression a mix of disbelief and sorrow. Coming to the worst part of all, I take a deep breath to steady myself. I recount how my mom was eventually beaten to death by one of her boyfriends, a man consumed by alcohol and drugs. The argument had been over something as stupid as money, yet it escalated into a lethal confrontation. The memory is forever burned into my brain: the sound of his fists connecting with her fragile body, the sickening thud as she hit the ground, lifeless.

The hardest part for me to relive is the moment I found her. I tell Veronica about walking into the room, my heart stopping as I saw my mother's body sprawled on the floor, her lifeless eyes staring at nothing. The shock, the paralyzing grief, the overwhelming sense of loss—all of it comes rushing back in that moment. I remember screaming, the sound tearing from my throat as I cradled her cold, still form.

Veronica reaches out, her hand gently squeezing mine, offering silent support as I finally lay bare the darkest parts of my soul.

Relief seeps out of me as I let everything come to the surface. I realize how truly special Veronica has become. I knew the time would come when I needed to be completely honest with her about everything. About me. I just didn't know how easy it would be to tell her.

Clearing my throat before continuing, "The guy—my mom's murderer—he's up for parole now. He could be out any day now, and I'm really struggling with it."

I look up and see tears welling up behind her lashes. She sniffles before reaching to cup my face with her hand.

"I'm so sorry about your mom, Ronan," she says.

She blinks slowly, her hand tenderly caressing my face. Her touch numbs the rage going on inside me.

"It all got me to where I am today," I say. "Still hurts like hell though. But I have someone who works with me, Sylvie.

She's practically the sister I never had growing up. You'd love her. She sees through people like glass. She's the kind of person who doesn't back down, doesn't soften herself to make anyone else comfortable." I laugh. "Honestly, you two have that in common."

Admiration shines from Veronica's eyes as she looks at me.

"I hope I can meet her one day, if that's something you'd want?"

I press my lips to her forehead.

"What about your family?" I ask, desperate to know everything about the woman before me. "I don't think I've heard you talk about them."

She rips her eyes away from me and looks down at nothing. "I don't want to talk about my family," she says, so quietly that I'm not sure if she even said the words aloud.

She sucks in a shaky breath before blowing it out via pursed lips. I can feel her hand trembling against my face. She drops it down into her lap and gazes at it. Her eyes return to mine, and she speaks low.

"I feel so stupid comparing my worst day to yours. It's nothing in comparison." Tears well up in her eyes.

I pull her hand to my mouth and press my lips against it.

"Good thing this isn't a competition," I say as a small smile curls across her mouth.

She dabs at a tear before it falls down her cheek.

"My childhood was complicated." Her voice breaks as she speaks. "I was a moody teenager, but honestly, isn't that what they say about every teen?"

She lightly shakes her head. Her lips twitch to one side as if she's contemplating what to say next. "It's hard to describe how I spent most of my childhood. I felt unloved, and I wasn't sure if I'd ever want children of my own. How could I trust myself to love my own kid when I'm not sure if I know how to love?

"At that moment, it was settled. I had other things to focus on, so I decided I wouldn't worry myself over having kids," she says, lifting her shoulders and then letting them relax back into place. "Then three years ago, things felt off, and I took a pregnancy test."

Her eyes go vacant, and she blinks rapidly as if she's trying to fight back her impending emotion.

"It was positive." She clears her throat, and I know that Richard is about to come up. He's a sore subject for both of us, given our current predicament.

"Richard was very vocal about not wanting children. That ship had sailed for him long ago. For the first time in years, I was excited, and I started to look forward to each day. I kept the secret from Richard, feigning an illness and staying in bed as often as possible. To me, it wasn't his baby. It was my baby. Mine and only mine."

Her voice is barely above a whisper as she says this last part.

"Then at my first appointment, they brought me back into the ultrasound room. They found the embryo, but they told me there was no heartbeat."

She purses her lips together, and I see them tremble slightly.

"In an instant, something I wanted for myself had been taken away yet again. It was like my own body betrayed me. I'd finally started to feel like I was ready. I found an unexpected purpose. But I miscarried alone a week later. And I never told Richard anything that happened."

She looks up at me, tears filling her eyes.

"I just kind of accepted that I'd always be alone after that." She sniffs. "I had started making plans to leave with the baby, like faking my own death just to get away from him. You know, all those unlikely scenarios that you see in movies. Blame it on the hormones, I suppose. I thought I could do it."

This piques my interest, that she always planned to leave Richard.

"You knew that you and Richard wouldn't last?" I ask.

She chuckles lightly, not with amusement but as if she feels uncomfortable. "Yeah. It's—uh, it's complicated."

Something passes through her eyes, that familiar yet unfamiliar glaze I've seen all too often from her. Something I still just cannot quite pinpoint. The mystery of this woman drives me crazy, keeps me on my toes. She's letting me in but not completely, I can tell.

"Do you want kids?" she says to break the silence.

These words spill out of her mouth, and I'm once again lost in the chaos of what I feel for her.

I hold her gaze. She takes my silence as her answer, dropping her eyes to her hands, fidgeting in her lap. She looks as if she recognizes that once again, life has dealt her a losing hand of cards.

I raise my hand to her face and nudge her chin up.

"To be honest, before I met you, no," I reply solemnly. It's the truth.

Her eyes quiver, and a tear slips down her cheek. After what happened to my mom and what we went through, how could I ever imagine myself as a father?

I cup both of my hands around her face. "I never thought I was worthy of having a family of my own."

Her mouth drops open, and she sucks in a surprised breath.

"I can't explain this thing between us, the way I feel when I'm around you." I intertwine my fingers with hers. "I've never really dated, and I definitely don't do...whatever the fuck we are." We both laugh at my confession. "The truth is, I don't think I can be without you at this point," I say. "I've lived so much of my life full of rage, and you're the first person who has gotten me to see past my anger."

Her eyes soften as she stares back at me.

"Veronica, I'm still not sure that I'm worthy of you, but I'd do anything to be. Being with you feels like coming home for the first time. To a real home. A happy home with a family."

I drop my mouth to hers in a passionate kiss. I said all I needed to say to let her know I'm in this, whatever this is. We'll figure it out together.

She pulls back from me and cups my face in her hands. "You are so much more than your past, Ronan," she says, green eyes bright. "There is so much about me that I want to share with you—"

I place my thumb to her bottom lip in response. "You'll tell me in time. We have nothing but time together."

My phone pings, and I see it's a text message from Mark, asking to meet. Hopefully, he wants to talk about the end of this contract so I can move on. His money isn't worth it anymore, especially now that I know he can't even trust people in his inner circle. Getting involved with him was a stupid decision, and I'm ready to wash my hands of him. I'll need to give him a heads-up about someone leaking information to Richard about the hit.

Maybe I can figure out a way to get rid of Richard without having to kill him. I don't need anything else weighing on Veronica's conscience. I can force Mark and Richard to be each other's prime targets.

"I know this is horrible timing yet again," I say, "but I need to go. I'll be back as soon as I can." I lean down and press a tender kiss to her lips.

In the car, I wrap my fingers around the steering wheel. My knuckles turn white from the added pressure. I feel a tiny bit of satisfaction in letting out my frustration. I shift into drive and pull away from my house and the woman I love.

I grab my phone to dial Sylvie.

"Sylvie, listen," I say as soon as the ringing stops. "I need some information on Richard."

I hear a sharp intake of breath from her end.

"Listen, I know it's fucked up, but I promise I'll let you know everything that's going on."

"Ronan—" she says, quietly.

"I know, I know, you've been telling me about this for a while. It's a bad idea, I'm a stupid fucking idiot. I get it, but listen to me, it's been a really shitty last two days—"

"Ronan—" she says again, this time her voice a bit louder.

"I don't need a bullshit lecture right now," I bite back, balancing my phone between my ear and my shoulder.

"Ronan, fucking listen to me," she pleads.

"Y—yeah?" It takes all the energy I have to say that small, stuttered word.

There is a pause after I speak, and I can feel the tension in it. Whatever is about to come next is not going to be good. I close my eyes and suck in a deep inhale to brace myself for the inevitable. I know what she's going to say before she even says it.

I hold on to the memories of the last few days with Veronica and our conversations. Because this entire day is about to be even shittier.

I'm about to risk everything in my life for revenge. And there is nothing anyone can do to change my mind.

"His parole was approved. He's being released today."

53

Veronica

My heart feels like it has been ripped straight from my chest. I'm still as I remain seated on his couch, recalling all the truths Ronan told me about his upbringing. It makes sense of why he is the way he is.

He told me all about his childhood. His mother was murdered, and he found the body. And now his mother's murderer is up for parole. Has it been granted so soon? My stomach clenches at the thought of what he must be going through at this moment. The familiarity with my own situation stings.

I think about the hardened man who was just sitting in front of me. The truth is that Ronan does scare me a little bit, but I'd be lying if I said it didn't excite me at the same time. The more time I spend with him, the less I have any idea what I'm doing. He has a tough exterior that only this cruel world can give someone, but

I know that feeling all too well. I know that he is a good person deep down, even if he doesn't believe it himself. I can see it when I'm with him; I can feel it.

Holy shit, I really am falling in love with him.

I can imagine Richard will retaliate after that phone call. I won't tell Ronan what he has said and done. Ronan might hurt him, but after everything, would that be so bad?

No. That's not what all of this is about. I'll take care of Richard myself. I don't need Ronan to fight all my battles. I need just a little bit longer to button this whole thing up. Then Ronan and I can start over fresh. No more secrets.

I collapse back into the couch pillows, letting my eyes roam the ceiling as I roll my head from side to side.

My phone vibrates softly against my thigh, and I cringe at the thought that it could be Richard, following up on our last conversation. I pick it up and glance at the screen.

New Victim Unearthed in Ongoing Serial Killer Investigation

My eyes widen as my palm covers my mouth. Immediately, I grab a nearby remote control, and my heart skips a beat as I flip Ronan's television to the local news channel. An impending sense of dread creeps over me.

The anchor's grave expression mirrors my growing anxiety as they cover the finding of a new victim.

"Good evening. We have a breaking update on the ongoing investigation into the horrific murders that have been gripping our community for months. A new victim was discovered this afternoon, buried in a shallow grave a few miles outside of the city, off Highway Twenty-Nine." Images of the gravesite flash across the screen. "Police have confirmed that the death is linked to the same suspect responsible for the earlier murders. Officials are urging anyone with information to please come forward, as they continue their relentless pursuit to bring this killer to justice."

Shock and disbelief wash over me as I sink further into the couch, eyes fixed on the screen, unable to process the identity of the latest victim.

On the screen, Miranda's face smiles at me.

54

Ronan

Sylvie's voice repeats in my head. She knew the impact this news would have on me.

He's being released today.

Few things can make me lose control of myself. The man who murdered my mom is getting released today. The man who abused me for years throughout my childhood. The man who made me into the killer I am today, in hopes of ridding the world of pieces of shit like him.

My fingers vibrate with adrenaline at the thought of finally being able to pay him back for all he's done to me.

"How?" This is the only word I'm able to voice in response to Sylvie's statement.

"His parole was expedited," she cries. "It seems like there might have been some pressure from someone higher up. Evidence was missing. It's a whole mess."

A growl burns deep in my chest. I know who was behind this. This confirms what I already suspected. There is only one person who has this much to gain from preoccupying me.

I sit in my car, waiting outside the prison. Right now, the area is completely empty. I keep my eyes trained on the large metal doors.

Waiting, I can hear his mocking laughter echoing in my mind as well as the slurred yells he used to direct at me and my mom. I can still feel his fists against my ribs. I still remember the look in my mother's eyes right before she left me. I see her body lying on the hardwood floor, battered and bruised. Her delicate fingers reached up and stroked my cheek before the light in her eyes went out.

The sound of the prison gate opening and closing feels like another taunt. I look up and see a figure approaching. With every step he takes, I tense further, feeling my fists and my teeth clench.

I had a feeling that no one else would be here to pick him up. I have no idea what his sorry ass plans to do once he's released, and I don't care. Even if he had plans, they've changed.

As he closes the distance between us, my first thought is that he's much skinnier than I remember. Deep lines are etched into his leathery skin. He approaches my car slowly, unsure who could be waiting for him.

He bends down to look through the window and freezes when he recognizes me. The tension hangs heavy in the air. Recognizing he has nowhere to run, he holds my gaze before bowing his head lightly.

John Martin. The guy who ruined my life and killed my mom.

He's finally out of the one place where I couldn't get to him after twenty years.

"Get in," I murmur.

There's a moment of hesitation before he squares his shoulders and steps closer to my car. He obliges and gently opens the door to slide into the passenger seat.

55

Ronan

My car's engine roars to life, drowning out the thoughts swirling in my mind. I speed away from the prison lot with no real game plan in my mind.

I'm taken back to twenty years ago. I'm a nine-year-old kid, digging my fingernails into my skin before the jury walked back into the courtroom after deliberating. I remember everything from that day like it was yesterday. The courtroom smelled musty, and every few moments, I would see a panicked glance in my direction. The jury found the defendant guilty of aggravated assault and manslaughter. There were a few audible gasps around the room, but my eyes stayed trained on the back of the man's head. The judge declared that the defendant's actions were reprehensible and had caused immeasurable pain to the victim's loved ones. He nodded his balding head in my direction as he said the last part, staring directly into my eyes.

The judge sentenced him to twenty years for manslaughter and ten for aggravated assault, ensuring he would serve a good part of his life in prison for his heinous acts of violence. As his gavel fell, I never quite understood why the justice system failed my mother and me. She wasn't alive anymore. Why did John Martin get to live?

After closing, the judge found me seated on a bench in the courthouse, alone. I didn't know where to go from there. I didn't have anyone anymore.

He placed a firm hand on my shoulder and assured me that I'd never have to see that man again.

I knew then as clearly as I know now: The judge was lying. Because here the man is now, sitting in my passenger seat.

John Martin is walking free.

My lungs tighten as I try to breathe in more air. I feel like I'm suffocating. My grip tightens on the steering wheel as I fight the urge to wreck my car and kill us both. He knows I'm on edge and unpredictable. He doesn't dare say anything to try to smooth this situation over. The silence fills my car with tension.

After about fifteen minutes of driving in no direction, I let my impatience take over and jerk the car to a halt on the side of the road. I don't know where I'm going, but I can't be around this motherfucker any longer. I pull the gun from the waistband of my jeans and bring the barrel to rest against his temple.

He scrunches his eyes shut and braces for impact. I notice the fingers holding the gun are trembling. I'm falling apart here.

"Out," I order.

His eyes widen, and he struggles as he tries to open the door. He all but falls out of the car. Using the opportunity, I get out and rush to his side of the car before he has a chance to stand up again.

His chin shakes, but he stands up slowly, both hands on the back of his head. "Listen, kid, I'm sorry," he rasps. "I did my time. I'm rehabilitated."

I stand there silently, analyzing his facial expressions. He has his regrets, but there is no way he is remorseful.

"A model prisoner, then, huh?" I laugh as I straighten my arm and press the gun closer to him. "Get up," I say. "Start walking." I point the gun in the direction of the woods.

"I'm sorry for what I've done," he breathes. "No words will ever be able to make up for the loss that you went through. I wish I could bring your mother back."

I see red at the mention of my mother. I step closer to him, pressing the gun into the flesh on his forehead. "Don't you ever fucking talk about her," I spit through gritted teeth.

He raises his hands further in the air and shrinks down, trying to get away from the gun.

"Go now," I say, and he slowly puts one foot in front of the other, walking between the large, bare trees of the forest.

He pauses for a moment and glances over his shoulder. "Listen, son. I'm the least of your worries."

Son.

It's a miracle I don't rain bullets down on him after hearing that word come from his mouth. I narrow my eyes at the man who took everything from me. The one who made me who I am today.

"You are the reason for all of my fucking worries," I spit through my teeth.

He drops to his knees, knowing this is the end of his miserable fucking life.

For a moment, I think of Veronica and the life she and I could build together. The children we talked about having. I realize how much she has changed me in such a short period of time because, even though it's brief, I think about doing the unspeakable. I think about letting this man go.

But then I remember the scared little boy I once was. The orphan I became when he killed my mother. The darkness he basically pushed me into. He gave me this life without even knowing it.

I think of people like him hurting other children.

Hurting *my* children. The children I admitted to Veronica that I wanted. With her.

Veronica deserves better than me, but I can't let her walk away from me. I'll be a better person for her.

But starting tomorrow.

Not today.

Letting those thoughts fuel me, I adjust my grip on my firearm, fingers hovering over the trigger, ready to squeeze. I know the only thing that will satisfy me will be seeing his warm blood spill down his corpse.

At the thought of finally receiving closure, alarm bells sound in my mind. I freeze in place. These pieces are falling into place too perfectly: I met Veronica, I discovered Richard was involved, the cops showed up on my doorstep, John's parole approval arrived on an expedited timeline, John was released to me so easily.

Someone orchestrated this scenario. Someone who has been pulling the strings all along. I've walked straight into a trap.

56
Veronica

My body shoves out another violent wretch, and only stomach acid lands in the toilet bowl before me. The shock of Miranda's body being found has left me devastated.

Was this my fault? Was she killed because I was trying to talk to her? I crumple to the floor, the weight of blame incapacitating me. She hasn't been seen since that night. That cannot be a coincidence. The person she spoke to before I saw her was Ronan.

My heart breaks again. Ronan and I are tethered together in a tangled web of passion, pain, and secrets. I wonder if the danger of our love is worth the risk of losing ourselves in its fiery embrace. This is another body added to the growing list since I met Ronan.

I peel myself off the bathroom floor and turn on the shower to a scalding temperature. I strip off my clothes and step inside, letting the heated water bring the feeling back to my body.

Stepping out of the shower, I grab the lush beige towel hanging from the rack to the side. I raise the towel to my face and inhale the comforting scent of Ronan. I need to talk to him. I need to tell him about Miranda and let him know I have a feeling that this has something to do with us.

I grab my phone and see Lauren has texted to see where I am.

Veronica: I'm at Ronan's. Are you okay?

Her reply pops up before I even lock my screen. Too fast, I stare at it for a second longer than I should before responding.

Lauren: Is he there?

Veronica: No, he left earlier. I'm here by myself. Again, are you okay?

Lauren: Stay there.

I scroll back up, trying to piece together the fragments of this conversation. Does Lauren know where Ronan lives? If so, how? I don't respond to her request. I put my phone away, like the conversation hadn't happened. It's probably nothing.

But maybe it's not.

Getting dressed, I hear a knock at the door, and I freeze. I quickly finish dressing, jumping up and down to pull up my pants before I rush down the stairs, trying to keep my footsteps light and quiet. I peek through the peephole and see a beautiful, brown-skinned female. Her eyes are a deep brown, and her black hair is curly and hangs to her shoulders.

"Ronan, open up," the woman calls. "It's serious."

She pounds her fist against the door a few more times, vibrating the frame against my face.

Without fully thinking through the situation, I throw open the door and meet this beautiful stranger's stare head-on.

"Veronica?" a soft voice asks. Her face has relaxed since I was looking at her through the peephole. She looked impatient before, but now she seems...scared.

I clear my throat as a tremor passes through my body.

"You're Veronica, right?" she asks. "Ronan has told me about you. Jesus, I'm glad to see that you're okay." She offers me a small smile.

"He-he's talked about me?" I manage to stutter out.

She huffs a laugh. "Yeah, girl, he barely talks about anything else."

My cheeks redden as I realize I was immediately jumping to conclusions about this woman, assuming she and Ronan knew each other intimately. My shoulders sag with relief at the mention that she knows who I am. I drop my eyes to look at my feet, hoping she doesn't read my eyes.

Her eyebrows furrow in slight confusion before her eyes widen in shock. She curls over, and her body is ransacked with laughter. "Oh, fuck no," she says through her laughter. "I know what you're thinking and trust me, I would never. You'd be more my type than he is."

I let out a small laugh.

Her eyes drop the length of me, and I blush further beneath her stare. "What can I say? I'm a girl's girl. He's like the older brother I never wanted." She gives me a bright smile and extends her hand to shake mine delicately. "I'm Sylvie."

Ah, the famous Sylvie. I should've known. "Nice to finally meet you, Sylvie," I say, returning her smile. "Ronan has so many good things to say about you."

"Don't bullshit me, I know he's an asshole," she says. "Speaking of our favorite guy, where is he?"

"He left earlier, said he had some things to take care of and would be back soon. I think I owe you a thank you, after making sure I was okay."

"I'm glad Ronan took care of those fuckers and that you're okay. Seriously, it's no big deal."

I glance down at my feet and shove my bare toe into the ground. Being taken care of is not a feeling I'm familiar with. Sylvie smiles at me again. Her eyes sparkle. She really is beautiful, but from what I've heard about her, she has a brain to match. I think back to the news segment earlier that rattled me. Miranda's smiling face looked out at me. I still haven't grasped the news that she's dead.

"I'm sorry, I've been a bit frazzled recently. Do you want to come inside and wait for him? It sounds like it's important."

At the mention of this, her posture straightens, and her eyes focus. When she speaks next, her voice is a bit louder than in our earlier conversation.

"Yes, but don't tell Ronan I'm going to drink something from his top shelf liquor collection."

I laugh as she marches through the door, acting like she owns this place. I already like this girl, and butterflies flutter in my stomach as I think about how easily we could fit into each other's lives.

But as Sylvie enters the house, her demeanor changes.

57

Ronan

My grip loosens on the gun, and my hands shake more violently. I take a deep breath in through my nose and let it out slowly through my mouth. My eyes are frantic as they dance around the area, afraid of seeing blue lights in the distance.

Backing up quietly, I tuck the gun back into my pants. John rests on his knees on the forest floor in silence, his head hung low in surrender as he waits for the bullet. As time passes, his body releases tension. I turn to walk away when his voice stops me.

"He said you'd probably kill me."

My spine straightens. That motherfucker. He's been one step ahead of me this whole time. He's the only one with the power to get someone like John out of prison this soon and this quick. He knew I would come for John as soon as he was released. He knew I'd kill him and that it'd probably be done sloppily. Then he'd have a body and sufficient evidence to make me the prime suspect.

"Honestly, that's what I've wanted for quite some time," he says, solemnly. "To die." His eyes look up at me as a tear runs down his cheek. "I thought I owed it to you to let you be the one to do it."

Every muscle in my body wants to wrap my hands around this throat and crush his windpipe. He's acting like he's doing me a favor by offering himself up.

"Get the fuck out of here," I say, disgusted.

Shock registers in his face as he pauses before slowly standing up, testing to see if I'm bluffing. His eyes stayed locked on mine, and they are filled with tears. Every moment since John was sentenced, I've been anxiously waiting for the time when I could get my hands on him. One day, it would've come on its own, I have no doubt about that. This is another aspect of my retribution that Richard has taken away from me. I'm fucking livid. This kill was supposed to be for me. For me to forgive myself and move on. He took that away from me. He tried to play God in knowing I would end this man, and then he would end me.

John backs away from me timidly before walking down a path of green grass and then running to disappear deeper into the forest.

My teeth chatter with the rage coursing through my body.

Richard has fucked with me for the last time.

58

Ronan

I sprint back to my car and fire up the engine before peeling off the side of the road. Something in my gut tells me that Richard is also looking for me, so I drive in the direction of the hotel, expecting him to be there, keeping an eye on Veronica.

As I get closer to my destination, my pace slows to a crawl. My eyes are frantically searching the area to see if I can spot him. Not giving a fuck if I get a ticket, I park on the street outside the hotel and quickly exit my car.

Entering through the revolving door, I look around to spot anyone familiar—Veronica, Miranda, Richard. Miranda still isn't behind the bar, and I think back to when Veronica asked me if I had done something to her.

I walk closer to the bar, positioning myself so that I can see everyone who enters the lobby or exits the elevator. I do a quick sweep of the area and take a count of everybody who's already here. It's surprisingly empty; those who are visible wear somber expressions. One girl even cries silently into her hands behind the desk.

What the fuck is going on?

If I can't find Veronica at the hotel, my best bet is to let Miranda know it's important she tells me what's going on. She can't hide her secrets anymore, especially if it involves me.

I walk over to the bar and place my elbows on top of it.

"Is Miranda coming in anytime today?" I say to the guy shining glasses.

His eyes bulge out of his head as he takes in my question, and I see his lip tremble.

"You-you didn't hear?"

"Hear what?"

"Miranda was found dead," he says quietly.

My mouth drops. "When?"

"I'm not sure. The news did a segment on it earlier today, and the manager let me know before I started my shift."

"Okay, thanks," I stammer.

It's the only response I can muster right now. Has Miranda been missing since I talked to her that night? Veronica saw us talking and then assumed I had something to do with her disappearance. My stomach twists when I think about the fact that this might be another way to set me up.

I let my mind wander for a moment before turning to leave. And then I come face to face with the person I came here looking for.

Richard.

He stops a few feet before me and adjusts his suit jacket.

My muscles tense, and I instinctively touch the gun at my waistband. He recognizes the movement and drops his eyes to my hand before raising an eyebrow slightly.

"Hello, Ronan," he says, a thoughtless grin plastered on his face. "I was wondering when we might finally meet in person." His tone is flat.

I stand up straighter, reminding him I'm at least half a foot taller than he is. Seeing him this close is disappointing. His stature holds nothing of the power he tries to show. Right here, he just looks like a sad old man.

"Richard," I reply, my voice steady, betraying none of the turmoil raging inside me. "What brings you here?"

His smirk widens, a knowing glint in his eyes. "Oh, just passing through," he quips. "I hear we have a mutual acquaintance staying here."

At the mention of Veronica, I drop my head slightly, and I fill with anger. I can feel his gaze boring into me, probing for any weaknesses. I refuse to let him know how much she affects me. I can't yield to him.

But I also can't kill him right here and right now.

Clenching my fists, I find every ounce of resolve in me. Steeling myself, I meet his eyes, silently daring him to make a move.

"Do we have a mutual acquaintance? I thought it was made clear on the phone the other day that she has been..." I clear my throat. "Preoccupied." My lips lift in a smirk as I say the final word.

He presses his tongue into his cheek and narrows his eyes at me. He's not as good at hiding his feelings. I'm satisfied with the pain I can deliver without being physical.

He adjusts his jacket again by grabbing the flaps below the collar before letting out a small chuckle as he rolls his head around, stretching his neck.

"Speaking of our friend," he says menacingly. "Where is she? I'm surprised she's not with you, but I figured you'd also be *preoccupied* today." At the reuse of my word, his eyes glower at me.

My blood runs cold as I realize what he just said. He assumed I would be preoccupied. That's the proof I need to confirm he was behind the expedited release of John Martin. He did it to occupy me and he damn near accomplished that. But what does that mean for Veronica? Why did he need me out of the picture today?

I turn to run out of the hotel.

Just before I exit onto the street, Richard's voice calls out after me.

"You're probably too late."

59

Veronica

I follow Sylvie into the house as a sense of unease creeps over me. Her mood has changed instantly in the five minutes we've been talking. As we enter the house, the air feels heavy, and my skin prickles.

"Do you know where he might have gone?" I ask Sylvie as I walk to sit on the couch.

She seems distracted, and it takes her a moment to acknowledge my words. She's searching around the room like she's looking for something.

I can't shake the feeling that something is wrong.

"No, I haven't talked to him since I called him earlier," she says.

Her voice sounds distant, and she never makes eye contact as she continues glancing around the room. She walks to the shelves and traces items with her fingers.

A nervous energy tingles through my veins, whispering that something is amiss, but I can't quite put my finger on it. Why does Sylvie seem so tense?

"Maybe I should call him."

I shift on the couch to grab my phone from my pocket.

At that moment, Sylvie whips her head in my direction.

"Oh no, I'm sure he's on his way home." She chuckles sharply. "I'll send him a quick message."

I offer a strained smile, hoping to mask my uneasiness. Her knowing look tells me that my facade is failing. She walks over to the messy desk in the corner of the room. She pulls out a small envelope from the inside of her jacket and places it delicately onto the desk. She offers a small nod to me before getting out her phone and tapping on the screen.

"I was surprised to see you here. I heard you and Ronan were planning to get out of town. When are you leaving?"

I look up at Sylvie, puzzled. Before I have a chance to speak, she puts her phone down, and I'm surprised to feel my phone vibrate in my pocket.

"Uh, yeah. Hoping to leave this weekend, I think," I lie.

I'm not sure what we're doing here, but I decide to play along.

Her face relaxes further in relief as she lets out a deep breath. I glance at my phone's screen to see a number I don't have saved. I look up to her as she gently raises her finger to her lips before pointing it at my phone.

I open the text message and a sense of dread builds in my stomach.

Unknown: *They're listening.*

My eyes jerk back up to meet hers and she gives me a knowing look. How does she have my number?

"Yeah, Ronan told me that you guys were planning a weekend to visit The Homewood Grounds and Vineyard, right?" Sylvie says.

Her head dips forward, like she's hanging on my every word.

The Homewood Grounds and Vineyard.

My eyes widen with realization at the message she's trying to convey. Is Richard the one who is listening to us? "Yeah, just a quick trip. Maybe we'll leave sooner."

Sylvie quickly shakes her head at me, letting me know my response isn't adequate. Fear rises in my stomach at the fact that I might've just made the situation worse.

"No, definitely wait until this weekend. Maybe on the way back from there, you guys can stop at this little place I told Ronan about."

She pulls out her phone and glances at the screen for a moment before she begins tapping on the screen again. I pull out my phone, and it vibrates in my hand.

Unknown: *Going to jam connection and then we need to run.*

My body tenses as I read her message, my phone gripped tightly in my hand. My gaze rises to meet hers, and I see her hold up three fingers in a countdown as her other hand works on her phone screen.

Slowly, she drops a finger each time until only her pointer remains. Just before her last finger drops, I hear a distant beeping noise before I sprint to the back door, desperate to escape whatever is coming after us.

60

Ronan

I sprint up my porch and through the front door, which stands wide open.

With every step I take, a sinking feeling settles in the pit of my stomach. The scene before me looks like a nightmare. Pieces of furniture are flipped, cushions are torn from the sofa, and drawers are pulled out haphazardly.

I move cautiously through the wreckage, scanning for any sign of the perpetrators who did this, but the silence notifies me that whoever was here is long gone.

Veronica was here, but she's not anymore.

I rush over to my security system and pull up today's footage to play it back. Each frame feels like an eternity as I scan through the recording. I fast-forward to after I left earlier today. I watch Veronica as she stays on the couch, mouth open at something on the TV, probably the news on Miranda. She disappears upstairs, then comes down after hearing something at the front door. She looks through the peephole before opening the door to Sylvie. They chat for a moment, and it seems friendly. After a few minutes, Veronica gestures inside and Sylvie accepts.

The interaction is weird as they enter the house together. Sylvie and Veronica both watch each other at different times. Sylvie navigates around the room like she's looking for something. She pulls out her phone before walking over to the same desk I'm standing at. She sets down a white envelope dramatically on the desk. I look down to see the exact one she placed there in the video.

Veronica gets a text message, and she looks up at Sylvie. They both look very uncomfortable as they continue their conversation. Sylvie asks Veronica about her and me taking a trip. Sylvie begins typing on her phone again, and she looks up at Veronica, who nods her head. Sylvie raises three fingers, a countdown. Right as she drops her final finger, the footage cuts to black as the signal is disconnected. So that's what Sylvie was doing.

When the camera comes back on, the living room is empty. Veronica and Sylvie are nowhere to be found. Shortly after, a man kicks in my front door and comes running in, another man right behind him.

I pause the recording to get a better look at the two men.

It's the two cops who came by my house a few days ago.

A few seconds later, the back door opens, and in walk three more men, but they're not alone. One man has his arm around Veronica's throat as he drags her across the floor. She's kicking and clawing at his throat. Sylvie's body is limp and thrown over the shoulder of one of the men. The two cops nod at the other men before they all exit through the open front door.

"Fuck," I yell as I slam my fists down on the desk. I missed it. The obvious details that would have unraveled Richard's plan—instead I played right into his hands.

My fury grows with every passing second, my mind replaying the scene in an infuriating loop. My oversight has put Veronica and Sylvie in serious danger.

My jaw tightens as I think about Richard's smug face, still a step ahead, predicting my next move.

I rip open the envelope and hope that Sylvie has come through for me yet again.

61

Veronica

The throbbing in my head is what wakes me. I pry my eyes open and almost black out from the pain pulsating in my temples. I shut my eyes tight, trying to drown out the light. The dehydration headache is killing me, along with the few blows I've taken to the head.

I move my hands to my face to ease the discomfort, but they are restricted. I struggle against what's holding my arms and find it unforgiving. My eyes shoot open as I try to piece together the most recent events. I look around the room, and while I should be surprised at where I've ended up, I'm not.

The silhouette of someone stands in front of me.

As the face becomes clearer, I see his lip turn up into a snarl.

"I told you that you'd regret this, Veronica."

I see three men behind him. Two of them are dressed as cops and I'm sure they're the ones who came into Ronan's house. I hear someone groan next to me, and I roll my head over to see… Lauren? A gasp escapes my mouth at the sight of her.

Shadows linger beneath her eyes, and her hair is damp with sweat. She's clearly been crying, and mascara streaks her face. Her arms are tied behind her back, like mine. Her head hangs heavy in defeat. I strain against the ropes in a desperate attempt to get to Lauren. Beside Lauren is Sylvie, who is also tied to a chair. She's not moving.

"Don't worry," Richard says, nodding toward Lauren and Sylvie. "They'll be okay, as long as you do exactly what you're told."

The metallic taste of blood pools in my mouth, and I spit it onto the floor at his feet.

"After all, Lauren is the reason I was able to get so much information on your comings and goings. She helped me make sure you were alone today."

My spine stiffens as I look at Richard, hoping to call his bluff. Lauren would never do that to me. Lauren begins crying. My eyes cut over to search her face.

"Veronica," she cries. "I had no idea! How could I have been so stupid?"

Panic shoots through me. There is no way Lauren would betray me. I'm about to ask what she means when the door creaks open and a tall figure steps into the room. It takes a moment for me to recognize him, but when I do, it all makes sense.

It's Liam. The guy Lauren met at the bar.

Lauren's cries intensify as she sees him. "You fucking betrayed me," she yells through her sobs.

"Liam was supposed to be another one of your dates, Veronica," Richard says as Liam holds my gaze confidently. "But it appears he was taken by your friend instead." He looks at Lauren with disgust. "Still, he was very helpful in keeping track of all your movements. Having a slut for a friend only made this that much easier."

I spit at Richard's feet as Lauren only sobs harder.

"I'm-I'm sorry, Veronica."

"Liam, please shut her up," Richard says before Liam walks over to Lauren and puts a piece of duct tape across her mouth, then plants a kiss on it over her lips. She squirms to get away from him, but he holds her in place before turning around with a disturbing smile.

Richard's attention turns back to me. "You thought I had no idea that you were the rat?"

He walks over and slaps me hard across the face. Hard enough that the spittle goes flying from the side of my face. I hear a muffled scream come from Lauren behind her duct tape.

I let my head droop to the side, and I see a line of blood streaming from my mouth and onto the floor. Lauren looks at me, eyes wide in panic.

"I can't risk things going differently than I planned again," he says.

I pull my eyes to look at him and spit the pooling blood in my mouth onto the floor in front of him again. "So, you've been the puppet master all this time?" I say. "Since I left the apartment, did you orchestrate everything?"

"What I couldn't have planned for was that you'd fuck the person who was contracted to kill me," he snaps, bitterness lining his tone.

His face twists in disgust, and my mouth falls open. My eyes widen at the realization that Richard knows that Ronan was hired to kill him.

"Should've known you'd open your legs for just anyone," Richard says. "But there is a lot more you don't know yet, my dear Veronica. And I suppose we don't have to wait for our other special guest to arrive to get the fun started."

62

Ronan

My tires screech as I slam on the brakes, my car barely making it into park before I'm out the door and running to the entrance. Sylvie had known something was going to happen today—she just couldn't reach me in time. In order to protect Veronica and me, she put herself in danger. If something happens to her, I'll never forgive myself.

I burst through the metal doors, hoping I'm not too late.

Before me stands Richard, surrounded by three other men I don't recognize. Behind them are three bodies tied to their chairs—Veronica, Lauren, and Sylvie.

Richard's eyes light up when he sees me.

"Ah, you made it," he says, clasping his hands together in delight. "I was hoping you'd find your way to us, eventually."

I burn with rage. Veronica is slumped over in a chair with her hair hanging down past her face. Her arms are tied behind her back, and there are bloodstains on her clothes. Next to her are Lauren and Sylvie, who look to be in a similar disarray.

"Lovely to see you again, Ronan."

With Richard's words, Veronica's eyes snap to me. My heart cracks in my chest at the sight of her. We haven't had a chance to speak since our last conversation. The one where we basically told each other that we were falling in love with one another.

"I was wondering how quickly you'd be able to figure every-thing out after I saw you at the hotel," Richard sneers. "I was just telling Veronica that it wasn't part of my plan to have her sleep with the guy who was hired to kill me." He shrugs as he says this.

I take slow steps closer to the center of the room, my eyes roaming over the setup to get the full picture.

"And what was your plan, Richard?" I say, masking any emo-tion that tries to show itself on my face. I know more about Richard's plan than he thinks I do, but it's essential I play along.

"So, you're not as clever as I thought." He sighs. "That's a damn shame."

It's all about power with Richard. He needs to feel like he's the one who has complete control. He takes a few steps closer to where Veronica is seated, and my body tenses up. Richard is too unpredictable. I can't let him anywhere near her.

"You see, my team and I concocted a deal. If we were to bring in one of the 'big bads' of the city, I'd be untouchable. This city would call me their savior. Plus, rumors were spreading about me being a dirty politician." He reaches behind Veronica's head and grips a strand of her blond hair, then jerks it backward to pull her face up in my direction. "Thanks to this one for spreading filth to the journalists."

He pauses for effect and keeps Veronica's face tilted upward toward me. Tears streak down her face.

"I needed a sure way to get the people back on my side. I had to find a way to convince them that I was making a safer place for them."

A door creaks open, and heavy footsteps begin approaching the light in the room.

My eyes widen as I recognize the person moving toward me.

Mark.

He comes to Richard and stands by his side.

"Lucky for Mark, he does have ears everywhere in this city," Richard begins. "He caught wind of my plan to bring him in and proposed an even more interesting solution."

I swallow as I recall my original meeting with Mark.

The only person in this city who could rival my notoriety.

"In exchange for leaving him out of your plan," I say, "he'd bring you someone else." My mouth is dry as I speak.

Richard's eyes move back in my direction as he smiles. "Ding ding ding," he chimes. "But that's not all."

My jaw clenches and my eyes narrow as he stares back at me. Everything makes sense now. "You needed someone to pin the disappearances and murders on."

63
Veronica

Ronan's jaw clenches, and his eyes narrow. I hear a slight growl escape his throat. My eyes fill with tears at the realization of what they've been planning. Setting Ronan up to take the fall for these horrendous murders that have been taking place. Making him look like the bad guy all along.

"Lucky for me, our state honors the death penalty." Richard laughs. "That'll be an easy case to wrap up. I can imagine anyone who sits on the jury will be eager to see you brought to justice."

His head turns away from Ronan, and he looks at me. "And now, you're tainted goods. I wouldn't touch you, let alone fuck you, after that piece of shit has been inside you." He shivers, as if his repulsion has taken over his body. I narrow my eyes at him.

His voice gets louder as his anger takes over, his frustration at how the events have played out, unlike how he had planned.

"You should've just taken my original deal. Fucked some young man like a good girl, and we could've moved on. But instead, you had to get involved with that piece of trash, getting right in the middle of my plan." His face is blood red. His gray eyes are unforgiving and cold. There is so much hostility dancing behind them. "I tried to steer you away from it, of course. But then you played right into my hands. I had to get even more creative. What could make this situation even better for me?" His voice is diabolical.

He clears his throat before clasping his hands together in front of his chest, emphasizing the moment he reveals we've been outsmarted. "What if the narcissistic vigilante hit man running amok in our city violently killed the district attorney's wife when he was trying to get to the DA?" Richard says. "What a tragic ending to a sad story. No one would ever question my stance on ensuring safety in our city." His sinister smile sends a chill down my spine. "I'd be free to move on."

I struggle against the restraints, knowing now how he wants this plan of his to end.

"I'm sorry to say that while I had planned to let you live, Veronica, your death benefits me more."

64
Ronan

The blood drains from my face as I listen to Richard recite the rest of his plan and how Veronica is involved. It's all my fault. Because of her involvement with me, he intends to kill her and pin it on me.

Focusing on something a little more predictable, I turn to Mark. "Thought you were better than this, Mark," I snap. "What will people say about you when they find out you've been conspiring with this piece of shit?" I nod toward Richard.

Richard throws a glare in my direction.

"Are you kidding me? This is perfect for business." Mark laughs. "We're untouchable. My business will be fucking booming."

"You're wrong," I tell him. "They'll think you're pathetic."

"They'll know I did what I had to do to protect myself and the business," he says, lifting his nose slightly into the air.

"But that's what you'll always do, right?" I say, raising my eyebrows. Richard tilts his head in question, curious about what I'm referring to. "You'll protect yourself above all else?" I glare at Mark, despite the blood obstructing my vision.

Mark's eyes narrow at the comment, and he glances in Richard's direction. They're nothing but two overconfident, hot-headed assholes.

"Isn't that right, Mark? You'll always do whatever it takes to protect yourself." I nod my head forward to Mark, trying to emphasize that they cannot trust one another.

They are both loose cannons, and the only way we may make it out of here alive is to get them to turn on one another.

That was one piece of information that Sylvie had left me in that envelope. She discovered that Mark and Richard were working together. She never trusted Mark from the beginning, and I should've listened to her. She was right in questioning his motives, and I should've seen it coming. All I have to do is get them to start second-guessing their partnership. They both have a history of stabbing people in the back.

Richard's eyes are a bit wild now, and they dart around the room, often stopping on Mark, who does not respond to my question.

Mark clears his throat to regain control of the conversation. "I did see you were smart enough to evade our other plan." He smirks. "And I'm impressed. I really thought you wouldn't be able to control yourself once he was released."

Behind him, the younger cop forces another person out of the doorframe and shoves them onto the floor by their neck.

It's John Martin, the man who killed my mother. I knew it. I knew it was a setup, and it almost worked.

"It's a damn shame you didn't kill him. That would've made this all very easy," Richard says, regaining control of his emotions. "Though once the body is found, it'll be obvious who killed him. You'll no doubt leave behind evidence, and we have clear security footage of you picking him up outside the prison. Case closed."

John's face is toward the floor. He can't bring himself to look up at me again. He really did know he was walking to his own death and let it happen. He knew I would be here to seek retribution. He welcomed it, knowing he had ruined my life and that he would meet his end with me.

"But the one kill I actually needed you to make, you couldn't do, could you? I guess I have to do fucking everything around here, huh?"

Richard pulls out a gun and points it at the back of John's head.

John looks up at me with tears in his eyes.

"I'm sorry, Ronan," he says, his voice breaking. "I'm sorry for everything."

He pinches his eyes shut, and with that, Richard pulls the trigger to a chorus of screams from Veronica and Lauren.

65

Veronica

His body hits the floor with a sick thud. Blood pools quickly beneath his lifeless form, and I fight the urge to retch. Richard holds up the gun toward the light.

"Ah, see this beauty? You know how fucking hard it was to find another one of these?"

Ronan's gaze narrows at Richard as he looks at the gun in his hands.

"No better way to get a solid conviction," he says, showing his teeth. "I present the murder weapon used for the most recent kills."

My head is still fuzzy, and this elaborate plan is too much for me to take in. I'm trying to digest all the moving pieces. So many people had to die for us to get here, and it seems like it's all my fault.

My voice is weak, but I find the strength to speak. "How are you going to pin the murders on Ronan with that gun, when all the other women were strangled?"

Richard's head whips at me. "Specifics aren't necessary, my dear Veronica. The public simply wants an arrest. I have enough people in the judicial system that a trial will be swift and thorough."

"But the murders won't stop," I add. "What happens when the killer keeps on killing?" I study Richard's face for a reaction, hoping I've pointed out the one loophole that could cause his whole plan to come crashing down. After all, he doesn't know who the actual killer is.

"That doesn't matter anymore," Richard says. "We have our suspect, and we have all the evidence we need right here. The murderer is long gone."

"Are you sure about that, Richard?" I ask.

His unsettled gaze lands on my face. I see his pupils moving back and forth quickly, between me and something else. His jaw goes slack, and a look of surprise dances across his eyes. Following his eyes, I see movement in the shadows. A petite figure, moving as if it's one with the darkness.

The figure steps slightly into the light, revealing itself.

Familiar gray eyes stare back at us.

"Hello, Father."

With only his side profile, I can still see the color drain from Richard's face.

Claire handles herself with brutal efficiency. She's already moving before anyone has a chance to react. She grabs the gun from the holster of one man, shoots him in the center of his chest, and then effortlessly turns to shoot the other two men in the head before I have a chance to blink. They didn't expect a threat to come from outside the room. They thought the only threats were here inside it.

The gunshot erupts in the small space, and it echoes off the concrete walls. Mark pulls his gun out and aims it right at Claire.

"Claire." His voice is low. Angry. "I thought you left again for Europe."

A smile crosses Claire's lips that reminds me so much of her father, it's eerie. "Not yet—I wasn't quite ready to leave."

Richard pauses, and I see the muscles in his jaw twitch. Claire isn't supposed to be here.

"I told you to get the fuck out of this city," he says through his teeth, an echo bouncing off the concrete walls.

She walks toward her father with slow steps, almost like she's dragging her toes behind her. "I thought about it. Trust me, I really did." She stops and bends her fingers and glances at her cuticles. "But I found something I wanted more," she says as she drops her hand to her hip.

I suck in an inhale as awareness settles over me. This was something I'd feared about my stepdaughter, but never quite let myself grasp. The scary feeling Claire has always carried with her. The dead animal on my pillow. The hatred for her father and her mother.

Richard's eyes darken, and his upper lip twists up into a snarl.

"So, Father, tell me why you are trying to pin my work on someone else?"

66

Ronan

I try to drown out the pulsing in my head as I digest the fact that Claire is the murderer. Richard's own daughter has been behind the murders, and he *knew*. He was covering up for his own daughter.

Glancing around the room, I realize how fucked this situation is. There are too many guns being held by unpredictable hotheads in one room. I focus my attention on Claire, in hopes of settling her and Richard down. They are the biggest risks to Veronica's safety right now.

I speak quietly but firmly, trying to defuse this fucking tense situation. "Claire, put the weapon down," I say as calmly and convincingly as I can.

Her head turns in my direction, painfully slowly. Her lips curl upward, and her eyes trail up and down me.

"Hello, Ronan," she says. "Nice to finally meet you in person. I've heard lots about you. You have some decent methods of killing but they're not exactly my taste."

Veronica is the next to speak. "Claire, please. You don't want to hurt your father or anyone else." Her voice shakes under her breath.

Claire lets out a harsh laugh. "I don't want to hurt my father? Are you fucking kidding me?" she spits. "I've always wanted to make his life a living hell, just like he made mine."

Richard looks stunned as he watches Claire closely. His mouth hangs open in surprise. This was a part of the plan he didn't fully vet out.

"Claire, sweetheart, please. We talked about this. You agreed to get out of the city, and I'd keep you safe," Richard pleads.

"More like you needed to keep your reputation safe. Why is everything always about you?" Claire tilts her head to the side and looks her father up and down.

"You knew she was the killer." Mark's voice is low. "Your daughter is the fucking killer?"

Mark is the last person we need in this room. At least everyone else has someone they care about in this situation. He is the one person who gives a fuck only about himself.

"Shut the fuck up, Mark," Richard says, pressing his fingers to his temple, trying to figure out this change in events.

"Oh, all of you, don't look so goddamn surprised." Claire laughs as she flails her arms out wide, gesturing to everyone in the room. "The troubled only child of a rich, asshole father turns out to be a killer. Sounds like the plot to every single horror movie."

I look at Veronica. She doesn't look as shocked as everyone else does.

"Why did you kill Miranda?" Veronica asks, her voice breaking in the middle, and I see just how much Miranda's death has broken her. My heart hurts at the thought of everything this woman has been through since she met me. She doesn't deserve any of it.

"Miranda?" Claire's head turns to Veronica, confusion painted across her face.

"Yeah, the bartender from the hotel," I reply. "Miranda. She was a good person and had nothing to do with any of this."

Through a shaky voice and his disbelief, Richard says, "The bartender was an unfortunate task that needed to be completed. She witnessed a few of my dealings that could not become public knowledge and started to put her nose where it didn't belong."

Veronica's mouth drops open as she gasps. "You killed her for talking to me?"

"I did what was necessary," Richard says. "I will always do what is necessary."

Veronica's face goes ghastly white, and her lips part slightly as she inhales a deep breath.

"She wasn't trying to warn me about Ronan," she says, looking at me briefly before turning her eyes back to Richard. "She was trying to warn me about you."

Trust me, I'm doing both of you a favor. Her words repeat themselves in my mind. She was trying to protect Veronica and me from Richard.

Richard had shown up at the hotel after I left to meet Mark during my and Veronica's first date. Miranda had known who he was, but not who Veronica was. She was trying to protect both of us, and it got her killed.

"You're a fucking bastard, Richard," Veronica shouts, more tears spilling down her cheeks. "You'll pay for everything you've done."

I hear the distinct click of a trigger being cocked. My eyes widen and frantically search to see who made the movement. Richard still looks stunned, and Mark's hands haven't moved.

That leaves Claire.

"Claire, wouldn't you rather watch your dad rot in prison like he deserves?" I say, trying to keep Claire from pulling the trigger and causing a bloodbath. In this tight room, any bullet could ricochet and hit an unintended target. I don't trust her control or focus. "Think about it—the reputation he's so desperate to reconcile will be destroyed."

"We can save you." Veronica's voice breaks as her eyes fill with tears. "Claire, you know you can trust me."

Richard's eyes are crazy, and they shoot over to Veronica, bouncing between her and Claire.

"You knew?" he shouts at Veronica.

"There is no saving me," Claire yells. Her eyes are vacant of any true remorse. She turns slowly back to face Richard completely, gripping the gun tightly with both hands. Her arms shake slightly under pressure. "You're a piece of shit," she screams at the top of her lungs. "You deserve to die."

Richard's chin trembles, and he fights back the tears building in his eyes. "Claire, what would your mother say?" he asks, desperate to save his own life.

It's obvious he's pulling out the last trick that could save him.

And with those words, whatever composure Claire still desperately hung onto fades completely. Her lips press into a thin line, and she tilts her chin slightly down.

"My mother?" She laughs. "You really don't fucking get it, do you?"

Everyone in the room looks puzzled and exchanges brief glances.

"Did you ever stop and think *why* I am the way I am? Why I found pleasure in murdering all those women?" she growls.

Richard remains silent, his hands shaking by his sides.

"You were supposed to protect me from her!" Her voice is erratic, and her head shakes as she yells.

Richard briefly opens his mouth to reply, but snaps it shut. His jaw clenches as he grinds his teeth together.

Claire chokes out a sob before readjusting her stance. "Besides," she starts, dropping one hand to her hip while the other keeps the gun trained on Richard. She lets out another laugh before nodding in Veronica's direction, a smile curling across her lips. "I would have killed my mother too, if Veronica hadn't beat me to it."

67

Lillian

Fifteen Years Earlier

"I need your help," I whisper. "I think I killed him."

The silence following my admission hangs over me like a black cloud. The alcohol still coursing through my veins no longer dulls my senses.

"Honey," he pauses. "What's going on?"

I take another slow step toward the unmoving body. The face is covered with lacerations and swelling. Bruises slowly make their way to the surface. Several limbs lie unnaturally, broken at different angles.

Something else catches my gaze, and my eyes shoot to the black car resting upside down, debris scattered around it. The smell of gasoline fills my nose, making me even more lightheaded. In the passenger seat of the inverted car, I see light brown hair swaying in the wind. The hair cascades down from a dangling head. My vision focuses on the face above the hair that originally caught my attention. It's covered in shadows and difficult to discern its features.

Then I hear something that stops me in my tracks. The sound is unlike anything I've ever heard before. It sounds like a gurgle, or more like a rattling noise.

I can't hold the sob building in my chest. I drop to my knees in the middle of the road, letting the bite of the concrete press into my bare flesh and bring me back to reality.

I try to speak but am only able to gasp out guttural sounds that do not sound human.

"Stay where you are," he barks. "Don't touch anything. Is anyone around?"

I shake my head, as if he can see through the phone. "No, it's an empty back road," I manage to say through my cries. I am now plagued with hiccups, a subtle reminder of the one-too-many straight-up vodka martinis I had tonight. "I thought it'd be empty at this time of the night and that I—"

"Are there any survivors?" He cuts me off.

Another sob tears through my chest. This is all the answer he needs.

"Listen to me, this is very important." His authoritative tone is familiar and somewhat comforting, in a bizarre way. Even the bad parts of your spouse can feel like home.

I hear him take in a sharp inhale of breath before speaking again.

"You need to get away from the scene of that accident as quickly as possible," he says. "I'm going to call and report your car stolen as soon as we hang up."

If anyone can fix this, it's Richard. I know he can. I've made a lot of mistakes, but Richard always puts the pieces back together. We'll get through this. We always do. His background in law can save me.

His voice continues in my ear, but I'm only faintly paying attention. I'm nauseated and unsteady on my feet—though it's hard to know if it's the alcohol or the adrenaline.

I pinch my eyelids shut, but I cannot erase the images of what happened here tonight. They are burned into my brain along with the sounds and the smells still lingering. The sounds of metal hitting metal, the smell of burned tires, the lifeless bodies in and outside of the car. A man and a woman.

I muster what little energy I have and begin to run in the opposite direction of the accident, heading toward the large brush of trees. I'll have to travel quite far, but once I get through the woods, I'll be close to a busier back highway, where he'll pick me up.

"Richard, I'm sorry," I speak through sobs and my increasing breath. "I shouldn't have driven tonight. I had too much to drink."

I glance back at the car wreckage one last time while my heart threatens to beat out of my chest. Through my tears, I can almost swear I see a little pair of eyes staring at me from the back seat of the car, blinking. Very much alive.

68

Taylor

Six Years Earlier

P anic erupts like wildfire in the clinic as the news of the patient's demise spreads like a dark cloud. Nurses scurry frantically, their once-steady hands now trembling with disbelief and urgency. The doctors exchange terse instructions amid the chaos, their voices strained with a mixture of sorrow and frustration. The main room is filled with hushed murmurs and anticipation from other patients and the rest of the clinic's staff. The air is heavy with disinfectant and fear, suffocating anyone who dares to breathe it in.

My hands, steady despite the chaos, give no hint of the guilt that should be coiling like a serpent in my stomach. I observe the crowd with a detached curiosity, analyzing their reactions with clinical precision. Every quivering lip, every furrowed brow, feeds into my facade of innocence, masking the truth that festers beneath the surface.

Surprisingly enough, among the scene, I glance up and see a familiar pair of gray eyes staring at me through the curtains of brown bangs.

Claire.

Instead of happiness, I see recognition.

I see anger like a predator who just lost its prey to another. I thought she might be happy that she got her wish. That her mother would never come home. But I believe I thought wrong.

Her face looks angry, like I took her kill away from her.

Behind her is an older man with his hands on her shoulders; similar gray eyes stare out above her head. It takes me a moment to realize that the eyes are staring directly at me.

His gaze feels like an unwelcome intrusion, piercing my skin with an unsettling intensity. I shift uncomfortably under the weight of his stare, my skin prickling and fear building in my stomach.

He knows. He knows it was me.

But then, as the moments pass and his gaze lingers unabated, a different realization dawns on me. The intensity of his stare morphs from predatory to lustful, his eyes alight with a primal desire that sends a shiver down my spine. His wife's body isn't even cold yet, and this shithead is already eye-fucking the next best thing.

I know he's the infamous Richard Sullivan, in the flesh. What a creep. He's made quite a name for himself as a prominent lawyer, specializing in prosecution. Of course, he's dabbled in defense cases as well.

Like the one where he defended his wife in a DUI hit-and-run. With his expertise, she was able to get off with two years' house arrest.

Two. Years. House. Arrest. For killing my parents and leaving me for dead in the back seat.

House arrest doesn't mean shit when you're rich, either. The punishment did not fit the crime. But I made sure to dish out the kind of punishment she deserved.

And in that moment, fueled by my rage, the fear of being caught gives way to exhilaration. I meet his gaze with a challenge of my own.

69
Veronica

The whole room stills, and the air feels thick. I see Richard's huge eyes look as if they're about to bulge out of their sockets. Everyone's eyes dart around the room, trying to assess the situation and see who is the biggest risk at this moment.

Ronan is moving before we hear the gunfire. The sharp, loud noise rebounds across the empty space as the air around us vibrates. He tries to disarm Claire before realizing the gunshot didn't come from her gun, it came from the other side of the room.

Mark stands there with his arm still in the air, a hint of smoke dancing from the barrel of his gun.

Ronan pulls back to look at her face, and I see the bullet hole right above Claire's heart, blood pouring out continuously. Finally ripping apart the restraints I've been so diligently working on, I run over to Claire, my hands pressing on the gaping hole in her chest. She tries to choke down air but only sputters up blood. Ronan stands up to act as a shield for Claire and me.

"Nonononono," I repeat. "Claire, please, stay with me."

I press my trembling hands harder on her wound, trying so hard to stop the bleeding. The blood, it's too much. Too much is coming out too fast.

Claire's eyelids flutter as she fights to keep consciousness. She opens her mouth to speak, but no sounds emerge.

"You killed my daughter?" Richard screams from behind me.

I turn my head over my shoulder to see the situation unfold further.

"She's a fucking psychopath!" Mark rebuts, taking a step away from Richard. "She was going to kill us all."

A second gunshot rings through the air, and I try to decipher which gun it came from. Both Mark and Richard stay with their feet grounded, staring at each other with their guns pointed.

After a moment, I see Mark's mouth drop open and he begins coughing before glancing down at his chest. He drops the gun and reaches up to place his hands over his stomach. He stumbles backward before colliding with the concrete wall. Sliding down to the floor, he leaves behind a smeared trail of blood. It takes only a few seconds before his face goes slack, and his body stops moving.

I turn my attention back to Claire, desperate to try to fix this situation. I press my hands further onto her wounds. "Claire, I'm so sorry," I cry, choking on my sobs. "It wasn't supposed to end this way."

Her eyes are distant and unfocused. She tries to reach her hand up to touch my face, but it collapses back to the floor.

"I was never—never going to make it out of here. It's okay." Her lips tremble, but she forces the best smile she can. "Remember what we promised," she says before her head rolls to the side, empty eyes staring right at her father. "Give him hell."

I use the devastation building inside me and the disarray of the moment to act. I'm up on my feet and running toward Richard before anyone has a moment to register what just happened. I feel Ronan try to grab for me, but he barely misses me as I tackle Richard with as much force as I can muster and try to wrestle the gun out of his hands. I wrap one hand around the cold metal of the gun and place my pointer and middle finger behind the trigger to try to delay the inevitable. The tension in the air crackles like static electricity.

Our eyes are locked on each other in a fierce struggle. Whoever gains control of this gun will not hesitate to shoot the other. My muscles are straining, and my heart is pounding. I fight against him with all my strength. Every movement is a risk, a delicate dance between life and death for both of us. The gun wavers precariously between the two of us, its weight a tangible reminder of the stakes at hand.

Richard glances into my eyes and I use that moment to over-power him one last time. I smash my forehead into his nose with a resounding thud, sending shock waves of pain through both of us. A breath escapes my mouth as I sit up atop Richard's body, warm blood spilling down my face. A smile curls at my lips as I lean closer to him and press the barrel of the gun, now firmly in my hand, into his forehead.

"Tell me, Richard." My inflection is flat, sinister. "Do you recognize me now?"

I bare my teeth at him as I press the gun deeper into his skin, watching as his flesh gives way to the metal. "Claire was extremely ambitious in trying to kill her mother, but unfortunately for her, I beat her to it. Only you would be married to a woman with multiple people who wanted her dead."

I do feel sadness about Claire's death. I tried to help when I could. I knew one day her true nature would come to light. She's always had some resentment for me since I killed her mom, but we both had mutual destruction in our minds, so we allowed each other to coexist. Though I wasn't sure about the murders, I always had a small suspicion—they often correlated with the times she was in the city. I couldn't prove anything, but I kept a close eye on Claire when I could.

Once Claire and I had a chance to finally speak openly, I convinced her that it wasn't worth it to let her father die. He needed to pay much more than that.

"Claire was owed more than that," I continue. "After all, Lillian did ruin both of our lives. The kill that mattered the most to Claire was the one she couldn't follow through on, so no wonder she became what she was. I mean, look at you. Your wife's body wasn't even cold before you decided to set your sights on me." I laugh. "You see a pair of legs with tits and only think with your dick."

His face twists in sadness, recognizing that he never once had the upper hand. Perhaps he did actually love Lillian in his own way, but I doubt he ever loved me.

"The tapping you've become so accustomed to? It's a neat trick my mother taught me. Morse code. I used it to remember the license plate of the other car that caused the accident that night. I didn't want to forget any vital information that would lead me back to the person truly responsible for the horrible accident that took my parents' lives."

I begin tapping out the sequence on his forehead. His eyes are wide with shock. He's watched me do this over and over, throughout the last five years, and was never smart enough to put two and two together.

"I hadn't really intended to get involved with you, but you made it so easy," I say. "My original plan was to take care of Lillian and move on with my life. But I knew you were the reason she was able to get away with a double homicide while driving under the influence. Tsk tsk, Richard."

His eyes widen in horror at the realization that he's been out-smarted.

"But don't worry, death isn't good enough for you. I'd rather see you rot in prison for what you've done. I'd love to see the headlines: *District Attorney's Daughter Revealed as Serial Killer While Daddy Aided and Abetted Her.*"

We're always taught to fear the loudest person in the room. But the truth is, you should be more afraid of the quiet ones. The ones calculating their revenge deep in the back of their minds, all while pasting a convincing smile across their lips.

A good woman is compliant.

The slight recognition in his eyes is all I need to feel a brush of satisfaction. This wasn't how I wanted things to end up, but I've been playing the game for far too long. I simply want to be rid of him, once and for all.

They thought they got away with what happened that night.

But money can't always save you.

No, I moved to the city with a plan, always keeping tabs on our dear Lillian, knowing she would end up back in the rehabilitation clinic.

It's not my fault that men are stupid, and Richard played right into my hands. Seducing him was easy, especially after I murdered his wife. After all, I would need someone to help fund the rest of my life.

Richard's life has always been about power and status, two things he won't have in prison when the world hears about what he's done, especially not after he killed Mark.

Lillian murdered my parents. Richard used his reputation to get her off squeaky clean. For both of them, the crime matches the punishment.

I'm aware of Ronan's presence behind me, but he doesn't intrude. He recognizes what this moment is for me and how long it's taken for me to get here. If anyone understands having someone you love taken away from you too soon by a bad person, it's Ronan.

We are two sides of the same coin. He just didn't know it until this very moment.

Over the last few weeks, he was analyzing the puzzle pieces, but he didn't finish the puzzle until now.

I look at him and I see it. Recognition of the darker side of me. One he knew was there but was never able to specifically pinpoint.

Ronan walks over to me and takes the gun from my hand, slowly, keeping it pointed at Richard, who stays motionless on the ground, panic still present in his face.

After Ronan takes the gun from me, I collapse against him, letting every emotion take over. The sense of release is indescribable. I've spent so much of my life hidden away, and now, the mask has been ripped away permanently.

Ronan lifts my chin to gaze into my eyes. "It's okay, baby," he says, his voice a soothing reminder that I'm safe. "It's all over."

With those three words, I fold into him, overtaken with relief.

70

Veronica

Three Months Later

Deepening our kiss, I run my fingers through Ronan's hair. I move toward his ear to whisper how badly I need him right now.

He leans back to look me in the eye before giving me another of those devastating smirks. My heart continues beating out of my chest as I peel the towel away from my body, letting it drop to the floor, and then his lips crash back onto mine.

Guiding me back onto the bed, Ronan reaches down and circles my clit with his thumb. I arch my back in pleasure and press into him before he lays me down. He stands up from the bed, grabbing one of my legs and pressing a delicate kiss at my ankle before trailing further upward. Once he's reached my upper thigh and he's right at the place that's dying for attention, he grips my waist and pulls me down to the edge of the bed so that my ass is nearly hanging off.

Wrapping his hands around my ankles, he presses my legs up so that my feet are planted on the bed with my knees straight up toward the ceiling. He moves my feet out to spread me further.

He flattens his tongue and licks me from bottom to top before pulling his mouth away to let out a long, slow breath on my clit, then presses two fingers inside me. My hips lift off the bed, and I suck in a breath of air at the intrusion. I reach down and grab fistfuls of his hair, and I press myself further onto his mouth.

He licks me with such veracity that I know it won't be long until I unravel. As I build higher, I glance down at him to see that his eyes are locked on me. The corner of his mouth tilts upward, and the sight of him almost sends me over the edge. I drop my head back to the bed and arch further into him. With a sudden gasp, I let my body descend into an earth-shattering orgasm.

He climbs up my body, pressing his lips against my skin as he goes. Once he reaches my face, he kisses me deeply, and the taste of myself sends me into another frenzy.

His responding kiss isn't gentle. It's a claiming, brutal assault, like he's marking his territory. Making me remember what he's capable of—and what he wants. With that, he grabs my shoulders as he rolls over onto his back to set me on top of him.

I lift up as he shimmies down his pants and briefs before kicking them to the floor. His dick presses against my legs, and I'm aching to be filled by him.

Holding his gaze, I slowly slide down onto him and he hisses in response as he presses his hips up to meet mine until he's buried deep inside me.

"Oh fuck," I cry out, trying to catch my breath once more.

He lifts to rest on one elbow and places his other arm around my waist. "Breathe, baby," he says as he continues to pump effortlessly into me, matching my movements perfectly.

He drops his head back in pleasure. "You take me so well like this," he grunts. He drives even deeper still.

My cries echo out in the room, and I swirl my hips in slow circles as he pumps in and out of me. His movements rub against my clit in a way that leaves me breathless. I swell further until I shatter, with him not too far behind me. I stop my movements, flexing my hips and spreading my knees further, as he pounds into me, and we ride out our orgasms together.

I collapse onto his chest and heave out deep breaths. I feel him press his lips to the top of my head, and I sink further into him. Slightly in awe that I'm here, we're still here together, especially after everything we've been through.

"Well," he says with a laugh. "I think that leaves us about five minutes before we need to leave."

"Shit," I say, pressing myself up to sit on him before jumping off. "I forgot, I forgot, I forgot." I hate being late, but I know if anyone will understand, it's Lauren and Sylvie.

Three months ago, my past finally came to the surface. After years of holding onto secrets, a wave of relief washed over me and soothed the frayed edges of my soul. I exhale a breath I've felt as if I've been holding for my entire life.

For years, I carried the weight of my secrets like a burden too heavy to bear, their whispered truths echoing in my mind. No longer do I have to weave intricate webs of deceit, masking my secrets. I am finally free from the shackles of my own making.

This was all set in motion fifteen years ago, when I was ten years old. The very night, a woman decided to drive after an evening of binge-drinking at some upscale event. What she hadn't planned on was falling asleep at the wheel and drifting into the other lane, going seventy miles an hour. It was late enough that the road was bare, except for one unfortunate car. One unfortunate car with three passengers. Two adults and one child.

My parents and me.

Veronica Taylor. My maiden name.

That careless, self-obsessed woman was Lillian. Richard's first wife.

Lillian killed my parents and got away with it. She snuffed out my entire life in the blink of an eye. My parents both died on impact—at least that's what I was told. An impact shearing brain bleed for both.

They also said it was a miracle I survived.

It was a miracle I hadn't asked for.

Given Richard's status in the state and his criminal justice background, Lillian managed to stay out of jail and was sentenced to two years' house arrest. If Richard or Lillian had only paid closer attention, they might've been able to recognize me as the teenage girl who vowed to make them pay. The one with such rage in her eyes after the sentence, that they should be afraid.

It would be a long game, but I would play it. And I would play it well. It's funny how easily men take to a wounded animal. Richard was easy. Lillian needed a little more effort and preparation.

A lethal man raises a murderous daughter. That's something even I couldn't have predicted. Poison leaks, and it's another instance where fate had a role in all this.

I had a feeling all those years ago when I first met Claire. The way her mother swore she had tried to kill her. I assumed she was exaggerating. Her years as an alcoholic permanently damaged her brain and caused her to turn on the ones she loved, wanting to rot in silence. But no, I had been right. I took away the one kill that mattered to Claire. That might be the one thing I regret in this life. If I had let her have that one, would she have moved on with her life? Could I have saved all those young women's lives? For that, I'm not sure I can ever fully forgive myself.

We had made promises to one another. I killed her mom, but together, we'd take down her dad. She'd keep my secrets, and I'd keep hers. We had to put on a show for the last five years, and I'd say we both played the part well. We slowly fed reporters information about Richard's dirty history in politics. With the connections Claire made from her life as a travel writer, we were able to make sure it got into the right hands and our anonymity would always be protected. I was able to get the evidence needed to prove our words went beyond rumors.

I always knew Richard was unfaithful, but I waited until the right moment to strike. That would be the last puzzle piece in taking him down. Who could stomach someone so powerful cheating on their precious wife with their secretary during the campaign? If they looked closely enough, they would have found that the referral to hire Olivia came from a nonexistent temp agency named VAT Staffing.

Veronica Ann Taylor.

I was sending Richard's exact type to him. Another trap that he walked right into. Now I get to watch Richard spend the rest of his sorry life in prison.

Thanks to Sylvie, she was able to intercept the spyware that was planted in Ronan's house when those dirty cops visited. She knew they were coming and wanted to help protect us. She basically made herself into a sacrifice. I'll always be grateful for her help in saving us. She made sure Ronan knew exactly where he could find us.

Surprisingly enough, Lauren and Sylvie have become quite close. After the whole thing with Liam and Richard, Lauren has sworn off men forever. "Not worth all the trouble they cause," she told me casually one day.

After a mad dash of getting ready as quickly as possible, we're only sixteen minutes late in meeting Sylvie and Lauren at the pool bar. How right is it that my best friend fell in love with Ronan's best friend? They make an insanely beautiful couple.

In the middle of Ronan and my game, I glance over at Lauren and Sylvie, who are cuddled up in the corner of the bar, acting like they are the only two people in the world. Sylvie tucks a piece of Lauren's hair behind her ear and smiles up at her. Sylvie leans in and plants a passionate kiss on Lauren's lips. I smile to myself but turn away at the intimacy in their moment. I can't help myself: I love seeing these two people healed and happy.

Ronan grabs my jaw and pulls my gaze to his, shaking me loose from my thoughts. We both thought he was the dangerous one in this relationship, but a woman's fury is patient. It's silent. It's cunning. What is that saying?

Hell hath no fury like a woman scorned.

"Are you paying attention to me, love?" he asks, a slight purr in his tone.

"Yes, sure, I'm listening," I jokingly respond.

He drops my face and picks up his cue stick.

"Corner pocket, bottom left, off the cushion, with a slight right spin," Ronan announces as he leans over the pool table.

He knocks the black eight ball with a steady motion. It bounces off the cushion with a slight spin to the right before falling into the left side corner pocket.

"Ugh," I groan. "You know I hate you, right?"

"Show me just how much you hate me, then," he says through a huge grin. He exhales deeply before his lips crash into mine.

No one can hurt us anymore.

A wicked smile curves at my lips as I press them into his.

Ronan and I. Cut from the same cloth.

Our worlds might've fallen apart before but in Ronan's arms, where our darkness finally matched, I found the only truth that ever mattered: I was finally myself.

And at last, the lies were beneath us.

71
Olivia

Happy endings? There are no fucking happy endings. I stand in the shadows, concealed from their oblivious gazes. A seething rage consumes me as I watch these two people carry on without a care in the world.

Smiling at each other like they've reached their happily ever after. Every glance, every casual exchange between them, fuels the fire of resentment within me.

The memories of what could've been flash before my eyes. My heart winces in pain when I think of him. Of my Richard. He was going to leave her for me, I know it. He only needed a little more time to get his affairs in order. After the election, we would have been together. We would have had the perfect life. Now, Richard won't even see me. I'm turned away every single time I try to visit.

Once again, this little blond bitch gets everything she wants. She didn't deserve Richard. She doesn't deserve to be happy.

Another surge of anger courses through my veins as I tighten my fists and I try to bury the overwhelming urge to confront them.

I just need to be patient. Let them believe they're safe, untouchable. The higher they climb, the sweeter it'll be when I rip it all away.

I want to be close enough to see the exact moment her world shatters.

Not now, but soon.

Acknowledgements

To my boys, Daniel and Owen. I'm forever sorry that my first published book is a spicy romantic suspense, and I didn't dedicate it to you both. It just felt wrong. I promise there will be many more, and everything I do is for you two. I love you to the moon and back.

To Joyce and Emily, this book simply wouldn't exist without the two of you. Thank you for being a huge part of my process, and for letting me send you puzzle pieces continuously. Your cheerleading helped me power through.

To Madison, let's hope you are my sister-in-law by the time this gets published (!!!!) because I said it and it's going to print. Sorry, Sam! Thank you for always encouraging me, and for just being you, from one author to another. Also, remember that time I wanted this acknowledgement to be a surprise, and I sent it to you in my manuscript draft? Yeah, that was cool.

To my mom, part of me hopes you never read this book be-cause... well, if you've gotten this far, then it's too late and you already know why. Thank you for always supporting my love for reading, and for encouraging me to write. Little "Nicole", who used to write books on lined notebook paper, staple it together, and sell it to Nana for ninety-nine cents, wouldn't believe how far she's come.

To my editors, Laura, Vicky, and Victoria. You all breathed so much life into my manuscript. Not only that but you truly changed me as a writer. I learned so much from you all and gaining that knowledge is unmatched. Thanks for taking a shot on a debut author with a pretty wild book synopsis.

To Alison, I'll never be able to put into words how thankful I am to have stumbled into Cleary's Bookstore on that random Sunday morning. You changed the trajectory of my writing career and for that, I don't think I'll ever be able to truly thank you.

To my beta readers—Allie, Avrial, Cecily, Lala, Jillian, and Sarah. Thank you for giving this book a chance. Your feedback and love for the story really kept me pushing towards my dream.

I've saved the most important acknowledgement for last—you, my lovely reader. Thank you for picking up my book and for diving into Ronan and Veronica's world. I was a reader long before I became a writer and without you, none of this would be possible.

www.ingramcontent.com/pod-product-compliance
Lightning Source LLC
Chambersburg PA
CBHW020014120726
47903CB00004B/1280